# PAINTER'S BEACH

## JESSICA RYAN

For the writer's group that gave me the courage
through critique and laughter.

For my best friend for being my biggest fan.

For my love for inspiring me.

For my family for their love and support.

You know who you are!

# PAINTER'S BEACH

*Lizzy,*

*My love, I hope you're settling in.*

*I hate burdening you with this move all by yourself. I wish I could be there to help right now, but when I get back, I promise to let you use me in any way you want. Please let the movers do their job, and that means ALL the lifting. I repeat… no lifting! At first, why don't you focus on getting your art studio organized?*

*I'm settling in with the new crew on here. I'm fortunate to have some really great mates. The food has been bland as usual, but it makes me dream of the meals we will make in our new kitchen together.*

*Astor Line has already proven to be a rather unhelpful company. I've been trying to nail down when we will arrive in the Gulf of Guinea. Calm seas so far, but it looks like there might be some weather coming. A little out of season, but I'm keeping an eye on it.*

*Don't fret, love, we will have everything we need and want very soon. I promise. I've got something big in store for us.*

*Miss you dearly. Need you desperately.*

*Give Chico some big pets for me.*

*Love you,*

*Your Capt.*

# PART I

# SUNDAY

# Aimsley August

**Sea grass unveils her house like a silk sheet.** As I walk next to the sand dune that guards her house, the sharp point of its Victorian turret pierces the sky, and the reeds sway down its pitched roof. My stomach flutters when the second-floor balcony reveals itself from the grass.

She's up there.

She sits beneath a floppy-brimmed hat and thick-framed sunglasses that are all black against her black wooden house. The fish scale cedar shake is slightly salt scrubbed, but the most distinguishing factor between the shades of black is her pale skin.

Tall, lengthy pine trees wall in her property like the house is hiding, even though it's steps away from all the other beachfront properties. I wonder if the pine trees in Oregon are anything like these. She told me she was from Portland. Maybe I'll ask her next time.

*Elizabeth Corey.*

I remembered her full name the first time I opened up her tab at Breaker's Beach Bar. My favorite customer. Mostly because she orders the same thing every time, and mainly because I find her incredibly attractive. Her dark apparel, tattoos and gauged earlobes don't fit the Painter's Beach aesthetic, but maybe that's why she interests me. She doesn't look like every other clone of a person on the island.

It's not even just her looks. She's different. She talks to me about things that my customers, even my friends, never talk about. Elizabeth likes to talk about how different phases of the moon affect our energy, or what it would be like to live in an alternative universe, or the power of aphrodisiacs, while she slides oysters down her throat in front of me. She doesn't talk about the new traffic light causing a fifteen-minute delay at dinnertime or how milk prices on the island are fifty cents more expensive than off-island.

I miss seeing my favorite customer. She hasn't been around in a couple of weeks, so I've been checking up on her. It's not like I could just shoot her a text to ask where she's been. I'd love to get to that level, get to know her better, be sitting on that balcony next to her, but for now, I just observe and hope for an "accidental" interaction. If she ever breaks her gaze from that damned ocean, maybe she'd catch a glimpse of me kicking the sand and wave me over. Invite me in.

I wonder what she's looking at. Sitting up there with her big fluffy dog at her feet. She looks out at the horizon. Almost beyond the sea. Like she's waiting for something to appear.

I too search the horizon, maybe to catch a glimpse of

something, but there's nothing in view besides the beach full of tourists endlessly searching for sharks' teeth.

"Auggie!"

I'm being called from the beach. Brooke shouts my name as her jog bounces the two bright pink triangles of her swimsuit with every leap. Her long, red, crimped hair wisps from side to side behind her. An absolute bombshell with tanned skin and long legs. My girlfriend.

I peer up to Elizabeth's balcony one more time as reality starts to sink my feet deeper into the sand. She's facing away towards the doors to go inside when she pauses. With a swift turn of her head, she lowers her glasses. It's hard to make out her facial expression in shadow from her brimmed hat, but I almost feel as if she's standing right in front of me, looking into my eyes. From the corner of her mouth, her lips curl into a devilish grin.

I'm frozen solid in eighty-degree weather.

I wonder if she knew I was here the entire time, or if my "accidental" approach coincidentally worked. Now it makes me nervous that she might have caught me in the act. What if she thinks I'm stalking her? But she did give me that grin, and I've seen it before from the other side of the bar. Every time I've set a drink down in front of her, her grin causes me to have the biggest, dumbest, cheesiest smile on my face. She doesn't ever follow the expression with anything. She just continues to grin deeper, and I'm forced to busy myself to escape my own awkwardness.

Sharp fingernails grasp into my shoulders, spinning me

around.

"Auggie, baby, where have you been?" Brooke asks.

I open my mouth, but before words form, she asks me why I wasn't at Breaker's yet.

"I'm ready to get shitty tonight!" She tugs at my arm to insinuate the direction she wants us to be walking. I look up one last time at Elizabeth's house.

"What are you doing over here anyway? Looking at that creepy lady's house?" Brooke pries.

"What? No. I was just on my way there, just walked up North Beach and back," I try to sound as convincing as possible, but before she can ponder, I bite my lip and compliment her, "Damn baby, you're looking fine today."

She cracks a sparkling white smile and pierces me with her violent green eyes. They feel like daggers stabbing into my brain for my wandering thoughts.

She spins around and throws her arms up, showing off her physique. She knows how hot she is. I'm not sure how I got so lucky or how I landed this girl. I feel like an idiot for being here instead of going straight to Breaker's like I should have. Like a good girlfriend would.

She looks me up and down with exaggeration. "You're always looking fine," she says as she circles my band-tee and board shorts. I don't see myself comparable in any way. Just a short, average-built woman with an untamable mane of mouse brown hair, but I'll take the extra love from her any day.

Brooke curls her finger for me to come hither, before taking off running. Commanding me to chase her, I run arduously after her like a zombie in need of brains.

"All right, all right, wait up girl!"

**Stepping under the awning at Breaker's is a relief to the scorching sand under my feet.** The bar is relaxed enough to get served without shoes, and where all my close friends take over the dedicated employee high-top table in the back corner. The patio is packed with full six-top tables and walk-ups at the bar waiting in line to order drinks.

"Auggie, get me a rum runner? You make the best." Brooke demands with a bitter sweetness before skipping over to our friends' table, and I do as I'm told.

She calls me Auggie, short for August, my last name. Funny because my friends all call me August, but no one ever bothers to call me by my actual name. Maybe they figure it's too girly for me, but I actually like it. Elizabeth calls me Aimsley.

Diverting my path to behind the bar, I squeeze in between Dean and the barbacks, trying to stay out of the way while mixing ingredients.

Dean was the unlucky one of our friends who was scheduled to work tonight. As bad as I feel for him, I'm relieved to be making a drink for fun instead. He casually dips behind me to grab a stack of cups. Shaking the blonde curls out of his face, he asks, "Hey, yo, August, you want a beer?"

Almost as soon as he asks, he pulls a freshly poured cold one from the tap and passes it over to me. Just as fast, he passes out four more beers at once to a group of customers and begins pouring again immediately for the next ones.

I raise my voice over the noise at the bar. "Thanks man!" I say as foam falls over my cup and down the back of my hand, "Not as good as your last brew, but I'll take it." I toss back a large, refreshing sip of what tastes like the summer ale on our menu. The cool liquid instantly brings my body temperature down and relaxes my nerves.

"Dude, I know that last APA was sick. I'm working on a new batch, can't wait to crack that baby open." Dean throws up the hang loose sign and clicks his tongue as he winks and smiles his bright white teeth at me. His skinny tank top reveals his broad tanned shoulders and one of his hairless pecks that have all the tourists and local cougars holding their breath.

"For sure. You know I'm always down. Cheers!" Dean pauses and raises a cup to clink against mine, splashing beer from the sides. Leaning into his ear while mugging the tourists lined up impatiently against the bar, I say, "And don't let any of these snowbirds give you a hard time."

Dean knocks his head back in a silent laugh. "No worries, these chickadees will be flying home soon!" He winks again and moves his eyes to his next customer at the bar and then back at me, chuckling at the older woman in her sixties with an animal print suit on, fake boobs and lips bursting with filler. I giggle myself, shaking my head side to side as I take the drinks across the bar to join our table of friends.

Being the last Sunday in April marks the end of tourist season. A time when things finally start to slow down and feel like real island life, but it also makes for a fun last weekend with all the extra off-islanders, or what we call the "outies". You never know what trouble you can get yourself into when the outies are still around. Although Painter's Beach is still considered a hidden Florida gem, over the last few years, tourism has really picked up after we were featured in a popular destination social media blog. And again, when we were ranked number three of the best island towns in America according to a major travel series. It was my fifteen minutes of fame, even if the show only recorded the back of my hair in a blurred-out scene of the bar.

"Nice of you to finally join us," Cameron calls at me from the table.

I shout a big "Hey!" in response, lifting my drink-filled hands in the air.

I place Brooke's rum runner in front of her, stealing a big wet kiss in exchange that has everyone at the table oohing and awing.

"I had to make my baby a drink," I say as I pull up a chair between her and Tiffany.

Tiffany's bony body embraces me in a big hug, like we hadn't just seen each other during yesterday's shift.

"Isn't it nice being a tourist for once? Nothing to do, nowhere to be. This shit is so nice," Tiffany says. Her slick ponytail almost lashes my face as the table collectively cheers to her statement.

"You know you guys...it won't be this way forever," shirtless Cameron says as he flexes one of his hairy biceps, "We are all amazingly talented and sexy. We'll show up these rich fucks someday!"

This conversation is a typical one at the end of the busy season. We all have bigger dreams for life in our thirties, besides being slaves in the hospitality industry. I want to publish a novel someday and be chilling in a beachfront house like Elizabeth. Garnet's already published and trying to sell copies while serving coffee. Jada stays up all night making art for the local markets when she's not waiting tables. Tiffany works days at the bar so she can support her wedding photography gigs on the weekends. Then there's the boys. When Cameron isn't trying to score a date with a customer from the bar, he's being a fitness guru, giving personal training lessons to rich ladies on the island. Dean crafts great drinks, but the homebrews he makes during his off time are brewery-worthy. My Brooke is practically an island celebrity when she's bartending, but when I ask her about her dreams, she always looks at me funny. She'll say she's saving up enough money to someday move the furthest away possible from her parents, and I don't blame her, because I don't like them either.

"Looks like my next market's going to get swept away by this hurricane," Jada morbidly claims, pointing to the bar TV.

A headline on the local news runs across the screen:

*Tropical Storm in Atlantic Upgrades to Category 1 Hurricane.*

"Oh, what a load of B.S.!" Cameron exclaims.

Jada, being fairly new to Florida, asks, "I know y'all are used to these hurricanes and don't take them seriously, but I just got an alert on my phone, so shouldn't we be worried?" She then reads from her phone, "This article says the tropical storm has been upgraded to Hurricane Amelia this afternoon with seventy-five mile an hour wind. That sounds really bad."

"Oh, maybe this means we'll have a hurricane party!" Brooke shrieks as Garnet joins her, clapping their hands together with devilish joy.

"Come on guys. Seriously?" Jada pleads. She shrinks her already short stature deeper into her high-top chair. Tiffany uses her chair to reach the volume on the TV above us, making it louder.

*"The National Hurricane Center is still showing two projected paths. The GFS model is predicting the storm will hook back out towards the Atlantic in a couple of days; however, the European model is still predicting a more direct hit to the Florida coast. Early on in this storm's path, residents and visitors need to keep in mind a possible life-threatening storm by the end of the week. Everyone needs to make sure they have their hurricane plan in place."*

"I should probably go pick up some water and canned goods," Jada says.

"A hurricane party sounds so fun. I'm so in Brooke!" Tiffany agrees, ignoring the look of disbelief on Jada's face.

"Oh Jada, don't even worry about all that. The news always tries to scare us during hurricane season, so we panic-buy a bunch of shit. It's a conspiracy." Cameron dismisses her concern and chugs more of his beer.

"Yeah, I wouldn't worry too much. It's too early for hurricane season anyway. Plus, the last time we had a hurricane hit the island was like a hundred years ago." I add to the conversation.

"I don't know guys. You know what they say about the curse." Garnet raises her eyebrows while she speaks.

"Oh, here we go," Cameron says.

"When the British colonists discovered the island, they took out a small group of natives, accusing them of using witchcraft. Before one of the so-called witches was killed, they cursed the island, saying one day the land would be taken away by a powerful storm, destroying the island and everyone who inhabits it."

"Dumb," Cameron states calmly, scoffing at the story, "I don't believe in that superstitious crap, but I hope we do get a hurricane so we can have the week off. This winter has been busy as hell."

"Cameron! Don't jinx it!" Jada swats his arm, and he retorts, chuckling at her fear.

"It's true guys! I read the story in the bookstore," Garnet claims as she sips the straw of her frozen drink.

"Guess we are all doomed then, better drink up!" I tease and chug the rest of my beer. It goes down way too quickly, so I wiggle my way out of the table to get another. I position myself in front of Dean as the bar front has calmed down from earlier.

"Ready for another?" Dean asks as he refills my beer. "So, what am I missing? Anything good?" he asks while wiping his hands on a bar rag.

"Oh, not really. Jada's just freaking out about the storm."

"Yeah, I saw that. You know what that means." Dean grins and springs his eyebrows up and down at me, handing me over the freshly poured pint.

"I know. Tif and Brooke are already planning the party." Our conversation is interrupted by a customer waving at Dean, drawing his attention to the other side of the bar.

I don't find myself bothered by the idea of a hurricane. I've lived here my whole life, and nothing bad has ever come of it. Sure, we've had tropical storm winds. We've had rain that flooded Main Street, but the world didn't come to an end. We simply woke up hungover and went back to work. Although there is always that gut feeling in the back of my mind that maybe this will be the year. I look out of the bar towards the beach, observing the houses, the palm trees and the rolling sand dunes, trying to imagine what it would look like in a hurricane. Guessing where the storm surge would reach. I wondered if it would come up to the bar, or even up to Brooke and my lower-level apartment a few blocks from here. I question how many feet above sea level our apartment is, but I doubt anything would get past the dunes. That's what they are there for, right? Elizabeth's home is right there on the beach, even with stilts, I'm not sure that old worn-down place would do well in a hurricane. I wonder if she knows about the storm. She only moved here a few months ago. Maybe I should warn her.

*Wait, no.*

There I go, letting my mind wander again. Thinking about this *"creepy lady"* as Brooke said. Elizabeth, this mysterious woman that won't leave my thoughts.

**The high-top table is now riddled with stacked cups and dried-up sour spills.** Dusk is creeping in as the sun settles behind the houses, and the full moon rises above the water into a soft pink sky. The moon displays boldly against purples that collide with the deep blue of the horizon. Waves lap against the shore in predictable ways, but in the north, a group of towering puffy clouds hangs low and flickers with lightning. A storm is coming later.

The group is becoming loud and belligerent with laughter. Tiffany starts making repetitive sounds, "Wee woo, wee woo, wee woo!" Garnet nearly spits out her drink as Cameron points to the window, looking into the bar's host stand where a man is waiting to be helped.

"Bad boys, bad boys, what you gonna do? Brookie's dad is gonna come for you!" Cameron chants.

Brooke looks over, letting out a large huff. "Oh, shut up!" She rises from her chair quickly, "Guess that's our sign to go to Slack Tides. C'mon! Let's get the hell outta here."

We all follow Brooke's lead like Mother Goose and her ducklings. In a row, our group exits the back bar onto the beach, waddling in and out of a single file line.

Heading south, we put a good distance between Brooke's dad, who happens to be the Chief of Police.

"I can't believe my Dad's out tonight. He's so annoying,"

Brooke says as she jumps onto my back and wraps her legs around me.

"Yeah, for real. He's probably out chasing tail," I blurt out.

"Aimsley!" She viciously jumps off my back and smacks my arm. "Shut up!"

I grab my stinging arm. "Damn girl! It was a joke. Gah!"

Brooke snarls at me and catches up to Tiffany, holding her hand. They skip further down the beach while Garnet and Cameron race each other the rest of the way to the bar.

I guess I overstepped in front of everyone, but all of us know what a douchebag her dad is. I wasn't joking at all, but I regret mentioning it if this means Brooke will be mad with me the rest of the night. Before we moved in together, she used to call me crying because of her parents fighting all the time. Catherine would accuse him of cheating, and Duncan would slam doors, punch walls and break things too frequently. Now a bad feeling sits in my chest.

Jada puts her hand around my shoulder and rolls her eyes. I know she can tell I'm in trouble. With encouragement she says, "Come on, let's go dance."

The bass is louder than the thunder rolling in as we walk up the boardwalk to Slack Tide's. On their multi-tiered outdoor decks, a band plays loudly for a crowd packed in like sardines. They sway left and right like the waves, and I jump right in. Jada nudges people aside so we get close to the front of the stage. A 2000s cover band plays familiar songs that bring back nostalgia for the whole crowd. People sing in unison and pull out dance moves I hadn't seen since high school. Surprisingly,

Jada pulls out the pop, lock and drop it, which makes me know she's definitely feeling the drinks. I laugh and bend my knees, swaying with the crowd. Strands of hair flow wildly around my face, and I feel genuinely so happy right now. The band members are smiling while tipping back a round of shots on the house. The people next to me are smiling and doing the Dougie. All I can think of is how fun this is, but also how much it sucks that Brooke isn't dancing with me.

I pull Jada close and shout in her ear, "I'm going to get a drink." She nods and mouths back, asking me to get her one too.

Scanning the crowd on the deck, I move to the nearest bar front, searching for the crown of Brooke's fiery red hair. She's nowhere in sight, so I move on to the top deck, where a smaller bar sits. Instantly, I spot the top of her red head and her bright pink bikini straps tied in a bow around her back. She's leaning over a man at the bar I don't recognize. It's probably one of her regulars, but hot blood fills my head as I see her hand resting on his thigh. She throws her head back in laughter. He doesn't flinch but places his hand slightly above her hip. Without a second thought, I charge over to toss the guy's hand away and stand in between them, staring angrily into her eyes. Brooke pulls back and gives me a look of disbelief. "Aimsley, chill!"

"What are you doing? And who the hell are you?" I ask, staring back and forth between them.

Receiving a look of confusion on his face, he replies with a chuckle, "Who are you?" His response boils my blood hotter.

"I don't give a damn who you are. And why are you

touching him?" Focusing all of my attention on Brooke now, the man swivels his chair in the other direction.

"Oh, don't be ridiculous," Brooke exclaims as she leans her elbows against the bar and looks away from me.

"C'mon, let's go home," I demand, gripping around her bicep to pull her away, but she fights against me. Her retort only angers me more.

"Dude, come on. It's getting late. I have to work tomorrow morning anyway."

She turns her head from me and says under her breath, "Well I don't."

"What's your problem?" My voice whines.

Brooke turns and explodes on me, "You! You're the problem! You come over here with that attitude like I'm doing something wrong. I'm just trying to enjoy my night, and you're ruining it. Maybe you should go home."

"What's that supposed to mean?" I ask, but she doesn't turn to look at me, and I can feel this conversation beginning to form into a circling argument. I stare at her for a few seconds longer, hoping she has it in her to apologize and make up with me so we can continue to have a good night together, but realistically, I know that there's no chance in hell. This isn't the first time I've seen this side of her. I can't have a good time now that the night has turned this way. I will only push and push to try to fix it when I know it won't happen. Gathering what pride I have left, I turn my back and walk away.

Down the stairs and onto the lower deck, I push and shove past the crowd I was smiling with only minutes ago. Onto the boardwalk, I stomp my feet. Jada yells for me, spotting me making an exit.

"Hey August, hey, are you okay?"

I stop for a moment to explain as a hot tear rolls down my cheek. "Brooke's up there with some random guy and told me to fuck off, so I'm leaving." As I look past Jada's shoulder, I can still spot her sitting next to him at the bar, and I wonder if she will sleep with him. Maybe I'm not really what she wants.

"You can't let her keep treating you like this. How many times?" Even if Jada's words are meant to be helpful, they're only making it worse.

"I don't know Jada, guess I'm just an idiot. I'm out," I say as I continue walking down the boardwalk and onto the beach. Jada still calls for me to come back. I think about the disdain on her face and know I might regret that comment later, but when I said it, all I was thinking about was getting the hell out of there.

The bass of the band begins to fade into the dull sound of rolling thunder. The moonlight on the water replaces incandescent lights in the distance. Waves recede and crash into the shore with longing, mocking my destruction of a relationship. At times like these, I just want to say fuck it. Call it quits on us, Brooke and I. Disappear into a new life. Even if I tried, the island wouldn't allow it. Everyone knows everyone here. I couldn't escape this life if I wanted to. I'm stuck.

After all the effort we've put into this relationship, her words rip me apart. I'm not sure my heart will recover from this one. She pulled it out of my chest, squeezed it dry and stomped it to death. Like the jellyfish I almost just stepped on in the tide. That jellyfish is me. Tossed ashore, left to dry up on the sand, completely helpless.

**My legs have grown tired.** The brisk tide washes over my feet, trying to pull me in. I imagine the relief of slumping over and letting it consume me. My body plops down in the sand. Water fills up my board shorts and falls back down my legs before it rolls on itself and does it again.

The storm is much closer now, blocking the moonlight. Until lightning cracked from behind me, I hadn't noticed the tall pine trees. The next flash of light reveals the pointed peak of Elizabeth's home. How I've managed to stop at this exact location baffles me, but it could be muscle memory at this point from all the stalking I've been doing lately.

Studying the house between flashes of lightning, suddenly, a silhouette of a woman and a large dog appears. Her dress trails behind her, billowing in the wind.

It's her. Elizabeth.

I wonder if my eyes are playing tricks on me, or if I've really passed out drunk on the beach and imagined this like a dream. She slinks down the sand dune and passes me closely. I'm still as a rock, besides a few curls of my hair tickling my face. Assuming she notices I am sitting here, to my surprise, she makes a beeline for the shore. The lightning is showing her movements in a compartmentalized way, like the flash of a camera, creating pictures in my eyes, seconds apart. Her dog is looking left as she is at the tide, then it's looking right as she's now knee deep, and then her dog's head is back as if howling for her as her arm is lifted in the air, raised one second, and then dropped, her body slightly slumped the next.

Buzzing comes from the pocket of my board shorts. Unlocking the screen, the bright white light of my phone blinds me. My eyes adjust to read a text from Brooke:

**Where are you?**

The timestamp is after three in the morning. Where has the time gone? I need to get home. I place my phone back in my pocket. Everything is pitch black. I stand up, almost losing my footing in the sand, but I catch myself with one hand and rebalance. In front of me, the shoreline is fuzzy, but I feel there is a stagnant figure facing me. Another flash of lightning. This time near the shore. I duck down to shield myself. Elizabeth and her dog are nowhere to be seen. I stagger slightly towards the shore, wanting to get a better look, but it's so dark, and another strike hits dangerously close. Pellets of rain begin to drop onto my head and arms. The sound of a wall of rain comes towards me. I run as my hair slicks against my face.

# MONDAY

## AIMSLEY AUGUST

**I reach for a blanket, but my hand falls off the side of the couch.** I never made it into our bed last night.

Shivering, I rise from the cushions like a vampire from my casket, touching my clammy feet to the cold terrazzo floor. Examining my surroundings, I'm still in my damp clothes from last night, and the coffee table has a half-drunk beer next to my notebook with a mystery poem scribbled on it.

*Can't wait to read that one.*

My perception of time is non-existent, but my head is throbbing, and my bladder feels like a balloon, so I have clear priorities. After relieving myself in the hall bathroom, I attempt to turn the handle of our bedroom. It's locked. Brooke locked me out. Which explains why I woke up on the couch.

As I'm making my way around the kitchen for a glass of water, I recall our argument and how I'm still angry about it, but I could just as easily go into that room and steal from Brooke's warmth.

The red digits on the microwave read 7:20 a.m., which means I have to be at my shift in less than ten minutes, only enough time for a brisk shower and to fish clothes out of the dirty laundry basket, thanks to my lack of a car. Breakfast will have to wait, even though my stomach is churning. I can't tell whether food would make it better or worse right now.

Armed with my trusty dry bag backpack and skateboard, I take to the sunny skies and relish in the cool breeze of an early Florida morning. Before heading downtown on my board, I send a quick text message to Brooke:

*Sry bout last night…had to blow off steam. Luv ya. C U after work??*

Not that I expect much of a reaction out of her, but it might lessen the blow to apologize first. I wonder if she will forgive me, but after last night, I question saving all year to buy her the engagement ring that's been burning a hole in my pocket. Why she wouldn't leave with me last night when she knows my insecurities about her bisexuality baffles me and makes me feel like an idiot. I wonder who the guy was. I don't remember seeing him around Breakers, which concerns me more with how friendly they were being. Maybe it's all in my head, but I'd beat his ass.

Letting my skateboard slam into the pavement, I kick off and glide through the neighborhood out to the main road downtown. I can feel the weight of my body wishing to lie flat from the lack of sleep, but I keep kicking. Neighbors tend to their lawns and pick up the newspaper. An old shirtless man walks in the direction of the beach to keep up his leathered tan. A couple on bicycles wearing tight spandex shorts race past me in the pedestrian lane. A group of people on a golf cart zooms around me and turns left to get to their morning tee.

Main Street marks the beginning of a one-lane cobblestone street lined with live oak and Magnolia trees, and the beginning of the sidewalk. I jump off my board to walk the remaining blocks to the bookstore.

Two- and three-story brick buildings sit on the sidewalks with different colored valances. The storefront entrances have large glass display windows trimmed in ornamented wood. The glass of the bookstore has an all-white logo that reads *"Book & Brew"* in a semicircle over an open book. Peering in behind the window display, I already see Garnet opening her station at the café counter.

Aromas of coffee, almond and vanilla float through my nostrils. I flip over the *"We're Open"* sign as I walk in one minute past eight o'clock.

"C'mon in!" I mutter sarcastically under my breath. The thrill of a hangover shift could kill.

Garnet waves at me from behind the chunky café counter on the left. Her cheerful appearance provides me with a small spark of energy I desperately need. The wall behind her is covered in dark wooden bookshelves, like the rest of the store, but her shelves are filled with sacks of coffee beans, tea tins, mugs and glasses. She works from behind a shiny metallic espresso machine atop the glass display of baked goods and pastries.

"Feeling a little rough this morning Aims?" Garnet blurts out, leaning over the counter. Her straight brown hair and choppy bangs frame her nose ring that wriggles when she laughs. Her judgment is playful.

"Do I look that bad?" I hide my face and check out the new display she's arranged this morning. A fresh stack of her published books sits next to other Florida authors. A spark of envy punches my gut, but I am proud of her.

She notices me flipping through pages of her book. "Hey, I have to shill my novel somehow, right? I am technically a Florida author now too."

"You sure are girl! You'll have to teach me about publishing when I'm ready."

"Duh! You have to get one written first!"

She's right. I do need to write my book. I'm just not sure where to start.

"You think the boss will notice I moved things around?"

"Nah, I think your book fits right in. Plus, I won't tell her if you don't mention I was late."

Garnet smiles in agreement. "Deal."

On the other side of the bookstore is my counter that is shoved tightly under a staircase that winds up to the second floor. The walls are covered from floor to ceiling with shelves and books. Between the café and my counter are a couple displays of classic and new novels, and a few café tables. I set my skateboard and backpack behind the counter and open the register. Counting money is the last thing I want to be doing right now, but I'm technically already behind on my opening duties.

Garnet comes over as I pull money from the drawer to count.

*20, 40, 60, 80...*

"So, what happened with you and Brooke last night? Where did you go?" she asks, leaning closely over the counter.

*10, 20, 30, 40...*

I shrug my shoulders. "Eh, I don't know. We haven't talked since."

*5, 10, 15, 20...*

"Oh no, that's no good. I'm sorry." She pauses, leaving room for me to vent. I don't really feel like venting, but I know she will only keep prying if I don't.

I put down the stack of five-dollar bills. "I'm just tired of arguing, you know? So, I walked up the beach, and then eventually it started raining, and I went home."

My mind drifts to the image of Elizabeth's silhouette in the lightning. I remembered I was outside of her house last night and how I could have sworn I saw her out on the beach. It's hard to tell if I was seeing things or if it was the booze.

"I'm sure you guys will work it out. You always do." Her genuine response warms me, but it doesn't necessarily fill the doubts in my heart. "I think you need a coffee!"

I follow Garnet to her side of the store, excited to see what concoction she has for me today. She always makes me the 'Special of the Day' before we have any customers, but my stomach still churns, and I worry about keeping it down. I happen to know one thing that always helps my stomach, but

I forgot to do it before I left the apartment. "What I really need is a big fat joint right now."

"Oh, sorry, I don't bring that shit to work," Garnet claims as the espresso machine hisses.

"Yeah, thought it was worth a shot, just in case you were holding out on me." I snicker. Getting stoned right now would help me focus and cure my stomach instantly. I'm kicking myself for letting it slip. If Brooke and I were on better terms, she would probably bring one to me, but she still hasn't answered my text from earlier. Guess I'll have to suffer through.

To the left of the cash register are dozens of coffees and two overfilled bags of pastries. "Hey, what's all this?"

"That's an order for the po-pos. They called it in when I first got here. Guess they won't be coming in as usual." She hands me a warm drink topped with a pile of whipped cream. Caramel drizzle and chocolate shavings pour over the sides of the mug. "Here. I made it especially for you." She squints her eyes and clasps her hands with anticipation, leaning in to see my reaction.

I take a sip, acquiring a moustache full of whipped cream in the process. The sweetness coats my tongue. Warm liquid fills my throat. "Damn, okay girl! This is what I needed. Wait, what is this?"

"It's a café con leche with almond milk, a pump of salted caramel and a teensy tiny bit of Mexican vanilla." She fawningly grins at me, awaiting a compliment after a long indulging gulp, but before I can respond, the bell at the front door dings as the first customers shuffle in.

"Can you believe it? In this town? Poor Jim!" The woman sighs and grasps her friend's arm. She's a regular at the bookstore with her tag-along who buys coffee every day, but I've never seen her pick up a book. Quickly, I go back to my drawer to finish counting in the off chance that this time she actually wants to buy a book.

The woman seems hysterical. Garnet rolls her eyes at me and asks her, "What's happened, Mary?"

*1, 2, 3, 4...*

She throws her arms over the café counter and bows her head, letting out a sigh and a whimper, "Oh, Garnet, it's awful! Jim, Jim Crowley from church. They found him early this morning. Laid out on the beach."

*Again, 1, 2, 3, 4...*

Garnet looks quizzical. "Oh, no. Really? Is he okay?"

*5, 6, 7, 8...*

"No, he's not. He's gone. Dead." Mary throws up her hands as I lose count again.

"Wait, really?" Garnet looks at her with surprise and side-eyes me.

"I know! I cannot believe it. I mean who would do such a thing? Jim is such a great guy. And his poor daughters. I cannot imagine. I just hope they can figure out who did this and why." Looking distressed, she leans on her friend and looks over at me, making a deep frown.

"That's crazy. I mean, that's really awful. Sorry for your loss." I'm not sure what exactly to say, but that's all I can manage to come up with on the spot. I don't know Jim, but I grow instantly curious and attempt to look for any news on my phone. "Wait, what's his last name?"

"You don't know Jim? You know he runs the weekly youth group at church." She stares at me, waiting for me to reply.

Does she really assume I know anything about some church youth group?

I begin to shake my head from left to right before she states his name.

"It's Jim Crowley. Spelled C – R – O – W – L – E – Y."

I look at my phone to open a tab and type in his name, but before I do, an article has already populated my newsfeed.

"I can tell you everything there is to know. I've read all the articles already. There's not much more information than that, dear." Mary starts to ramble on about what she knows as I tune her out and read the first article:

### Body Found at Painter's Beach

*Early this Monday morning at approximately 5:15 a.m., a local man walking on the beach discovered a body near the popular Breaker's Beach Bar.*

*The man was identified as 42-year-old Jim Crowley, a long-time Painter's Beach resident. Police believe an incident could have occurred between the hours of 3 a.m. and 5 a.m. this morning.*

*At this time, no further information has been released by the police North Beach will remain closed for investigation until further notice. Please avoid this area if possible.*

*If you or anyone you know has any information regarding this incident, please contact our police hotline.*

"Wow, right outside work," I say. I feel a shiver run up my spine. My sour stomach feels nauseated.

"You mean outside Breaker's? We should text Tiffany. Is she bartending today?" Garnet looks intensely at her phone, while Mary chats on to her tag-along friend about the incident in the background.

"Were you out on the beach last night?" Mary asks, scanning both of us with a serious intent in her eyes.

"Yeah, of course we were at the beach. Everyone on the island was there. But we were down by Slack Tides, actually," I respond.

I can't help but feel like I'm being interrogated by this woman as she hums under her breath with suspicion.

"Well, if you girls hear anything, and I mean *anything*, please let me know. I am actually very close to their family. I practically raised his girls. Ugh, I cannot imagine how they must be taking the news. It's breaking my heart! I want to help in any way to get this man some justice," Mary declares and pulls a couple of cards from her purse, handing one to Garnet and walking the other over, handing it to me. "Here, please take my card. Y'all contact me if you hear anything."

Her card reads:

*Mary Pearly*

*MaryPearly.FHCPB@yahoo.com*

*Servant of God/ Treasurer for The First Holy Church of Painter's Beach*

*Board of Directors President for the Painter's Art Alliance*

*John 8:32*

*"Have a blessed day!"*

"Thanks," I say and put the card in my pocket while I wait for her to leave the counter in front of me. She continues to look at me for a little longer, making me uncomfortable. I feel her judgment of me like an X-ray of my bones. Maybe I'm paranoid, or maybe she's bothered by the way I look and dress. She seems like the type of woman who would be bothered by someone like me, someone who doesn't fit in a box like everyone else. A masculine lesbian. A sinner in her eyes.

"So, ladies, what can I get started for you this morning?" Garnet's question breaks up the tension, and Mary stuffs her nose into the air as she struts back over to the café counter. As Garnet fills their order, I take a moment to sit down and gather my thoughts.

I was on the beach around three o'clock in the morning, not too far from Breaker's. Not too far from where a body was found.

I should have gone home, but I wasn't the only one on the beach early this morning.

**The unboxing of freshly printed books feels like unwrapping presents jon Christmas morning.** They smell of newly pressed paper. It's a strong scent of freshly printed ink, a chemical but dreamy smell. Their crisp pages are wrapped in hard covers. Some have slick plastic sleeves with embossed lettering. My favorite book jackets are the ones that are velvety to the touch.

I think of all the ideas I've had for stories, and how I'd wished I were unwrapping my own novel from this box. I hold one of the new books, caressing its spine, imagining my name as I trace the raised lettering. I flip open the hardcover and see the image of this newly released author on the inside sleeve, picturing my portrait looking back at me.

If only I could stick with a single story from start to finish. Find that one great inspiration that would take my words and run with them across hundreds of pages. I unhook the sides of my backpack, unrolling its watertight seal to pull out one of my notebooks that's scribbled with ideas, characters, possible story lines, even full scenes of books I haven't figured out the actual story to yet. Flipping to a blank page in the notebook, I grab a pen and write:

**From beneath the storm, she walks with great urgency to the tide, her wolf keeping a watchful eye.**

I pause as a person stands over me at the register, clearing his throat. Quickly, I close the notebook, shoving it back into my backpack. Looking up, it's an officer and one I recognize. Standing in front of me without saying a word, he holds both sides of his vest near his chest, waiting for me to say something.

"Hey, Officer Macon."

"Mornin' Aimsley. You still, uh, writing? Uh, what are you writing about?" Officer Macon is a young officer. Although we're close in age, in his mid-thirties, his position of authority makes him feel so much older. We could have been in the same classes growing up, but he moved here from New York. I guess he found more luck landing his first police job. It seems the Painter's Beach Police Department always has openings for officers. Maybe the pay isn't great, or maybe people don't want to work for Chief Duncan. I know I wouldn't.

Macon always makes a point to stop and have a conversation with me when he comes in for coffee. He's not quick to judge me like most islanders. I guess people from New York tend to be more open-minded. He's always friendly and chipper, though his demeanor seems slightly dim this morning. Something's off.

"Oh, I was just scribbling an idea down. Nothing really." I fidget with my pen.

"Cool. Cool. Been busy in here today?" He bobs back and forth. I was hesitant to ask, but curious if his dimly lit appearance had anything to do with the body found at the beach this morning.

"No, not really. How about you?" He perks up and stops bobbing, letting out a big sigh.

"Yeah, actually. I'm fetching coffee for the rest of the unit. Uh, we had an early morning call. All hands."

I scrunch the side of my face with sympathy. "Yeah, I just saw the article."

"Yep. I, uh," he pauses, "was the responding officer."

I'm not sure what to say as the silence is eating up the room. He looks lost in thought. "Wow, that must have been tough."

"Oh, well, you know the academy tries to prepare you for this kind of thing, but when you see it in real life, it's a little different."

"I can't imagine."

"Trust me, you don't want to."

"That bad, huh?"

He diverts the conversation and looks at the shelf behind him, picking at some of the new arrivals.

"Hey, uh, you know I'm still reading through that series you suggested a couple weeks ago. I'm on the second book already. It's pretty good. I didn't expect that twist at the end of the first one. I was telling my wife about it, and so she's reading it now."

"Oh, that's awesome. I'm glad you're enjoying them."

Macon has been coming in for years, getting book recommendations from me. We often spend time in the mornings discussing different series and talking about ideas for books. He knows I want to be a published author someday, so he's always encouraging me, saying things like, "Don't stop writing, kid," and "Look, everybody, it's Painter's most famous author!" He even had me sign one of his napkins before, saying he would keep it for when I'm a "big fancy author someday". It's disheartening to see him in bad shape like this.

A buzz comes from my pocket. I think it could be Brooke finally texting me back, but when I look, it's from Garnet:

*Ask him about the body!?*

*Whaaat…naw.*

*Come on plz…*

*I'll do it for a bagel lol*

*Yess…with extra cream cheese…*

*Promise?*

*DO IT!! Plz...*

"Hey, Officer Macon?" As I ask for his attention, he turns from browsing books, giving me his full attention.

"I thought I told you to call me Rodger."

"Sorry. Hey Rodger..."

"Yeah, what's up, kid?"

I quickly try to think of a mild way to ask him about the body without being too pushy. I come up with, "Was it a rip current?"

"Huh?" He looks at me confused.

"From the storm last night, did he drown from a rip current?"

Rodger's eyes widen and then look down as he says, "It wasn't a drowning."

Shocked, I say, "Oh, I just figured."

He shakes his head back and forth, "Look, I can't really talk about anything, with it being an open investigation and all."

"Right. Of course. Sorry, I didn't mean to...I shouldn't have asked."

"No, I get it. You're curious. This isn't something that happens here. This town hasn't seen a murder in over twenty years."

"Wait, he was murdered?" My jaw drops, and I look over at Garnet, who is eavesdropping and lets out a small gasp, covering her mouth with both of her hands.

Rodger points his finger at me. "You didn't hear this from

me, so don't go telling a bunch of people. We don't need a panic," he looks around in either direction, checking to see if anyone is in audible distance, "but between you and me, it was a gruesome sight."

He looks off to the back of the bookstore, zoning out as if he's reliving the memory.

"I got the call when I was out this morning, just started my shift. They paged me, saying a guy found a dead body on the beach. So, I pull up in the parking lot of Breaker's and start walking out towards the ocean. It was pretty dark still. I couldn't find the man who called it in. So, I'm just out there walking around, wondering if it was a prank call, before I almost tripped over the guy. Sprawled out in the sand, like he was making snow angels, right there by the shore. I pulled a flashlight on him, and that's when I saw. He was as white as a ghost. Had a bullet hole, right in between his eyes," Rodger makes a gun with his index finger and thumb and holds it in between his eyes. He flicks down his thumb, like pulling a trigger, and says, "Execution style."

My palms are becoming sweaty. A rush of blood falls from my face and down my body. My mouth starts to water, as I try not to become sick.

"The tide just kept sweeping over his face. Blood was coming out of his head and washing out to the ocean. The waves were red. That's something I'll never get out of my head." His eyes remain glossed over, like he's deep in thought before looking back to me. The coloring of my face must be fading a few shades because he immediately apologizes. "Sorry.

You didn't want to hear all that."

I take a gulp of my watering mouth and look down at the counter, processing all what I just heard.

"It sounds like something out of a thriller novel." I awkwardly chuckle.

"Yeah it does, doesn't it?" He remains quiet for a second then purses his lips into a half smile, before clapping his hands together. "Welp, good seeing you kid. Keep up the writing. Got to get back out there. Us cops need their coffee and donuts, you know?"

I let out a half smile back. "Okay."

"Okay. See you around. And stay safe. I mean it." The undertone of worry in his voice was not reassuring. There is definitely more to this body being found than I initially thought.

Officer Macon grabs his order of coffees and bags of pastries off the counter from an extremely quiet Garnet and proceeds out the door. As soon as he drives off in his cruiser, she rushes over to my counter.

"Wow! Can you believe that? Like what the actual fuck." Garnet lifts up her thin arms and holds her hands to her temples, holding air in her cheeks and letting out a big puff. "I can't believe someone shot him execution style. Like, who does that? And why?"

"I have no idea. I feel bad for Officer Macon having to see that. I mean, can you imagine if you almost trip over a dead guy in the dark? That's terrifying."

"Yeah, he did not seem like himself. He was definitely

shaken up. His fingers were trembling when he picked up his bags."

I ask her, "Did you know that guy, Jim?"

She shakes her head. "I mean, I might have seen him at church on Sundays, but I didn't know him."

The air feels thick. Even in the chilly bookstore, it feels humid and stuffy, causing me to break out in a constant sweat. I can't tell if it's from the news or my hangover.

"That's so crazy," is the only response I can manage.

"Tiffany texted me and said Breaker's is closed for the day."

I wonder how long after I was there last night this occurred.

I try to picture the church youth group leader kneeling in the sand in front of a gun while the rain pours down and the lightning strikes into the sand.

I think again of the figure of Elizabeth walking around by the shore.

We were both out there. Both of us were on the beach around that time. What if we were the last ones out there before it happened?

I need to talk to Elizabeth, but I'm not even sure if I was imagining seeing her there or not. It was so late, and I was wasted. I want to believe it was only my imagination, but it felt so real, and as I reimagine it now, I know that it was. And I know she saw me, too. And right now, she is probably thinking about me. She is probably thinking about how her and I are the only ones who were there right before Jim was killed.

# Elizabeth Corey

**The pain behind my eyes feels like the lobotomy I've always needed.** Sharp stabbing of my corneas comes from the light seeping through the single-pane windows of my living room. I haven't had the chance to hang those damn curtains yet.

Blinking my eyelids open in the burning light, something dark pools on the floor beneath the couch I fell asleep on. This dark something trails across the living room and into the kitchen. Slowly, I lift the weight of my head, pressing my palms into my sockets as the pain thumps against them. The left socket feels wet and sticky. Pulling it away from my face, I discover a large, deep cut on my hand, dried and congealed. The pool on the floor beneath me and traced throughout the room is blood.

Managing to pull myself up halfway, my vision spins the room around me like I've been on one too many carnival rides. The real thrill ride was making my way through an entire big bottle of red wine last night. The empty bottle lies on the floor like a victim, not far from where I had lain my head.

I fall back to the couch cushion, cradling myself into a fetal position. My hand stings deeply, yet the pain in my head is paralyzing me from getting up. Suddenly, the bottom of my foot becomes damp when I realize it's being licked.

*Chico, my baby boy.*

I force open one eyelid and meet my eye with his. He stares back, positioned over me, wagging his tail with his jowls drooping heavily. He whimpers, and then when I don't move, he barks. I know he needs his breakfast and to go outside. It's time to get up. I must, for Chico.

The moment I shift my body to get up, Chico jumps from the couch and trots into the kitchen. He sits in the doorway, waiting patiently, like the good boy he is.

Supporting myself with random objects on my way into the kitchen, I see the floor is coated with more than a few measly drops of blood, but also a large traipsing of red paw prints. The crime scene is laid before me, leading from the lightly red prints by the doorway to the crimson mess below the sink. Inside the copper trough lies the evidence: a shattered wine glass. Thankfully, none of the glass was anywhere but inside the sink. The blood on Chico's paws was only from my leaking wound.

*I seriously need to switch to plastic.*

Carefully, with squinted eyesight, I remove the glass from the sink and wipe off Chico's paws with a wet dishcloth. Obliviously joyful, Chico's tail wags through the whole mess.

I take him out back to do his business and then fill up his bowl with kibble.

My hand desperately needs doctored but washing it and loosely wrapping it with a kitchen towel works for now. Calculating by the amount of blood on the floor and the weakness of my legs, I'm in need of replenishment.

I gather the eggs, butter and bread from the fridge, shoveling grounds into the coffee maker with no haste, wait for the pan to get hot and the toast to brown. I like it burnt.

*Black like my soul.*

Flipping eggs and scraping the butter onto the hard, charred, sourdough, I'm tempted by the idea of the knife in my hand and how easily it would puncture my skin. Not that I didn't already give myself quite the injury last night, but it was a failed attempt the moment I opened my eyes today, still breathing. I feel a scraping down my leg. Looking down at my feet is my little saving grace. He may be barely mentally there, but he's holding it all together for us. He's a gorgeous fluffball, with ice blue eyes and a brindle coat; my Native American Indian Dog, Chico.

"What would I do without you, my Chico baby? My handsome boy."

He looks up to me with large prying eyes.

"Your mommy is a mess this morning. What are we going to do?"

He tilts his head at my question as the room spins slightly.

"I know all you really want me for is eggs and you know you'll get them," I chuckle at the thought of being used by this creature for eggs, but he has to endure all of my problems. At least we are both using each other.

I place some of my eggs into Chico's bowl and he scarfs them down before I even get a chance to sit. My small corner table facing the beachside windows fills with warm light. Another hot and sunny Florida day makes for crap napping weather. It's nothing like the rainy days in the Pacific Northwest. But thinking of the rain only makes choking down this plate of food harder as I peer towards the ocean. I used to enjoy stormy weather. Now all it does is remind me that he's gone. The thunder sparks my imagination. Forces me to picture my own version of how tragic it must have been. The sea chopping up, the lightning flashing, seeing the waves crashing into his ship until they get so large they engulf him whole.

A warm tear falls down my cheek. This is the reason I began drinking last night. The same reason I drink every night and every day. I can't bear to picture the agony on his face, the helplessness in his eyes as he reaches out for me, calling my name, water filling his mouth and his lungs. A lump forms in my throat so large that it's not going back down. I run for the trash can and wretch the few bites of breakfast and bloody red pile right on top of the broken glass.

*Fucking merlot! I might as well have thrown the bottle out before I drank it.*

I hold my stomach as I painfully creep into the guest bathroom, swishing some mouthwash from beneath the sink. I try to rid the smell of bile from my mouth, but it still rests in my nose. The room spins as I grip onto the counter for dear life. I look in the mirror. A pathetic image of what I once was stares back at me. My hair has thinned, looking knotted and stringy. My eyeliner is smeared over puffy bags under my eyes that I can't seem to recover from. I lift my shirt to examine my visible rib cage and think about how different my body would've looked now if things were different. As much as I want to take a shower and freshen up, all I can do is make my way back to lying down.

I plop my body onto the purple velvet lounger away from the bloodied floor near the couch. It's my favorite piece of furniture in this house, an antique I reupholstered a lifetime ago. Once upon a time, in its original condition, may have lain a prima donna, a woman of status, dressed to the nines. As I lay here, a shriveled image of what I once was, I imagine my ladies-in-waiting by my side washing me with warm clothes, combing my hair, lacing up a fine corset for dinner, while telling me stories, preparing me to dine with my lover. On my back against the lounger, I rest my forearm across my head and let out a large sigh. Unfortunately, the ladies-in-waiting are not coming to bathe me or dress me or read me sonnets. *And my lover is dead.*

**I'm unsure of the time or how long I passed out for.** The only thing I am sure of is that the pain in my head is not as sharp as it was, but the pain in my hand is. Chico lies splayed out on the floor beneath me, basking in the sun coming from the windows. He'll sunbathe in the air conditioning, but he hates the Florida heat as much as I do. The air conditioner barely works with the poor insulation in the walls. The cool air comes in just as quickly as it goes out. The windows need replacing, just like almost everything else does in this god-forsaken home. The roof leaks, the toilet runs, the lights flicker at night, and you blow a breaker when more than one appliance is running at any given time. I used to be excited about all of the projects in this house. I used to be blinded by the old charm emerging from its rickety bones. "Like polishing a penny, it'll be good as new," Christian would say to me.

And it's still true. With enough money and elbow grease, this place could be immaculate. There is much to fall in love with a home from the early 1900s, such as the original wooden staircase with ornamented spindles, wooden-framed doorways, built-in shelving and pantries. There's an original fireplace, crown molding around all the ceilings, even an antique chandelier, and stained glass in the front door. The outside of the house definitely needs a new paint job. I often picture what it could look like when it's all finished. Our dream home.

It was a brilliant investment, if only he were around to help me fix it up. I can't do it alone. Sure, I was left with the money, but it all overwhelms me now. Ever since he left, I haven't had the drive to fix anything. Not even the simplest of things. I peer over to the paint cans resting in the corner of the room. The painting tarp is still spread out on the floor underneath the wall that I painted a small color swatch on, the week I moved in. The living room is pale blue, and the swatch is a deep navy.

Maybe I am just waiting, hoping, even though I know there is no point. He was supposed to come back. Christian wasn't supposed to die.

"Ugh!" I let out a frustrating groan and began to sob.

Chico jumps up and curls in my lap. The weight and warmth of his fur from sunbathing brings me comfort.

Between feeling sorry for myself and crying into Chico's thick mane, I realize I haven't seen my phone in a long time and that I am expecting an order today. Everything arrives by delivery now. I don't enjoy going to the store and socializing with the people of this island, with their colorfully dressed, turned-collar snobbery. I do leave the house occasionally to walk on the beach with Chico. Sometimes, I walk down to the beach bar to get drinks when I see that Aimsley's working, since she's the only nice islander I have met. She's very easy to talk to, but I'm sure it's just her job to listen and put up with me, just like Chico does. I can't call her a friend, but she might be the closest I have to one right now. I wondered if Aimsley was working at the bar tonight. Not that I'm in any condition to go, but some human interaction could be nice.

*But first, where is that damned phone?*

**"*You're such a lush, Liz,*" is what he would say to me.** I know he was worried about my consumption, but what else was I supposed to do while waiting out those long stints in between ports? How was I supposed to sober up after months of waiting for him to come back from the sea? I was upset with him from the moment he came home till the moment he left again. Never getting the time I thought we deserved. I loathed our time apart, dreading the wait, but we always made it through the long distance because our love was thick and stuck with me, as it still does. I guess that's what I get for loving a ship captain.

My throat burns from retching, feeling the acid creep up again at the thought of him.

*"You need to hydrate, Lizzy,"* he'd say.

*I know, I know.*

I consume a whole glass of water, gulping hard, while Chico follows me around the house like a shadow.

Not having any luck locating my phone in the couch cushions or in the kitchen, I pace about the living room and retrace my steps, all while clenching my wounded hand as it continues to sting deeply.

"Let's see," I say, placing my index finger to my mouth, tapping it, as if the gesture will help me remember.

*Yesterday... First, I let Chico out to potty in the backyard. Then, I came in to have a bite to eat. I made coffee and sipped it on the lounger. Then, I started my cross-stitch and cracked open the first bottle. Chico wanted to have his daily layout, so I took my drink to the balcony.*

I face the French doors out to the balcony when suddenly a loud "Clink! Clank! Clink, Clink!" sounded from the glass, along with shouting coming from the beach. As I crack the balcony door slightly, I hear a group of teenagers at the beach screeching as small objects are hurled over the dune, past my head and into my living room. I duck and see the porch floor is littered with broken shells.

"Witch! We know what you did!" one of them shouts.

Shocked and confused, I throw the doors open to yell back, but the objects stop coming, and the noises from the teenagers fall silent. They must have run off.

*Fucking ungrateful brats.*

I lean down to pick up shell pieces that scatter the deck and check the glass panes for any cracks. Luckily, they didn't do any damage. This house already has enough unfinished projects; I don't need another.

Peering over the balcony, I find it strange that the beach appears to be empty. Then I spot what looks like yellow caution tape strung up just north of the house. Several police cars are parked in the sand, with officers standing around. Off to the south, more caution tape is strung up.

Before giving this scene a thought, I notice a black rectangular-shaped object on the arm of my chair, lying in a puddle.

*Shit! No!*

I left my phone in the storm last night. Now soaking wet, I grab it quickly, trying to wipe the water off.

*Great! Now, how will I track my order? Smart, Elizabeth!*

Attempting to turn the phone on after blowing into the charging port several times, the screen remains black.

Ever since Christian left for his last trip at sea, it's been this way. One bad occurrence after another. It feels like I can't do any of this without him. He was always good at helping me keep my head on my shoulders. I can still feel his arms around them. I can still see the same big cheeky smile. One he wore the first time we met, and on the last day I saw him. Like he never had a worry in the world when he looked at me.

I met Christian in Portland. At the time, I was dipping my feet into the online dating pool. I didn't have much experience with it. I swiped right on people's profiles I probably shouldn't have. Like this twenty-something-year-old boy, who had a hot, grungy look and a cat named "Pippy". I can't even recall his name now, but I called him my Skater Boy. After we matched and chatted back and forth for a week, we agreed to meet for a date at a local dive bar. It was a warm summer night in Portland. The bar was past this hole-in-the-wall pizza joint across from the donut shop, underneath a large marquee sign. It must have been converted from an old theater. Inside was swanky and dark with red lighting. The bar was small, so I crammed in, taking a seat and checking my phone constantly as our meeting time began to pass. He seemed nice enough through our messages, but thinking back now, he was a total loser. I was young and naive, just ready for a possible hook-up or maybe a Skater Boy love story.

When he didn't show up, I was pretty upset. It must have been easily read on my face because the man next to me offered to buy me a drink. They didn't serve good wine, so I ordered a staple of mine. "An Old Fashioned?"

I twirled the large square cube around the glass and took a hefty gulp, letting the whiskey replace the burn I was feeling in my heart.

"Bad day?" the man asked.

"Not yet," I replied. I peered over sheepishly at a man saddled back into his barstool with one arm dangling over the backrest. His legs are propped up and open, facing me. I check him out from head to toe. His boat shoes are firmly placed on the stretchers of the chair, supporting strong thighs that peeked at me from beneath the hems of his shorts. A silver anchor pendant dangled from a chain in the center of his navy collared shirt, just below that big cheeky smile. His brown eyes and long, red, flowing hair had me instantly intrigued.

"Not yet?" He chuckled. "That's dark."

"Yeah, well, welcome to Portland. City of disappointments."

"Thanks. I actually just got in." He adjusted his posture to take a swig of his beer. He appeared to be relaxed and confident, but not cocky, merely comfortable in his own skin.

"I thought you looked out of place," I said.

Smirking at me, he says, "Oh, I can be any place."

He seemed to be enjoying my dry humor, as I was enjoying his sarcasm, so I figured I'd continue to entertain the conversation.

"Thanks for the drink. What are you drinking?" I gestured towards his beer.

"Irish stout. Now, I would have ordered a Tom Collins, but every time I order one, no one makes it right. Watch this." He waved his hand at the bartender, who walked over to us.

"What can I get ya?" the bartender asked.

"Yeah, can I get a Tom Collins, please?" he asked.

"Sure thing." The bartender turned around and started to make his drink.

"Ok, so it's the simplest drink." He presses his thumb and index finger together, checking off each ingredient, "Gin, lemon juice, simple syrup, club soda. But they always mess up the garnish. It's supposed to have a lemon slice and one maraschino cherry. Very simple, you'd think, but no one ever gets it right." As he finished his explanation, the bartender placed his drink in front of him and walked away.

I chuckled at the garnish, a lemon slice, but no cherry. "Well, that's unfortunate."

"Thank you." He responded sarcastically.

"Unfortunate that you're probably in the wrong bar for that."

"Oh, am I? Well, you'll have to show me the right place to go around here," he flirtatiously admits before swigging down the rest of his beer.

"Maybe I would take you up on that, if I wasn't already meeting a date," I say brazenly.

"Ouch. So, where is the lucky fella then?" He turns to look around the bar while I feel my cheeks start to redden.

*Who does this guy think he is?*

I looked at my phone again to check one last time to see if Skater Boy messaged me, but he hadn't. I shrugged my shoulders, knowing I'd been stood up. Just when embarrassment or disappointment may have settled over me, I felt an impulsive reflex in my brain when our eyes met. They glared into mine. His dark, devious eyes sparkled, like a demon attempting to infiltrate my soul, scratching to get in. Our connected stare lasted long enough that it might have made someone else uncomfortable, but I was hooked when his cheeky smile began to soften more into a grin.

When the staring didn't feel like it was going to stop, I blurted out, "What?"

He continued to look at me as his hand floated from the bar top and into my personal space, offering a formal shake, "Your name is?"

I hesitate, then offer up my hand to cup his and say, "Elizabeth."

"Elizabeth. Can I call you Lizzy?"

"Uh…" I was taken aback at his immediate nicknaming, but before I could oppose, he started talking again.

"Listen, Lizzy, you know it's his loss, right?" At this moment, I realized he hadn't let go of my hand. His hand was cupping mine, and he brought his other hand to hold it. I felt I should be mad at him for his forwardness, but I didn't retreat. His hands were large and soft, firm as they held onto mine, but his fingers were gentle as they caressed the back of my hand.

I couldn't tell if it was the drink I had downed or just that moment, but my head flooded with heat and fuzziness. My eyes moved. I looked into his eyes, and then down at our hands and back to his eyes again. He softly released his grasp and said, "Have you ever felt like you've always known someone you've just met?"

Feeling like I'd melted into my chair, I wondered if he pulled this on all the women he met. But, for whatever reason, there was a sense of familiarity with him. Something easy and comfortable.

I plucked the cherry from the bottom of my glass and splashed it into his.

"There. One perfect Tom Collins."

Thinking back on that moment now makes me miss him even more. We spent every day of that week together, until he had to leave for the sea. He was a captain only passing through. Although he told me it might be too hard on me with the distance, it didn't stop me. I fell in love and fell in love hard.

He told me he loved me the night before he had to go to the ship. Even though he said it first and begged me to say it back, I told him I wouldn't. Every time he left for the sea after that, I wouldn't tell him I loved him, because he had to come back to hear it.

I never told him I loved him before he left, because he was supposed to come back.

*You were supposed to come back.*

**My black phone screen finally lights up.** After unlocking it, a new notification pops up from my news app:

**Body Found at Painter's Beach**

Along with another notification from my local neighborhood app Vigil:

*Keep your eye out for a suspect. There's a murderer out there!*

My mind pictures the yellow crime scene tape on the beach.

I click on the notification for the Vigil app to find out more information. The post was trending at the top of the feed. With many likes, hearts and shocked-faced emojis, it reads:

**Mary Pearly, South Island**

*4 hours ago*

*Lock your doors tonight! The police are on the lookout for the murderer who took the life of our dear friend, Jim Crowley. Jim was a youth group leader for teens at The First Holy Church of Painter's Beach, a loving family man. Together, let's bring the perpetrator down quickly to give justice to his grieving family. Rest in Peace, Jim. Let's all say a prayer for him.*

Just reading the name *Mary Pearly* makes my fists clench, even though it pains me to do so. When moving to Painter's Beach from Portland, I had hoped to get away from news like this. I had hoped to become a part of a new art community. Being a resident artist of a town with the word "Painter's" in it seemed perfect. I had hoped to fit in here, and I might have, had it not been for Mary.

When I first moved to the island, Christian had assured me I would be a success. "Your art is amazing, you'll kill it in that small town," he would say. Unfortunately, he didn't make it here. And he wasn't able to find out that this island is full of dull, stuffy people who have no real sense of what good art is.

We couldn't close on this house in time before his last hitch, leaving Chico and me to make the cross-country journey on our own. We got into the car and drove all the way in my restored matte black 1969 Ford Mustang. The trip took us a week from coast to coast. We cruised slowly across the country, stopping at places along the way. We drove through mountains, desert and plains. The trip was extremely beautiful, inspiring a new sketchbook of ideas to work on for when we arrived at the new house, where I would make one of the rooms into my dream art studio.

I rolled the car windows down as we passed over the bridge to Painter's Beach. Chico stuck his head out of the window, and so did I, both of us smelling the ocean. The scent of salt, citrus and a not-so-pleasant smell of rotten eggs from the low tide filled our nostrils.

We pulled into the driveway of our new home. It looked just like the pictures, worn down and in need of some serious TLC. Luckily, the movers had delivered all our things before we arrived. Each room of the house was filled full of boxes and wrapped furniture.

The first thing I did was take a picture of Chico and me in front of the house to email to Christian, the only way we could communicate when he was on the ship. It was a step up from postage at least. I don't know how people did long-distance relationships during the pre-technology era.

I spent the first week unpacking my art studio. I was grateful to have a room specifically dedicated to all my textiles, needles, string and all the art pieces I've ever made. Finally, everything was all in one place and organized. I was so excited to have this space. I finally felt like my art career would take off soon.

I began working on a new art piece using some foraged items from around the house and property. I built a frame with small pine tree twigs I found in my backyard. Inside, I wove black and navy threads that intertwined and circled from the outside edges to the very center, where I stitched in a dead moth I found on the bathroom windowsill. I also added some small shells I found on a beach walk that had near-perfect holes in them to dangle from under the moth. At the time, the woven mandala that centered around the dead moth spoke to me as a new beginning. It was a representation of working with what I was given, trying to make this new house and this new town into a beautiful new life. However, something about the piece still felt dark. I wonder now if I was doomed from the start. A new beginning I never wanted. *Did I will this?*

In the spirit, I filled out an online application to be a vendor in the Painter's Art Alliance's weekly Sunday Art Market. I photographed each one of my art pieces, ordered a market tent and some display tables while I waited patiently for a response. I placed my little oddities made from collected pieces of bone and the wings of butterflies into miniature shadow boxes. Some weavings I framed, others I tied up with string to be made as wall hangings.

When a week went by without a reply to my application, I thought there must have been a mistake. Maybe their website listed the wrong email. Maybe it was best to meet in person first. As much as it killed my introverted soul, I worked up the courage to go to the Painter's Art Alliance and apply in person. I thought it would be beneficial anyway to make the in-person connection, but as soon as I stepped foot in the door, I felt instantly uncomfortable. Mainly because the woman at the front counter gave me an up-and-down judgmental look. I guess she had never seen someone who wore all black and was covered in tattoos, but in Portland, it's totally normal. After I peered around the front desk, into the gallery, the artwork made me just as uncomfortable. I noticed all the beach scenes, the seabirds and the sailboat paintings hung decoratively. Everything was painted in pastel colors. Blown glass vases in the shape of fish sat atop podiums. Jewelry hung from busts, daintily adorned with seashells and bright jewels. The only textile piece was hung on the back wall. It was felted into the shape of a sea turtle, of greens, blues and silver fibers. Everything in the gallery felt like something hanging from a grandmother's beach house. I had expected more variety.

When I introduced myself and asked if I could talk with someone about being in the markets, the lady at the counter stuck her nose up at me and told me they weren't accepting more vendors. She didn't even offer to keep a copy of my application or that they would let me know if a space became available. I asked her if there was anyone else I could reach out to. The lady gave me the email address of the Board of Directors President, who happened to be Mary Pearly.

Although I was feeling discouraged from my experience at the gallery, I tried not to let it bring me down. I still had hopes. Maybe the lady at the desk was having a bad day. Maybe if I reached out to the person in charge, they would be more receptive or even helpful. I typed an email with a copy of my application and portfolio to Mary Pearly, letting her know I had applied online and asking if she would consider me for any art opportunities in the future. While I waited to hear back, I typed my love an email to let him know I had moved in safely and started to settle. I asked him what he thought if I painted the kitchen walls hunter green. I didn't mention my experience at the gallery. I didn't want him to worry. We were so excited to move here with the opportunity to fix up an old house and to be part of a new community. A new life of our own together.

When I finally received an email back days later, Mary wasn't any more helpful than the lady at the desk. And worse, she completely rejected my artwork, commenting that the content of my art was not appropriate according to their association standards. My assumption was that the content of my art was full of oddities and dark colors instead of kitschy beach themes and pastels, so in their eyes, it wasn't a good fit.

I replied to her email with some rather unsavory words:

*Mary Pearly,*

*Thank you so much for finally responding to my application to show in your Sunday Art Market. However, I don't appreciate your immediate dismissal of the content of my artwork. I would have hoped there would be more consideration and inclusion of artists within this community. It has made me feel extremely disappointed and unwelcome as a new resident artist on the island. But, as an artist, I will not choose to lower my tastes to meet the tacky standard for what you consider to be fine art. Sorry if you can't appreciate anything that doesn't look like my grandmother threw up all over my living room.*

*Sincerely,*

*Elizabeth Corey*

After hitting send on the email, I felt a brief second of regret. But besides the opinionated comment about the beach art barf, the rest I felt was appropriate in my own defense. I was offended. I was hurt. And seeing her name on the neighborhood app brings all of those feelings flooding back.

Unfortunately, even if I were accepted into the art markets, I'd have been too drunk to make art. Wine's been my best friend ever since the loss of my love. I attempted a cross-stitch piece last night, but after picking it up off the living room floor next to the couch, I know it's problematic. The wooden circle hoop contains woven lettering reading *"Dead Inside"* surrounded by a skull and roses. Even though the context feels appropriate to me, potential customers might feel it's a bit too early for Halloween décor.

Although my art experience thus far has been a disappointment and I find Mary Pearly repulsive, I still moved specifically to Painter's Beach for a reason. Yes, the summer Florida heat is excruciating, and most of the people here suck, but I still love the sounds of the waves, the smell of the ocean air, drinking at the little beach bar and this old rickety house. And there is nothing that I love more than watching the moon rise over the ocean. Back in Portland, you had the chance to see sunsets if you drove out to the beach, and you were lucky enough to be there on a day it wasn't overcast. But the main reason we moved here was to be close to my mother.

I thought it would be smart to live near her when we decided to have a family. She could help me raise a child when my love was away on the ship. Regardless of the situation she put me in as a child, leaving me with pop, things were different now. There was no way I could raise a child around my father, *the skunk-bit*. Or as my mother refers to him now as *"the drunken bastard"*. I can thank him for passing down his alcoholic traits, but he wasn't always like that. When my mother gave me up, I moved across the country with him. My father had almost an excitement in his soul. He tried to turn a terrible situation into an adventure. Just pop and his little girl, surviving out in the mountains. We would camp and hike, take long scenic drives, and stop in small towns to explore haunted locations. He was actually really fun back then, but I did start to notice a progression in his drinking. He seemed down on his luck in finding a partner. Instead of trying, he kind of just gave up and married the bottle instead. It was hard to leave him behind. Especially now, knowing the purpose of this move ended up being all for nothing.

*Speak of the devil.*

My mother's name came across my phone screen. I hesitate to pick up her call at first. It's already been a weird day. I'm not sure I can manage her, too. I look at Chico, who stares at me like he's telling me I should pick up.

"Hello?" I answer the call.

"Hey, honey. Are you okay?" She sounds panicked.

"Yeah, why?" I reply.

"Did you not hear the news? Someone was murdered on the beach right by your house." Before I can answer, she continues, "Have you been out of bed today? Have you eaten? You know it's almost dinner time."

"Yes, Mom. I'm fine. I just heard the news. I was getting ready to check on my grocery delivery, actually." I open the grocery delivery app and look for the status of my order.

"Shit!" The app informs me that the order was delivered two hours ago. It must have been delivered while I was napping.

"What? What's the matter?" Mother hastily questions me.

"Nothing, Mom. Will you chill out? I just need to go pick up my order. It's been sitting at the front door, I guess." I slowly walk over to the front door, still weak, and my palm pulsing. Chico follows closely.

"I don't understand why you don't just go out to the store yourself."

"Because you know I don't like going to the store," I reply.

As soon as I grip my good hand around the front door handle to open it, I am startled by a loud knocking on the door from the other side. Chico begins to bark, alerting me, even though I clearly know someone is there, seeing a figure blocking the light from coming through the stained glass.

"Hold on, Mom. There's someone knocking."

"What? Who? Be careful. Don't open it to strangers!" she demands as I let go of the handle and hush Chico to stop barking.

I tap my pointed nail onto the small metal shade and move

it to the side, peering into the peephole where I see a man who begins aggressively knocking on the door again.

Chico barks loudly.

"Mom, I gotta go. It's a cop."

## Aimsley August

**I'm still not ready to go home and face Brooke.** She never texted me back. There's no indication that she wants to talk about last night or that she wants to see me when I get off work.

My day shift finally comes to an end. Garnet shouts, "Catch ya later!" and jogs out the front door of the bookstore. I flip over the *"We're Closed"* sign and turn the lock behind her. As I make my way to the back of the store, I dim the display lights and turn off the rest, when my pocket buzzes. It's a text from Jada:

Wine night?

A feeling of relief washes over me. Jada's providing me with an excuse to stay away from the apartment. Still receiving the silent treatment from Brooke feels like a ticking time bomb I want to avoid. I reply to Jada:

*Read my mind. Just got off. Be there soon.*

The drive off the island to Jada's is not too far, except for during dinner traffic. On my skateboard, it will take about the same amount of time. I skate out of downtown and onto the main road off the island. The trek up the bridge can be long. It's easiest to walk up, then once I reach the top, I can cruise my board all the way down the other side of the bridge to her house.

I take the first right after crossing the river. She lives on a hidden drive that winds down to the marsh's edge. Her quaint wooden house sits tucked back underneath large oak trees covered in Spanish moss. It's an old 1800s bungalow painted white with burnt orange columns and teal window frames and ornamented with eclectic signs and statues. I jump off my board as the paved road ends at her gravel driveway and walk the rest of the way up to her door. As I knock, her doormat reads *"Hope You Brought Wine & Catnip!"*

Jada opens the door for me in her overalls that are adorned with specks of wood stain.

She shouts, "Hey! Come on in!"

Her ash brown hair is tied up in a bun that bobs from side to side as she walks into the kitchen. Indie music blares from inside.

Oscar, her fluffy grey cat, purrs against the side of my leg as she takes a wine glass down from her cabinet, pouring me the end of her bottle.

"What up, girl? Am I in time for happy hour? I need that

hair of the dog right about now."

"Same! I cracked this open a while ago, so you made it just in time. I was getting ready to watch the sunset on the lanai."

"I'm glad you messaged me when you did. I was so ready to be done with my shift today. It was brutal," I replied.

"Yeah, I bet, after last night. Spill the tea!" Jada gives me a hard look while leaning over the kitchen island, picking at a charcuterie board of meats, cheeses, olives and crackers. "Girl dinner!" She winks at me and slides the food closer to me.

Dressing a cracker with Gouda cheese, I start to feel the first sips of wine warm me into the conversation about Brooke that I knew was to be had. Jada always has my back when it comes to my Brooke troubles, but not without the usual grain of salt.

"Let's just say I was happy to come hang out over here tonight because I'm not sure where Brooke and I stand after last night."

Jada chews through a slice of prosciutto as she responds, "She's always pulling this shit on you. And I'm sorry, but it's not okay, gaslighting you about her hanging with those regulars from the bar. I don't like it. You deserve better."

Still defending Brooke, I explain, "I really think she just had too much to drink. I'm sure everything will chill out."

"Yeah, but Aimsley, this is repetitive behavior. She will only continue to do it."

I know she is right in some way. However, it's hard to hear it or to picture a solution. Plus, there is something else on my mind I really want to talk to her about, and I think she reads it in my body language.

"Let's go out to the porch. I want to show you some of the new stuff I made for the market tomorrow. Plus, we have to take in the beautiful view before my house gets blown away." Jada laughs. Although it's a joke, I can hear worry at the end of her words.

"Oh, the hurricane. I'm sure it'll be fine," I assure her.

"You Floridians and your lack of concern for storms bewilders me."

Walking back through the living room, she opens the French doors to the porch that overlooks the marsh that almost tickles the house with salt grass and tall reeds. They frill in the soft breeze, framing the edge of the creek running parallel to the river where a small sailboat passes under the bridge. The water reflects the pink sky of billowing clouds, as the burning orange sun starts to tuck behind the line of cypress trees on the other side of the river. A great blue heron picks on critters in the low tide. I sit in a wooden rocking chair under the string of Edison lights dangling from the rafters. Jada sits in the rocking chair beside me.

"You know they're saying it's coming this way. It's upgraded to a category two now, and the path is still coming right for us." Jada sounds worried.

Unsure if I should worry too, all I can say is, "I know, but even when it seems like they're coming here, they turn away at the last minute."

"Well, either way, I'll be doing some prep tomorrow if it's still coming this way."

I hate to admit that she's being a total outie, but this is

exactly what they do whenever it's hurricane season. Everyone panics and makes a huge deal of it. In all the years I've lived here, I've never prepped for a storm. Sure, we keep some water around and some perishable food, maybe a few candles, but nothing more.

Jada hands me a large, round cut of wood and says, "So, anyway, this is what I'm working on. It's inspired by my time out West."

I hold up the piece of wood, examining the burned image: a natural stone archway with a female figure laid out in the middle between a pair of cacti. The cacti have three large flowers, painted pink and dusted with gold leaf.

"The desert landscape was so inspiring, and I was particularly drawn to the saguaros there. Did you know their flowers only bloom for twenty-four hours?" she asks.

"Wow, this is awesome! No, I've never been out west before. Hell, I've barely left the island."

"Well, we need to get you away from this little island life sometime. There's a whole other world out there, you know?"

She pulls out her wood-burning tool. The end of the wand-like tool sizzles as she presses it into a fresh square cut of basswood. I watch in awe, smelling it smolder as the image of a rattlesnake comes into view with each passing stroke.

"I don't know how you do it, but your artwork always amazes me," I compliment her.

"Aw, thanks. Try telling that to Mary." She laughs in disgust and continues explaining, "She's giving me a hard time at the gallery. Says she wants my pieces, but when I showed her my western-inspired stuff, she says she has to think about it." Jada gestures quotation marks with her fingers.

"Mary?" I ask.

"Yeah, Mary Pearly. She's the head of the Painter's Art Alliance. Just because I didn't bring her anything with a fucking pelican on it, it's not good enough. It's such bullshit, but whatever. I think the people at the markets will buy them as long as they don't have the same stick up their asses."

"You wouldn't believe, but Mary was at the bookstore this morning, going on about that murder."

"Oh, really? Yeah, I heard about that on the news. What did she have to say about it?"

"Well, before shoving her business card at me, she was asking questions and saying he was murdered and went on and on about how she was close to the family." I pull the business card from my pocket and hand it to Jada.

Jada reads it and chuckles after her next sip, almost snorting her wine from her nose. "Yep, yep. That sounds about right. Miss know-it-all."

Jada rests her burning tool onto its holder, taking a big drink of her wine.

"Officer Macon also came into the bookstore this morning and was telling me all about the crime scene. It was pretty messed up." I tap my foot anxiously against the porch floor, thinking about his gruesome description, then back out to the sun that disappears suddenly beneath the line of cypress trees.

"It's funny you mentioned Mary, though. I didn't say anything when she was asking me questions, but she made me think about it. That I was there."

"Yeah, we were all on the beach last night. I think we were lucky nothing happened to us."

"No, but I mean I was like right there, around the same time they said it happened on the news."

"Really? Did you tell Officer Macon that?"

"No, I didn't mention it. You're the first person I've told. You know that woman, the one who moved in not long ago in that old run-down beach house?"

"Do you mean the weird one that always sits on her porch with her huge dog?"

I roll my eyes and say, "I was up over by her house and saw her walking to the ocean. But it started to storm pretty badly, so I left."

"Whoa, do you think she had something to do with it?" She leans towards me.

I gulp down a large lump in my throat, "I wouldn't know. I couldn't tell. It just creeps me out that I was there, right before."

I let out a big sigh, rocking back into my chair, my wine glass now empty. "You got some more wine?"

"Do I have more wine?" She tosses her head back in laughter. "Of course I do. I'll get us more." Jada walks into the kitchen and shouts, "So what if you're the only one who saw that lady out there, right before she killed him?"

"I really don't think Elizabeth had anything to do with it. She walks her dog on the beach at night all the time." I scoffed.

Jada comes back to the porch with full wine glasses in hand.

"Wait, how do you know that?"

"Well, I see her. She comes into the bar; she's kind of my regular."

"Oh, okay." She hands me the glass of wine, and I take another sip.

"Thanks." I want to tell Jada that I have been feeling curious about Elizabeth. I want to spill my feelings of intrigue and attraction to her, but I am afraid she might not take it well. And it doesn't feel like the right timing, but the wine has loosened me up quite a bit. "Yeah, she seems really interesting, not like most of the people on the island."

Jada picks up on my energy right away. "Oh, my god. Are you crushing on her?"

"No! I mean, not really. I'm just curious about her."

Jada gives me a sly smile, then straightens up before saying, "I know you and Brooke got in a fight, so maybe your mind is wandering. But don't forget."

"Forget what?" I am genuinely curious as to what I am forgetting.

"The ring? Or did you give up on the proposal?" She crosses her arms and sits back in her chair. Waiting for me to explain.

*Of course, I didn't forget.*

How could I? Do I have reservations now? Sure. It's not the only fight we've had, giving me reservations; it's a culmination of things.

Although I plan to pop the question soon to Brooke, I guess you could say I'm not thrilled at the idea of becoming wed into the Duncan family, especially after our dinner over there last week.

My mind wanders, recalling it. I can still feel the tension as I was sitting in their dining room. The simmer began with Brooke's mom, Mrs. Catherine, deciding to tell us about her trip to the   grocery store that day. I was instantly put off by her tone when she said to me, "I met the nicest lesbian couple at the store today. They offered to let me take the very last pork roast. I wonder if you two know them. Well, wait, I never caught their names. Anyway, can you believe this was the last roast they had? How lucky is that?"

*Yeah, because all lesbians know each other.*

A large eye roll was what I wanted to do, but I smiled and nodded, "Oh yeah, Brooke, I wonder if that was uh, what were their names, you know that other lesbian couple we know?" Brooke kicked me under the table for the smart-ass remark I had made. I widened my eyes and raised my brow in contest, but she ignored me and turned to her father.

"Daddy, how's work?" Brooke asked.

Duncan looked up from his meal, shoveling in a mouthful of pork.

"Oh, Brookie," he smacked his lips and swallowed, "you know my job can be very stressful, but this week it's been quiet. Maybe a little too quiet." He forked in a few more mouthfuls, chewing on a thought. "Just dealing with the same ol' drug head townies. I'm sure you know them, Aimsley. Scott and Tommy. Didn't you use to hang around them?"

The comment was a jab at my character, which I didn't feel I deserved. I stewed, but remained calm, waiting for Brooke to have my back.

"Those guys are losers, Dad. Aimsley doesn't know them," she assured.

"Oh, really? Then who'd you get that little sack from?" He clamped his lips together, referring to the time I got busted for a minuscule amount of pot last summer. I glared in his direction, biting my tongue as a smirk crept on the side of my face.

"Oh my god, Dad! Will you drop that already? It was only a small amount."

He threw up his finger and pointed it aggressively in my direction, the same finger he had just used to pick pork from his teeth. "Yeah, well, I don't appreciate my daughter hanging around a bunch of drug bags. Because that small amount turns into a bigger amount. And sometimes marijuana turns into a small amount of heroin, cocaine, and methamphetamines."

"It's just pot, Dad," Brooke exclaimed.

"Just pot?" He rose slightly off the seat of his chair and leaned into the argument. "Marijuana is a gateway drug. You think I don't know what happens? I've seen it. You'd better remember, Brookie, I'm the Chief of this town. I know what happens."

The room became silent and extremely awkward as I heated like a kettle, ready to scream. Duncan's cell phone started ringing as he excused himself to take the call in the other room.

"Officer Duncan," he answered.

Mrs. Catherine only deflected from the tension, asking us, "Who wants pie? Key lime?"

That dinner had been on my mind all week. I felt Brooke could have had my back more, but her dad is also an asshole, so maybe she couldn't have done anything. It's hard to imagine him being my future father-in-law.

I tell Jada about the dinner, and she agrees with me that he is, in fact, an asshole, but also that I shouldn't be concerning myself with Elizabeth.

"She seems like trouble to me. Even if I think Brooke is being deceitful to you, it doesn't mean you should stoop to her level. At that point, you're both just being toxic."

"Yeah, you're right." I agree, but deep down, I know I cannot get Elizabeth out of my head. Maybe I don't want to. Maybe this whole proposal is a bad idea.

Checking my phone, I see I finally received a text from Brooke. She mentions she's staying at her parents' house tonight, but doesn't offer up more than that.

"Hey, is it cool if I crash here tonight? Brooke's over at her parents," I ask Jada.

"Of course. I'd hate for you to be at home by yourself tonight. There is technically a murderer on the loose." We laugh at the dark joke. I do feel more comfortable, knowing I won't be home alone if there is still a murderer out there.

I think about last night as I fade out to the sounds of music and birds chirping as the sky begins to darken. trying to recall what it is I really saw.

As I try to recall what it is I really saw, I pull out my notebook from my backpack and write the next line:

*The shy one followed close behind the dark figure, with caution and curiosity, afraid she'd consume her whole.*

# Elizabeth Corey

**Tightly bracing Chico's collar with my uncut hand, I open the front door just a crack.**

A police officer speaks, "Ma'am. I'm Officer Flint with the Painter's Beach Police Department. If you have a moment, I have a couple of questions. Can I come in?" He turns a sour lip at Chico, who's barking viciously. Looking back over my shoulder, the mess of bloody dog prints paints the floor.

"Uhm, hold on just a moment," I shout, closing the door on him. Instead of trying to clean up, I corral Chico into the downstairs bathroom and try my best to wipe the smear of eyeliner from under my eyes. I unwrap the kitchen towel from my wounded hand. It's no longer bleeding, so I conceal it beneath my crossed arms.

"Hello?" The officer shouts, "Open up!"

I yell back to assure him I am coming, hurrying my frail aching body through the cracked door and quickly shutting it behind me. The sun is scorching and bright on my porch. I wince my eyes.

The officer looks me up and down as I say, "Sorry, you've just caught me waking up from a nap. I'd invite you in but I'm renovating. The house is a mess."

Surely, he had hoped to get out of the heat, but I wasn't letting him in. No way.

"This will only take a second," he states.

"Okay, what's this about?"

"I'm sure you have heard the news. There was an incident on the beach last night, in close proximity to your home."

"Uhm, yeah. I did see the news on my phone a little bit ago."

"Right, so I am surveying the neighborhood for any possible information that could help us."

I nod in agreement, wanting this to be over before it began.

"Did you happen to hear or see anything out of the ordinary between the early hours of three to five o'clock this morning?"

All I can recall from early this morning was that I was blackout drunk. Suddenly, it hits me like a wall of bricks. I do remember something. I remember walking out onto the beach. It was storming, and I saw someone. I saw the bartender. Aimsley. The memory comes to me like a quick flash, blurry and jumbled. I can't be so sure of what I'm recalling with confidence to tell the officer. I'm not even sure why I was out there or what I was doing. Maybe I had taken Chico out to potty.

"Ma'am?" Officer Flint rests his hands at his hips.

"Sorry. No, I don't remember seeing or hearing anything. I do remember it was storming pretty badly, but I was most likely sleeping."

His eyes flick down to the pile of groceries outside the door.

Pointing at them, I say, "I have to bring these inside before they go bad."

He pinches his nostrils at the rotten smell, then looks down at my side, at my hand. Quickly, I tuck it back under my arm.

"What happened there, to your hand?"

"Oh. It's nothing. Like I said, I've been renovating?"

He begins writing things down in a small notepad.

"So, you weren't on the beach at that time?"

"No," I say sternly.

"Alright and what is your name?"

"Elizabeth. Elizabeth Corey."

He scribbles more onto his notepad and asks, "You just moved in here, didn't you?"

"Yes, actually. A few months ago."

The officer huffs and then asks, "Does anyone else reside in the residence? Can someone confirm where you were last night."

"No, it's just me and Chico."

He looks up from his notepad. "Chico?"

"Oh, sorry, my dog, his name is..."

He scoffs and cuts me off mid-sentence. "Might want to keep a tighter leash on that animal. If he had come after me, I'd have the right to shoot it."

My mouth drops, and my eyebrows furrow. My fingernails grip my crossed arms to hold back from bursting. All I want is for him to get the hell off my porch.

"Will that be all?" I snap.

"For now, Elizabeth Corey." He folds up his notepad and sticks it in his chest pocket. "It'll be in your best interest to have someone confirm your whereabouts last night. You can have them call into the office or stop by the station."

I slam the door shut before he has a chance to exit the porch.

*What a heartless piece of shit.*

I give Chico lots of pets after I release him from the bathroom. How could that officer say that about him? People judge him for his size and bark, but he's a sweetheart and is only doing his job to protect me from an intruder. He probably smelled the bad vibes emitting from that officer. This whole town needs a good smudging.

My phone buzzes in my pocket. Once again, my mother is calling. Her voice in panic, "What happened? What is going on over there?"

"Everything's fine. The officer just wanted to know if I saw or heard anything last night."

"Oh no! This is serious. I think I should come over there and stay the night."

"What? No. I'm fine, Mom." I've already had as much social interaction as I want today.

"Let me come over at least and make you some dinner."

It wasn't a bad idea. My entire grocery order needed to be pitched from sitting out in the heat for two hours. It's a nice gesture, but I can't help but feel she has an agenda. My mother is not the kind to just pop in and make dinner unless she wants to lecture me or gossip about island drama. With hesitation, I agree, but tell her I need some time to take a shower and clean up.

I fill a mop bucket with clean water and soap, ringing the mop and then smearing it over the bloodied floors. The labor is causing me to feel lightheaded again from lack of food in my stomach. The red-stained water sloshes in the bucket when I imagine it: a body, laid in the tide, bloody water rushing from his head, mixing into the waves. My sight starts to twinkle and fade to black. On the verge of passing out, I manage to steady myself until the twinkling in my sight stops.

What was Aimsley doing outside of my house last night? She's always on the beach, but wandering around at those hours in the morning seems strange. I thought I was the only one who did that. I wonder for a second if she's been stalking me. Two times outside of my house yesterday could be a coincidence, but it is a small island. I can't rule that out.

I need to gather more information about what happened last night so I can clear my head of all of this. I'd check to see if she was at the beach bar tonight, but I'm too weak, too hungover and in desperate need of food. I've decided that I am grateful to my mother for offering to make me dinner despite whatever her underlying intentions may be. I don't think I'd have the strength to cook anything myself at this point. If I don't get any food in me soon, I may shrivel to nothing.

I finish mopping and bring the trash outside to throw away the spoiled groceries from the porch and the trash containing the broken glass vomit from the kitchen. The smell of the groceries going bad is testing my gag reflexes. I cup my hand over my nose and hurry down the porch to the outdoor trash bins sitting next to the mailbox. As I toss the bag into the bin and let the lid slam back down, I hear a murmuring. In the street, a handful of neighbors are gathered around a golf cart, all looking in my direction. A few of them have their hands on their hips, and others lean in to whisper with one another. I run back into the house to observe them through the peephole. One of them points directly at my house. The group shuffles around, getting back onto the golf cart before petering out down the street.

What a bunch of nosey old bags.

Between the clearly nosy neighbors, the rude ass police officer and the teens throwing shells at my windows, I am beginning to think everyone assumes something of me that I don't know about. Remembering the words they yelled at me, "Witch! We know what you did." Is that what they think of me? A witch? What could they possibly have on me? I didn't do anything. Maybe they are picking on me because I'm new to the island. Maybe they think I'm a devil-worshipping infestation trying to blight their holy Margaritaville lives.

*Ha! Let them.*

I don't want anything to do with anyone on this island anymore.

Has Aimsley told people she saw me at the beach last night? Is someone I thought to be a friend, really just as soulless and full of themselves, like every other person on this island? I don't want to believe it, but then again, there have been more surprising things that have happened in my life.

**Chico follows me down the stairs.** The back door lets out underneath the stilts of the house. When I open it, he darts out like a participant in a greyhound race to do his business. The backyard has a small, fenced area between the house and the sand dune. It's nice and private, out of view of any unwanted attention, but unfortunately, not free from children chucking objects. There's an old, weathered hammock hung from the stilts and a rusty fire pit with chairs. Weeds are slowly consuming objects in the yard. It's impossible to see the brick walkway and an old stone fountain that I had hoped to restore. The tall pine trees give enough shade that a garden was hopefully going to be in my future plans, but looking at it all now overwhelms me.

I call out for Chico to come inside, desperately needing to shower before my mother shows up. He doesn't come right away, and I can't see him, so I call out to him again.

"Chico!"

I strategically step through the thick weeds in the yard, trying not to imagine what bug or snake may be hiding underneath them. Sand sprays up into the air from behind a pine tree.

"Chico, come! Stop digging and come here!"

He's not listening to my commands, forcing me to investigate. Maybe he's caught the smell of a lurking creature from under all the weeds. "Chico! Stop! What are you digging for?"

I pull back on his collar, the hole surprisingly deep in such a short time. He tries to lurch for the hole again but finally trots off. Looking into the sandy hole, I see something black peeking out of the bottom.

*What has Chico found?*

Maybe a large fossil. A hidden megalodon tooth or a piece of an old pirate ship? Whatever it is, it's sort of shiny and doesn't appear to belong with the coarse sand around it. I lean down closer for a look, poking it with a stick. It feels hard, like metal. I dig around it a little bit like an archeologist. I must preserve my treasured finding. I curve the stick around an oval with a small opening.

"Wait, is that a..."

I look down in shock at what lies in the hole before me. In the center of the oval is a trigger.

*A gun?*

It's not just any gun. I recognize it. My brain pictures the locked gun case under my bed.

*How did this get here? Why is it here?*

I don't remember much about last night. First, I find out someone was murdered on the beach, and now I find my gun in the backyard.

*Could I have...?*

"Elizabeth?"

I feel the vertebrae in my neck contorting. My teeth clinch into themselves as my skull thrashes upwards from being startled. From the balcony above is my mother. I must have forgotten to lock the front door after taking the garbage out.

"Damn it, Mom!"

"What are you doing down there? I've been knocking."

I walk out from behind the tree.

"Sorry, I had to let Chico out."

"Chico, my good boy! How's my grand doggy!" Chico whines, looking up to the balcony. He always gets excited when his grandma comes over. She makes her way back inside after shouting, "Come help me get these groceries."

My hands are trembling. My knees feel weak. I hastily kick sand into the hole and try to take a mental picture of its location so I can remember where it is before I rush back inside. I run down the hallway and up the stairs before my mother sees me.

Chico chases behind me, thinking we're playing a game. I turn the lock on my bedroom door and dive under the bed. The black box sits back in shadow. I pull out the gun case, punch in the code and lift the latch to reveal its contents. It's empty. My heart stops. My breath stops. The gears in my mind begin to turn, picking up speed like a belt sander.

My mother knocks on the door, "Elizabeth? Are you alright?"

I inhale a deep breath, exhaling slowly. I don't want her to worry or suspect anything. She can't know about this. Another deep breath. I speak into the closed door, "Yeah, Mom. I'm fine. You got here so fast. I still need to shower."

There is a silent pause. I can hear her grip release from the door handle. "Okay, honey. I'm making your favorite. Fettuccine Alfredo! So, hurry up!" Her footsteps disappear down the stairs.

I wonder if she's on to me. Wonder if she knows there's something off, and that's why she's here. Acting overly nice to me. Making my favorite meal. Then, I remember she has a reason to be worried about me. I look out the window, facing the backyard. I can see the tree where I know down in a hole lies the gun behind it. Then, I look out at the ocean. The waves gently lapped the shore. It's more than this. It's losing my love. Losing Christian. Losing everything. My complete lack of motivation or concern for my life and my drinking. Then this murder. She's just concerned for me. Isn't that how mothers are supposed to feel for their daughters? Sure, but I can't help but think she's here for another reason. She doesn't want me to embarrass her or have me taint her reputation in her perfect little island town, where she's become quite the socialite. If she knew what I found in the backyard. But she won't. No one will. I just have to get through this dinner, and I'll get the gun, I'll dispose of it. I never liked the thing anyway. I always told Christian they seemed like more trouble than anything. He's always had guns and wanted me to be able to protect myself. I wonder what I'd done with it. How it ended up in the backyard. The thought is too large to ponder.

I focus on the task at hand, peeling off my dirty clothes. I haven't had the energy or interest to take a shower or change clothes in a while. Who am I doing it for anyway? If my love were here, I would be all cleaned up. But without him or any friends to hang out with, there's no one to see and nowhere to be. I can't justify the reason for taking a shower. Sure, I know I do feel better after one, and I always think I need to do it more often. It's just hard. I've been in a dark place for so long now. This is just the way it's been.

Chico comes into the bathroom and curls up on the mat beneath my feet. I kneel down and take a second to pet his fur. I grab hold of his fluffy, warm body to pout into. He nuzzles me in return. With my anxiety high and my mind racing, I step into the hot shower. The water stings my skin in a comforting way.

As I grab the bar of soap and circle it in my palm, creating suds, I think of my love. We would always take showers together. If I were having an especially rough day, he would step in with me, testing the water temperature, knowing how warm I liked it. He would suds up the soap and run his hands over my body, washing me gently. He made me feel loved and comfortable. Each passing of the soap over my skin, I think of his large hands gliding across my chest. Then he would kneel to wash my feet and up my thighs, all while I was watching him. I'd run my fingers through his hair, feeling like the luckiest girl. When he was done washing me, there was no escape from his grasp, or his hard body against mine, and his soft kisses on my neck. The thought of him is still on the tip of my tongue. I still can't believe he is gone. It feels impossible. I let out a soft moan, and tears come from my eyes, burning my face. Everything feels so incredibly messed up right now.

*Why me?*

I shampoo my tangled hair through sobbing and pulling small clumps from my head, knowing my hair is thinning. The stress is killing me, and now surely it will only get worse. I'll be bald before I know it. I have to get that gun. I have to get rid of it no matter what.

*What have I done?*

I imagine the man standing on the beach, facing the tide. I can feel the gun in my hand and my finger on the trigger, lifting the weight of the barrel, aiming at his head. My vision becomes starry, watching the man fall into the water. The shower water swirls beneath my feet, red from the cut on my hand opening up again. Red like the tide.

*I killed a man.*

Could I really be capable of doing something like that? Have I completely lost my mind?

I know I blacked out last night, but I don't think I could ever do something like that... murder someone, kill someone. Right now, I'm scared of myself. The blank frames of time in my memory terrify me. And I have no one to tell, no one to ask. I'm the only one who knows the truth, but I can't remember anything. All I can do right now is finish this shower, get dressed and face my mother. I need so desperately to eat something.

I get out of the shower and dry off with a towel. I comb my hair out some more and throw on a black cotton dress, trying to appear somewhat put together. From under the bathroom sink, I take out my first aid kit to bandage up the cut on my hand as best I can. There's no avoiding the conversation about this; it's too obvious, but I think I can blame it on unpacking. Anything to avoid my mother knowing the true depth of my despair. I don't want that kind of attention from her; she'll never leave me alone.

As I walk into the kitchen, Chico runs up to my mother, who is in full chef mode. She's wearing an apron she found in my pantry over her bright, cheerful attire. Her thick, long, dark hair is wrapped up in a clip. I'm envious of it. It's how mine used to look. She's so tiny in my kitchen, thin and lengthy, but no match for the high ceilings and towering cabinets. If I can't reach them, neither can she.

A couple of pots heat on the stovetop as she rolls out fresh noodles on the kitchen island. Clapping the flour dust from her hands, she leans over to pet Chico. Then she gives me a once-over as I tap my nails against the kitchen counter.

"Well, there you are. I was beginning to worry about you," she comments.

The kitchen looks tidier than before, even with all the cooking. Maybe I was in the shower a little too long. The aromas of freshly chopped garlic and warm bread perk up my stomach into a growl.

"Smells good, Mom."

I tear off a piece of bread and dip it into the olive oil and herb mix set on the counter. It's the first thing in a while to hit my taste buds. It melts in my mouth.

"You know, I was out at the club pool this morning with the girls when we all heard the news. One of them said, 'hey isn't that right by your daughter's house?' And I thought, 'Oh no! I have to check on her!' It's just unbelievable that something like this could happen here. This is a safe town. No one gets murdered here. It's ridiculous!"

"Yeah, I thought so too," I agree. I, too, think a murder here is unbelievable. I have a glimpse of an image in the back of my mind. A dark one.

"Did you know the guy?" Knowing my mother is the social butterfly she is, I figure she might know more.

"Jim? Not too well, but I know his wife, Heather. She's part of the bitchy wife club."

"Mom, that's awful," I say, dropping my jaw.

She waves her hand to the side, "Oh, please. Don't get me wrong, no one deserves to lose their husband like that, but I'm not terribly fond of her and her little posse." My mother isn't the most sympathetic of people, so even though it feels a little harsh, her comment doesn't completely surprise me.

"You should hear some of the rumors going around. You know, she was on the news earlier today, weeping like crazy, practically screaming, but she never had anything nice to say about her husband. She was always hitting on the lifeguard at the pool and the caddy boys at the golf course."

"Well, maybe she's feeling sorry about being a bad wife?" I know very well that people grieve differently, sort of like how I remained quiet, to myself and self-loathed when my lover was gone. I bottled my emotions inside, crying only to myself. I wondered if I had been a good partner to him. Maybe this is Heather's version of grieving.

My mother abruptly changes the subject as soon as she eyeballs the bandaging on my hand. "What happened to your hand?" she shouts, lowering her brow.

"Oh, I accidentally cut it while unpacking."

"Jesus, Elizabeth, you need to be more careful. It looks bad, let me see it." She rushes over to grab my hand, but I tuck it under my arm.

"I'm fine. I cleaned it."

She looks at me with concern. "Young lady, you need to shape up a bit. This place was a mess when I came in. You look frail as a reed! Not to mention all the empty wine bottles dispersed throughout the house," she insults my lifestyle while putting noodles into boiling water. I remain silent, annoyed at her lecture, even if she's right. "You know, you're going to have to learn to move on. I know you don't want to hear it, but..."

I cut her off because I know I can't handle hearing this right now, "Don't, Mom. Please."

"Oh, honey. I'm just really worried about you. I want to see you thrive here. I know things aren't the way you pictured they would be, but you can't just stop living." She plates up the dinner and delivers them into the dining room. I take the moment to reach into the wine cabinet and open up a bottle. Although she nags me about drinking, she drinks every day, so I know she won't oppose.

I hope the few bites of bread I had are enough to coat my stomach to drink this glass of wine. I gulp down the first couple of mouthfuls. The sweet cherry and vanilla flavors pierce my tongue as the wine falls down the back of my throat with a dry finish. My belly warms, and my face becomes hot. It instantly soothes my nerves, so I take another big gulp, finishing the glass and pouring a new one before Mother comes back into the kitchen. I pour one for her, too. She takes the glass of wine naturally as I float towards the smell of fettuccine alfredo.

-

**This dining room is too lonely for one person.** Normally, I eat while sitting on the couch, on the coffee table, or sometimes out on the balcony. The dining room is still painted an ugly pale blue. I had pictured it would be more of a warm grey, against the pale white crown molding and ceiling. There's an original chandelier that could use a polish and repairs. It hangs directly over the heavy, dark wooden dining table. The chairs need reupholstered with new padding. When I sit down, I can feel the bones of the chairs pressing into my pelvis. I know it's not comfortable, but I loved that the house came with original furniture, and I was going to fix them all.

*Too many projects.*

The light coming from the chandelier is not great as it's missing a few bulbs and is caked in dust. With the sun going down, I decide to light a few candles. Mother sits in the seat across from me. The setting might be considered romantic if I were sharing it with my love. I start to twirl noodles on my fork, shoving a large bite of pasta into my mouth.

*Finally, real food.*

My stomach is more settled now, unlike my mind. I think about the gun lying at the bottom of that hole in the backyard. I can't figure it out. No matter how hard I try to, I can't recall what happened.

Deep into my bowl of fettuccine, my phone buzzes next

to my plate. A notification pops up on my lock screen for the Vigil app with a new trending post:

*RIP JIM CROWLEY*

**Mary Pearly, South Island**

*15 minutes ago*

*To all residents of Painter's Beach. I wanted to open a discussion for the public safety of our community through this app. I will be updating with all of the information I know and find out, daily, hourly, or even by the minute. It will require a lot of coffee and the grace of God, but together, we will find the truth about who has murdered Jim Crowley.*

*Please donate something if you can to the family of Jim. He left behind his wonderful wife and two daughters. I will be sending a link to the donation page. Please keep them in your thoughts and prayers during this difficult time.*

"Mary has really taken it upon herself to be the Painter's Beach vigilante," I say as I scroll through her updates.

"Yes, I have been seeing the posts on Vigil all day. She's been posting non-stop."

"I just think an investigation should be left up to the police department," I say. I keep scrolling, reading the concerned neighbor's comments and the latest from Mary's posts:

*I am working with the family to organize a memorial at the Painter's Beach Marina, where we will be lighting Chinese lanterns and floating them out to the sea in memoriam. Tomorrow at 8:30 p.m., for anyone who can attend.*

"Chinese lanterns?" I scoff, "Seems a bit like cultural appropriation to me."

"Oh, honey, let them do their ceremony. I think that sounds lovely. I know you don't like Mary, but at least she's doing something nice for the family."

I huff, "Yeah, that lady is nowhere near nice."

"I thought she was nice when I met her," Mother states as she twirls her fork in her pasta.

I drop my fork and look at her to say, "She's the one who wouldn't accept me into the art markets. I've told you that."

"Well, I keep telling you that you should try making some more ocean-themed art. You know what the tourists like: shark teeth, shrimp, seabirds."

I can't even reply to her comment, otherwise my anger might flip this whole solid oak table over. My mother doesn't understand art. She doesn't realize how offensive that comment is to me. Instead of arguing with her about the difference between decorative crap and actual art, I chug my glass of wine and offer to pour another.

"Sure, just don't have too much tonight. You've been drinking a lot lately. A glass or two won't hurt. You know, I'd hate to see you end up like your father."

I've suddenly lost my appetite, and I hope that after her next glass of wine, she'll leave. In the kitchen, I chug the rest of the bottle straight from the neck and open another to pour her a glass. I don't want to drink my life away, but her comments are not making it easy right now. This entire day hasn't been easy. It'll be easier to drink up and just forget the rest of the evening at this point.

I hand her the glass of wine as she continues the ever-so pleasant dinner conversation. "I think us girls are booking a rental off the island next week, if you want to come stay."

No way.

I would never dream of staying the night with her girls. All they do is one-up each other, gossip all night about uninteresting social qualms of the island, and watch trash television shows.

"What's the occasion?"

"Well, Hurricane Amelia, of course."

I give her a confused look, not sure what she's talking about.

"You know we're expecting a hurricane by the end of the week. Elizabeth, don't you watch the news?"

I look over to my living room where the wall across from the couch is empty. Ever since my love was all over the news, I took the TV down. I couldn't stand watching it anymore. The headlines ran for weeks, and I watched them obsessively.

"I don't watch the news."

My mother knows these things, but she tries to play it off like she's forgotten all about it, her idea of moving on, but I haven't. *Nor will I ever.*

"I'm sure it's nothing to worry about, dear. It's kind of exciting, actually. Your very first hurricane." She holds up her wine glass from across the table in a cheers motion. I lift my glass, giving her a cheers back with a sarcastic smile on my face, chugging the rest of my glass.

"Usually when it gets bad, we just go over to our friends'

condo, who live on a really high floor, or we rent a place off the island. Sure, it's not as nice, but there are a few decent hotels if you book early. I know it might seem scary, so if you're more comfortable, you can come stay with us. But I'm sure you'll be just fine, unless they start evacuations, which then you'll need to leave the house."

I hadn't ever thought about being in a hurricane. I'm used to worrying about wildfires and bad air quality, but not hurricanes. Either way, I would let a hurricane be the death of me before spending the night with my mother and her girlfriends.

I reply, "I'm sure I'll be fine."

We finish our meals and clean up in the kitchen. I thank her for making dinner. We hug at the front door where she pets Chico one last time and then leaves. The day couldn't have been more brutal. More brutal than most. I've been waiting for her to leave so I can go dig out the gun from the backyard, if I can even find it now in the dark.

The wine I drank, even though I ate most of my carb-loaded dinner, was going straight to my head. It feels like I'm intoxicated to the level I was the night before. Before stumbling into the backyard to search for the gun, I chug one more glass of wine, murmuring to myself, "You should try making more ocean things, what tourists like, seabirds... Oh, fuck off! Turn out like my father, well, thanks, Mom. I think I understand why he turned out that way."

My mother made me angry. She always does. She's an impossible person to get along with. I knew with the support of Christian here, she wouldn't be as much of a bother. He was great at distracting her from picking on me. He was great at talking to everyone. Dealing with all types of personalities was his job as a Captain. The diplomat.

Chico scratches at the back door downstairs to be let out. I walk down them slowly with a tight grip on the railing, one step at a time. It's dark outside now. Only the moon provides light. I rely on my eyes to adjust. I try to remember the exact spot where Chico dug up the gun.

I get on my knees and push my hands into the sand, combing through it. The coarse grittiness is warm, but it turns cool as I get several inches deep. I feel like a child playing in a sandbox, searching for a plastic toy as I recklessly claw the sand with my fingers. I feel ridiculous and chuckle to myself. The hilarity of the situation is less comical but more absurd. Could I really have killed a man in my drunken stupor? What if I really did? How insane would that be?

My dark thoughts swirl around me as I dig through sand, getting it all over my lap. My body becomes limp as I slur myself deeper into the sand. The wine has really gotten hold of me. I feel a buzzing in my dress pocket.

"Great! Probably another update from the famous sleuth, Jr. Detective Pearly."

The buzzing continues, not stopping, when I realize it may actually be a call. It's probably my mother checking in on me again. I stop digging and lift up the phone. The screen is blurry. My sight is becoming less legible. I see the green phone icon and manage a swipe to answer.

"Hello?" I manage to whisper, but no one answers on the other end, "Hello?"

Thinking maybe I didn't answer it right, I check the screen, but see I have picked up a number I don't recognize.

"Hello? Who is this?" I ask.

"Lizzy?"

For a second, I think I hear my name, but I can't be too sure. The connection is poor, and I'm very drunk.

"Sorry, who's this?"

"It's me." As soon as I hear the voice a second time, I think I recognize it. But that voice, it can't be. It's impossible. Someone is playing a joke on me. A prank call.

"Wait, who is this?"

"Lizzy, it's me."

The sound of the voice on the other line terrifies me. It sounds like him. Like he's come back to haunt me. I hang up and throw my phone.

*Someone is fucking with me. Why? Why are they doing that?*

I curl into a ball and begin to cry violently, closing my eyes as I sink into the sand. I feel its coarseness on the side of my face. I can hear the sound of the ocean waves ebbing and flowing. My cries slow into sobs, and then my mind goes dark.

# TUESDAY

## Aimsley August

**"Do you want this table here?" I ask, pointing to the side of Jada's market tent that is set up along the sidewalk.**

"Actually, can you put it along the back of the tent, under the sign?" Jada directs me.

"Yep!"

"Thanks for helping me set up," Jada says.

"Of course. It's the least I can do for letting me crash last night."

Main Street is lined with ten-by-ten-foot white canopy tents on either side of the street, and people stroll leisurely where cars would typically be driving. It's warm and very sunny today. Jada's lucky to have scored a spot under the shade of a large magnolia tree. Lucky for me, her tent is located almost directly across from the bookstore, so I know that after setting up, I can have Garnet make us some coffee.

Jada sets out wooden coasters, key chains and bookmarks. Circle cuts of wood hang from the sides with burned images of sea life mixed in with her new desert scenes. We set up a pair of folding chairs behind the display table, finishing with time to spare before the market begins. "Be right back. I'm going to get us some coffee." I pass through tents selling things like candles, cotton dresses and photographs. I walk into the bookstore and wave to Garnet standing behind the café counter. "Hey! Can I get two specials?" I ask.

"Of course! You out walking around?"

"Actually, I helped Jada set up her tent just now. Going to hang out a bit before my shift tonight."

Garnet busies her hands behind the café counter, scooping ice and pouring things and squirting syrups. "Aw, well, that was nice of you."

"Yeah, we hung out last night, got into some wine at her place. Nothing crazy like Sunday." I huff and roll my eyes as Garnet giggles.

"Still haven't made up with Brooke then?"

I let out a deep sigh, knowing I still haven't been able to talk to her about what happened between us. "I'm sure we will talk it out, but she went to her parents' place last night so..."

Garnet passes over two takeaway plastic cups with lids and straws and says, "Iced today, to keep cool out there."

"Awesome, thanks! I'd better get back over there. I'll see you around."

"Yeah, enjoy it! It's a beautiful day!"

She's right about that. It's the perfect day for walking up and down Main Street. I remember when I was a kid, I'd run around with my friends during the markets while the parents were shopping and drinking. We'd chase each other through the tents, sometimes go skateboarding along the waterfront, or beg our parents to get sweets from the ice cream shop. Back when life was simple. Back before I had to work two jobs and have serious conversations with my girlfriend or worry about murders and hurricanes.

Handing over Jada's coffee, I hear a voice calling my name from behind me. Officer Macon says, "Where's your author tent, Aimsley?"

Turning around, he winks at me, and I chuckle.

"I was helping Jada set up her tent. You should check out her stuff. She's a really great artist! You out shopping?" I ask, even though I know he's on duty, dressed in his full uniform.

"No, I wish. But maybe I'll pick something out for my wife," he says as he scans the table and smiles at Jada. "Talented."

Jada thanks him before he gestures his head towards the street, for me to talk with him.

"Yeah, today was supposed to be my day off, but they have everyone working overtime to locate the suspect."

"Oh, do they know who did it?" I ask.

"No, they don't really know much, to be honest. We're waiting for the autopsy results, but there's been no witnesses so far and no leads. Seems like this happened when no one was around."

Hearing him say this makes me wonder if I should tell him what I know, but I don't want to incriminate myself. I know I didn't do anything. Elizabeth could be a potential witness. I wonder if she'd come forward to say anything, or worse, mention seeing me. I wonder if it'd be better to say something now than have to explain myself later, but I'd rather stay out of it. Keep my mouth shut.

A silence passes between us before he asks, "You going to the memorial tonight?" I give him a confused look, and he explains, "They organized a Chinese Lantern Memorial for the victim at the Marina tonight. I'll be on duty out there."

"Oh, I can't. I have to work at Breaker's."

"Ah. Well, I can't see you having too much business tonight, being so close to the scene. Might have scared people away, unfortunately."

"Yeah, we'll see."

Before walking off, he shoots me a warning, "Keep your eyes peeled, kid. You know what they say. The murderer is likely to go back to the scene of the crime, or even to the memorials. I'll be looking out for the bastard tonight. In fact, why don't you give me a call if you see anyone suspicious? Let me get your number."

We exchange numbers, and Officer Macon purchases a wooden bookmark with a dolphin burned into it from Jada's table. I can hear him tell her how he and his wife love to read. It's nice to see her smile, making a sale.

I know it's time to head back to my apartment to get ready for my shift. I have to go face Brooke and have a conversation with her. As much as I'd rather go skateboarding by the waterfront or grab a scoop of mint chocolate chip ice cream, I know it's time.

I tell Jada good luck and walk out of the market area, leaving downtown. I skate the rest of the way back to the apartment. I take a couple of deep breaths and go inside. It's dark. Brooke is sitting on the couch, wrapped in a blanket in front of the TV. A cup of tea sits on the coffee table in front of her. I turn on the lamp by the door and cautiously address her, "Hey, baby."

"Hey," she responds with an even tone.

"Are you okay?" I ask as she shifts deeper into the couch and curls the blanket up to her nose before looking at me. Her eyes are watering. "Are you crying? Look, I'm sorry." I sit next to her on the couch, and she burrows her head into my shoulder, sobbing. *Damn, I really made her this upset?* "Hey, what's the matter? I'm here now, we can talk about it."

She shrugs and then pulls her head back from my damp shoulder. She manages to blubber words through tears. "It's not that. I had a bad night."

"What do you mean? I thought you went to your parents. What happened?" I ask.

She nods her head, "I was at my parents'."

A tear rolls down her cheek. I can sense pain behind her eyes. I've seen this look before. Instantly, I knew that her parents were fighting again. I hate seeing her cry, but I hate that her parents cause it even more. And to think I could have been with her last night if we hadn't been fighting. I let her cry and wait for her to speak about it.

After a few minutes, she says, "He's cheating on her again."

Asshole.

"I guess my mom found a burner phone in his car," she explains through sobs. "They spent the whole night screaming at each other, and I had too much to drink, so I couldn't drive back."

"I'm so sorry. I wish you would have called me." I rub her back, but she pulls away from me like she doesn't want to be touched.

"You couldn't have picked me up anyway."

She's right. No argument there. I never saw the point of getting my driver's license since I could walk or skate to everything on the island, except in times like these.

"Who was he cheating with?"

"I don't know. He took the phone back from her before she could really figure it out. The messages were under the nickname *my pumpkin*. So fucking gross." Brooke makes a gagging sound.

As we sit on the couch and become lost in the noise of the TV show playing, I can't help but feel guilty about everything. I'm almost relieved Duncan's cheating has derailed our conversation about Sunday night, but it doesn't feel right to keep avoiding it, or eventually this will be fuel for a bigger fight at a later time. I'm tired of the same pattern of avoidance and fighting. I wonder if the conversation is truly worth bringing up, but the image of a man's hand on her thigh enters my thoughts, and I blurt from my mouth, "Who was that guy?"

Brooke tilts her head, "What guy?"

"The guy from the bar the other night. Who is he? Do you know him?"

Brooke looks at me in disbelief. Her sad, drooping eyes slant inward.

"Jesus, Aimsley! I don't want to talk about this right now." Deflection.

"I just want to know who he is. Can you answer me that?"

She scowls deeper. "No. I don't know who he is. Some random guy."

I might regret saying it, but my mouth speaks quicker than my thoughts, "You seemed awfully friendly with him to be some random dude."

She glares at me like I'm something vile and asks, "Don't you have to be at work?"

The time is inching awfully close to my shift. "Yeah, I do, but I need to know why you were hanging out with him and if you're not telling me something." I tap my foot on the stone floor, but she turns her head to the TV, ignoring me. I can feel the heat rise in my stomach. The anger I had on Sunday is returning. I stand now, towering over her, to demand an answer.

"Oh, my God! I've never seen him before. He was telling me some random story, and then you came up and freaked out on me. He was actually looking for his girlfriend. So can you drop it?"

Jealousy fights to burst through my chest, even if what she's explaining to me might be true. It's difficult to trust her. She's beautiful. She's hot. The hottest girl I know, and she's flirtatious. I should be able to trust my girlfriend, but I am somewhat of a hypocrite myself. Because as I stand here questioning Brooke's intentions with this random guy, I'm thinking about my shift tonight and how I really hope Elizabeth will be there.

# Elizabeth Corey

**Chico licks my face.** The sun is high in the sky. My skin starts to bead with sweat. My tongue sticks to the top of my mouth, dry with thirst. I feel grittiness in my teeth. Sand. Sand all over the side of my face, in my hair, on my clothes. And I'm itchy. Extremely itchy.

This is a first. I must say, I have yet to pass out in the sand until now, and I'm surprised any piece of me is left from the sand flies gnawing on me all night. I wonder how long I'd have to lie there before they consumed me whole.

In the daylight, I can quickly discern that the dig site from last night was behind the wrong pine tree. Instead of rising, I army crawl to the next tree and shove my sandy talons down deep. I shriek with pain as the tip of my fingernail hits something hard. I found it.

After attempting to flick the pain away in my finger from breaking a nail, I dust the sand off the gun and release the magazine. Even though I loathe weapons, my love taught me how to use them. How to operate and clean them. I can picture him at the range, lifting up my arms to help me aim. "Both eyes open. Loosen your grip. Control your breath," I can hear him tell me. More importantly, he taught me gun safety. To keep them unloaded and locked in the case. To never touch the trigger unless I'm ready to completely destroy whatever's in front of me. He would be disappointed in me right now. I just know it.

With doubt in my mind and an uneasiness in my gut, I take the gun inside and put it back, securely locking it into its case underneath my bed. My hands shake from the nerves. I couldn't have put it away quicker. Holding it scares me, feeling the weight of it. Not knowing what I've done. Not remembering how it got there. The whole situation makes me feel nauseated.

Chico stares at me, lounging on the bed. I hadn't slept in our bed since I found out Christian was gone, but Chico does. I think he can still smell Christian's scent.

The black case stares back at me.

*I have to get rid of you, but how?*

I'll get rid of it tonight, but while I wait, I have to get away from it. It'll drive me mad. It'll be the death of me; I just know it. I'm going out.

In order to go out in public, I need to be presentable. I'm on a mission. I'll go talk to Aimsley, see what she knows. I'll get some food and drinks, too. It'll be a good distraction while I come up with a plan to get rid of the gun.

In the bathroom, I remove the bandage from my hand.

Beneath it, the cut is still open. I can see the fleshy parts of skin turning to muscle and feel the grains of sand stuck deep in it, grinding against tender flesh. I know I have to clean it, otherwise it could get infected. Inside the shower, I let the warm water run over the wound, stinging as I feel the heat enter the inner layers of the cut. I bite my lower lip, bracing for pain as I pour soap over it, scrubbing at the opening with my pointed fingertip and scooping the sand from inside it. My head feels light. My tongue recedes, blocking my breathing. My throat feels as if it's dropping into my chest.

A new, clean bandage covers my palm, and I comb through my dark hair, trying to ignore the clumps in my brush. Looking in the bathroom mirror, I press my eyelid down and drag eyeliner across it. I brush my eyelashes with mascara and paint black lipstick over my open mouth.

I pick through my closet and decide on a black satin slip dress. It fits me snuggly against my chest and hips. Lace trims the neckline and a small slit on my right thigh. Lastly, I buckle into a pair of chunky platform sandals that make me feel tall.

I look at myself in the full-length mirror in my bedroom. I almost feel pretty, besides the massive bandage on my hand and the bug bites scattering my extremities like polka dots. I turn to the side and hold the dress taut against my stomach. I hold my hand underneath my belly, where a baby bump would be, if I had one.

"You're beautiful, my dark moon." It's almost as if I can hear him tell me clearly. Suddenly, my peripheral catches a shadow moving past the door frame.

Quickly, I peek into the dark hallway, grabbing the door frame and bending my neck to investigate both directions. For a second, my heart flutters, contemplating that someone could be there, but there's no one there. I back up, stepping my foot into the bedroom. Something touches my leg. I scream and turn around. Chico stands alert in the doorway. I had almost tripped over him.

"Chico! You almost gave your mommy a heart attack." His head faces the hallway. His legs are locked, and his tail is still. He begins to crouch, lowering his head. He raises one of his paws, and the hair on the back of his neck furls up slowly, rising in a line all the way to his eerily still tail. He lets out a low growl.

I pat his bottom softly, "Chico, what is it?"

He quickly turns to me, lowering his paw. Then his tail begins to wag as if nothing happened.

Again, I look down the dark hallway. A heavy shadow rests at the far-left end, leading up to the tower. My eyes must be playing tricks on me. The shadow is fuzzy, but the center is not. I flick on the light, expecting to be met with another being, but no one is there.

It's not the first time something strange has happened in this house. It's over one hundred years old. It wouldn't surprise me if it were haunted, especially with how cheap it was when we bought it. I told Christian that it had to be.

I remember searching online for houses like it was yesterday. It was a frigid winter day in Portland. We were snuggled on the couch beneath a blanket I had crocheted, in our tiny apartment living room. His hand played with my hair as I scrolled through listings on my laptop. We had just started entertaining the idea of moving to Florida. I had no idea we would find the house so quickly.

"It has to have a large studio space for my art."

"Well, of course, babe. That's a given. We need a master, a guest bedroom and an art studio. Three bedrooms?" he asked as he grazed my thigh with his fingers.

"Four bedrooms. We need one for the baby." I looked at him with a smile, excited about growing a family together.

His eyes widened in agreement. "Wait, so you actually plan on having visitors? That doesn't sound like my introvert girl. I assumed the guest bedroom would also be the baby's room."

"Just because I'm introverted doesn't mean I might not make a friend or two. Plus, my mom might need to stay the night. You know, when you're away."

He gives a pouted lip, knowing his job wears on our relationship when he's gone. It saddened us both that he would have to spend time away while I was pregnant. He'd miss milestones in our baby's life because of work. But this was the way it would be.

Under the blanket, his hand rested on my thigh, and he squeezed as he talked, listing more of his house wishes. "Of course. We will also need two and a half baths at least, and a large kitchen. Oh, and at least a two-car garage."

"Yes, for your woodworking stuff."

He always wanted to have a space to work on projects like making furniture and custom shelving. For my birthday last year, he constructed a special wooden chair for me out of my father's garage, the beautiful Adirondack chair that sits on our balcony now.

The grip on my thigh started to move upward as he slid his fingers between them. "Let's see what results you get with those filters," he says.

A heat rose from me, a tingle of sensation between my thighs. He teased me while I tried to focus on the search. I checked all the filters we wanted for our dream home. Many houses popped up on Painter's Beach, but I hadn't adjusted the price. Even though Christian made a great salary, we weren't in the million-dollar home bracket like most of the beachfront property listings. As I scrolled, he nuzzled my neck, pecking at it softly, then kissing it harder and nibbling. My head fell backwards. "Christian! We are never going to find a house this way."

He retreated from my neck and took his hand away from my thigh. He looked at me sheepishly. "Sorry, my love, I just can't help myself around you."

Being away from each other for long periods of time had an effect on us. It was difficult to keep our hands off one another, especially knowing his time off wouldn't last forever. Knowing we were starting a family together, looking for houses and building our future was exciting.

"Here, let me look." Christian sat back against the couch and scrolled through the listings for a few minutes before he said, "Ah!"

"Did you find one?"

"I think I found it, love. Here. What do you think?"

Christian handed the laptop back to me so I could look at the listing for an old, tattered house. It had four bedrooms, three bathrooms, a two-car garage and a fenced-in backyard for Chico.

"It needs a lot of work for this price."

"Yes, but love, look at the location."

I scrolled to a photo of the back of the house, sitting on top of a sand dune. A tall peaking turret towered from one side of the two-story house. An ocean-facing balcony. The view of the ocean from that balcony. "Is this on the ocean?"

"Yep!"

"No way!"

Christian's hand slid up the front of my shirt, under my bra. He leaned in to kiss my lips while whispering, "I think we found our dream home, Lizzy." I set the laptop to the side, grinning through kisses.

"It looks kind of haunted. Don't you think?" He pushed me back onto the couch and climbed over top of me, lowering himself between my legs.

"Then it'll be perfect. Dark, just like you."

After living here in this house for several months, I'm not sure I enjoy the feeling of a haunted house or the idea of ghosts anymore.

# Aimsley August

*Mystery trailed behind her, leaving spores of sweet demise, so tempting that her feet lifted from the ground for a drink.*

"Can we cash out?" a couple of my regular customers ask while drinking the last bits inside their novelty glasses.

"Sure. Would you like me to give those a quick rinse for you?" I close my notebook and take the plastic squall glasses from them and rinse them in the bar sink.

The sound of the TV overhead talks about the hurricane. The couple's eyes glue to the headline:

**Life-Threatening Storm Hurricane Amelia Now Category 3**

The man is already holding his card out while still looking at the TV. I swipe the card and place the tablet in front of them.

"Just need a signature on here. Thanks for coming in, guys."

The man selects a tip and signs with his finger in one quick swish motion. "We'd love to stay for another round, August, but we'd better go secure a couple of things in the yard. We might need to go out to get some supplies. It seems like everyone else had the same idea," he says, looking around the empty bar.

"Better to be safe than sorry." I smiled and waved them off.

I'd like to think part of the reason no one is at Breaker's right now is because of the homicide that happened very close to here the other night, with a murderer still at large, but maybe it's a combination of the two. In my opinion, in comparison to finding a murderer, the news is really starting to blow this storm out of proportion. It's hard to picture a hurricane coming when the sky is clear and sunny, with little wind. It looks like any other evening from my vantage. I haven't prepped in the slightest. I haven't had the time to worry about securing things or buying things to prepare. There's been far more concerning things on my mind than Hurricane Amelia, but by the look of this empty bar, maybe I should start to worry.

The pace of this shift has made time go by painfully slow. Watching hurricane updates on the TV is like watching paint dry when new information is only reported every six hours. All I have to look forward to is the next update, at eleven o'clock, five hours from now.

Dean and Cameron mosey over to the bar, wanting refills to add to the pile of empty glasses on the staff table. I wipe the counter of the bar down where the customers just vacated and dunk the wet rag back into a bucket of sanitizer.

"Damn! I haven't seen it this dead in a while." Dean grabs a chair behind the bar and rests his arms over the wet counter I just cleaned.

"Yeah, sucks you won't make shit for tips tonight." Cameron states as he smacks the counter with both his hands and turns his head, scanning the patio for any evidence of life.

"Oh, thanks, guys. Your words are encouraging." I pour two more of the same beers they have been drinking on since this afternoon and slide them over. Dean pulls out a crumpled wad of cash from his swim trunks and shoves it into the tip jar. It's a nice gesture, knowing very well that this shift has been a total loss. My bank account won't be happy, especially after I've depleted it by buying the engagement ring. I wonder if I should return it.

"So, where's ol' Brookie tonight?" Dean asks.

"At home, chillin'." Luckily, talking with the boys is simple. They don't ask too many questions.

"Lame." Cameron blurts. "Have a beer with us! You'll probably go home early anyway." Looking around the bar, it doesn't take long for me to agree and join in on a cheers.

"Are you guys going to that lantern memorial tonight?" I ask.

"Nah, I gotta get up early tomorrow for a private training sesh." Cameron says.

"Since when do you have a bedtime?" I chuckle.

"Hey! I can be responsible."

"Sure, but you're still training in a hurricane?" I ask.

"These ladies will do anything for a snatched waist."

"Anything, huh?" Dean elbows Cameron suggestively.

I roll my eyes at both of them.

"Hey yo, but can you believe that shit happened like right there? Someone was murdered right there, dude." Dean points over to the shore.

We all look over when a dark figure approaches.

She's here.

"Oh shit!" Cameron laughs into Dean's shoulder, a quiet mockery. They are both pretty drunk at this point. Seeing Elizabeth, I'm half tempted to kick them out, but to my surprise, her presence seems to push them away naturally.

"Looks like you got another customer after all. Good luck with that. Imma head out." Cameron chugs the rest of his beer and hits Dean on the arm, indicating to follow him.

"Yeah, me too," Dean says.

"Alright. Stay outta trouble." I suggest, as they exit the patio and take off South, most likely to continue their stupor at Slack Tides. Normally, I'd feel a hint of jealousy. I'd want to join them, but not this time. I'm exactly where I want to be. As Elizabeth passes them, Cameron turns around, and from behind her, he sticks his tongue out, his pointer fingers standing upright behind his ears to make devil horns, before the two of them burst out laughing. Luckily, Elizabeth doesn't notice.

As Elizabeth approaches the entrance to the patio, I try to look busy, cleaning the bar top again. My stomach flutters. I have to clench my jaw from dropping onto the floor as she walks up. A tattooed tentacle of an octopus comes down her thigh from the slit in her black dress. I try not to check her out, but it's nearly impossible. I keep my eyes on her face, which is hidden behind her large-brimmed hat and thick sunglasses. I shout a friendly *"Hey!"* as she approaches, to fill up the time it takes her to reach the bar.

She gives a slight wave and grin. Her dog's tail wags cheerfully.

"Did I scare everyone away?" She throws up her hands and looks around at the empty bar.

"No, actually, the place was reserved just for you. Sit anywhere you'd like," I say jokingly as she turns and pulls out a chair at a table far away.

She looks at me and giggles before coming to sit down at the bar in front of me.

My palms are sweaty. "Long time no see," I say.

Elizabeth's light blue eyes are striking. She brushes a long strand of hair from her face. Her cat-eye eyeliner and long lashes bat at me. I'm left staring at her lips; you never see anyone wearing black lipstick around here. Even though she looks great with all the makeup, I can still see bags under her eyes and exhaustion in her posture as she slumps into the chair which signals me to make her a drink.

As I grab the whiskey from the well, I ask, "Old Fashioned?" Even though I know it's what she wants.

"Yes, god, please." She sighs and rolls her eyes.

I can tell she must be having a tough day, but I wait for her to open up to me. I focus on mixing the bourbon, bitters and simple syrup, even though I can feel her watching my every move. I pour the mixture from a beaker into a glass with ice and fish a cherry from the fruit bin. Then, I rim the glass with an orange peel, twisting the rind over the drink before dropping it in. As I slide the drink over to her, I'm met with her gaze.

She's smirking at me.

I manage to ask, "How's your day been?"

Her smirk fades into a pouted lip. "Ugh. It's been a crazy day. Just have a lot on my mind. Which is why I came to see you."

*Wow, she came just to see me?*

Is she insinuating that being around me makes her day better?

"You make the best drinks. Cures any bad day." The pouted lip is replaced with the smirk again. Of course. The drinks. The drinks make her day better. Not me. She picks up her glass, twirling the ice cube around, and inserts her long fingernail into the cherry, pluck it out. She dangles the cherry stem over her tongue and bites down, all while maintaining eye contact with me. I look away quickly, to appear as if I hadn't blatantly noticed how heavily she is flirting with me right now. Elizabeth has always been a tad flirtatious and mentioned a few insinuating things, but I've always brushed them off, thinking it was all in my head. But the forwardness of that move, I'd be crazy not to assume it meant something. Is she gay? Sweat begins to pool on the back of my neck.

I notice her itching at her arms. Upon further inspection, I notice all of the small red marks covering her skin. The itching becomes violent as she gouges into them while in a trance. Some spots begin to bleed.

"Are you okay?" I ask.

Elizabeth stops itching immediately and tucks her arms beneath the bar. "Yeah. Sorry. I got bitten up last night. I was, uhm, sitting in the sand."

"Ah! No-see-ums got you. Try not to itch them. It'll only get worse."

"Oh. How do you know that?"

"Unfortunately, I've been a victim of no-see-ums, too. Little bitches hurt. They normally are the worst in the sand during sunset or sunrise." Elizabeth examines her arms and then takes a big swig of her drink. I do the same with my beer. Her eyes seem to examine everything very closely, as if she is thinking about a lot of things all at once.

"So, I have a question," she says.

I brace myself, "Yes?"

"Are you a student?" Elizabeth points to my notebook just when my mind started to race to what she might ask me, actually hoping the conversation might turn to the subject of something wicked. I shouldn't feel this way, but the tightening of my stomach and butterflies in my head are egging on the feelings I dare to embrace.

"Oh, that? No, just writing some stuff."

"Like you're a writer?"

"I'm not sure I'd call myself that, but yeah, I'm working on writing a book."

"Oh wow, that's really impressive." Elizabeth smiles at me

while swirling her drink. I blush, but just when I think she'll pry more into my creative endeavors, she switches the subject, and the tightening in my stomach twists further.

"Were you on the beach Sunday night, like, kind of late?"

*So we did see each other.*

My long-anticipated curiosity is coming to a head. If only I could avoid coming off as a fool.

"Yeah, I think I saw you, maybe?" I respond.

"Ok, I thought so." She stares off in thought for a while, but I wait for her to talk next as I can't come up with anything to say.

She empties her glass and tilts it towards me, "Can I have another, please?"

"Of course!" I busy myself with making another Old Fashioned.

"I was walking Chico. I've told you before that we go on night walks."

"Yeah, totally." I agree with her. The space between our conversations is verging on awkward. The silence between us is killing me, so I swallow down the saliva in the back of my throat and begin to explain myself. "My girlfriend and I got into a fight at Slack Tides on Sunday night. So I was walking aimlessly and drunk on the beach. I hadn't noticed I stopped near your house until I saw you and Chico out in the tide."

Elizabeth nods her head, as if recalling the situation, then says, "I do remember seeing you, but I also had quite a bit to drink that night."

"Well, I saw you in the tide, and then you disappeared. The

storm started getting bad, so I ran home."

"Ah, okay." She remains silent, her eyes shifting back and forth as if she's searching for more to the story. I wish she would spit out what her thoughts are about that night. Maybe a few more drinks will loosen her up. This conversation lingers slower than a gopher turtle getting back to its burrow.

I set another freshly made cocktail in front of her, but before I can remove my hand from the glass, her sharp fingernails graze the outside of my index finger. I withdrew quickly, causing a scraping of my skin as I pulled away.

"Ouch!" I hold my hand and shake off the pain.

"Oh, I'm sorry," she apologizes and then leans slightly over the bar towards me, as if to tell me a secret. I try not to look down the inside of her shirt as she does so. She looks to the left and to the right and then back at me. I lean in slightly.

She whispers, "Between you and I, I'm a little freaked out about being on the beach that night. You know, because of the murder."

"I feel the same way, actually."

She sits back in her chair while I let go of the breath I was holding.

"I'm glad you said something. I wasn't sure how to bring it up. I wasn't sure if you knew anything more than I did." A long sigh passes out from me, as I am feeling the relief to get it off my chest. I feel we now share a secret, and I've unlocked a new level of connection with her, beyond bartender and customer.

"Storms really upset me," she takes another sip of her drink, leaning back into her chair now. I can see she's about to open up to me. Her hands become jovial as she tells me her story. I can't help but smile, but her story is heavy, so I try my best to tame my excitement as she continues, "I lost my partner to the sea a few months ago. A bad storm took down a ship he was on." Her eyes well up with moisture as she continues. "We bought the house here, thinking we would start a new life together, grow a family, but without him, I've been a wreck. Between dealing with my grief, having no one to talk to but my awful mother. And with my failed connections with the art community on the island, and any island people for that matter, you're really the only person I talk to. I know that might be a little much, and I know you're just my bartender, and I'm sure listening to me is just you doing your job, but I appreciate you letting me vent. I've been having a terrible time lately. Yesterday, it felt like the neighbors were all judging me, the cops were questioning me, and these little shithead teenagers were throwing shells at my windows, calling me a *witch*. I mean, you're here at the bar and probably talk to a lot of the locals. Have you heard anything that they are saying? Are people talking about me, or am I just going crazy?"

Elizabeth's eyes seem to darken as she looks at me with vulnerability.

I realize that she's alone, and she's dealing with so much. My heart breaks for her. All I want to do is hold her and tell her everything will be alright, but I know I can't do that. I want to say the right thing.

"First of all, you're not crazy, and I'm really sorry you're having that experience here. I know the island can be tough on outsiders. I personally have always thought you were a really interesting person, and I look forward to when you come sit at my bar. You're the only customer I have that has anything interesting to talk about, more than surface-level shit. But no, I haven't heard anything.  People seem to be curious about who you are and why you bought that house, but I'm not exactly the person they would be venting to about someone they might not think fits in. I mean, look at me."

Elizabeth's eyes circle me, and a slight smile comes to the corner of her mouth.

"Maybe we were the only two people on the beach Sunday night. Maybe they are having trouble coming up with any witnesses, and it's scaring people. The first people they will blame will be outies."

"Outies?"

"Yeah, like out-of-towners. Obviously, you are a resident here, but just a new one."

"Well, joke's on them, because technically, Painter's Beach is my hometown. I was born here. I just moved away when I was little."

"Oh, really? No way!"

My pocket buzzes with a notification, pulling me away from our conversation. I received a couple of texts from Officer Macon:

*Hey Kid. How's it going at Breakers? Anyone suspicious?*

I look up to the empty patio of the bar. Only Elizabeth sits in front of me, also looking at her phone. I have no suspicions of her at all. I fail to see what anyone would have against her, and I pity her situation and the way the island has been unwelcoming to her. Her body and her soul appear so frail. Deep down, I just want to rescue her.

"Shit!" Elizabeth's jaw drops, and she covers her hand over her mouth. She looks at me with widened eyes as if she's discovered something horrible.

"What's wrong?" I ask.

She anxiously stands up from her stool, grabs her hat and glasses from the bar, and says, "I have to go."

# Elizabeth Corey

**New Evidence Found!!**
**Mary Pearly, South Island**
*Now*
*A suspicious object was just located on the beach next to the crime*
*scene. It's some sort of witchcraft or devil-worshipping object of pure evil!*
*I never thought I'd say this, but we have evil forces operating right here, in*
*our own backyard. Does anyone recognize it? If anyone knows anything,*
*please come forward. Together, we will find the person responsible!*

Paired with the post is a picture of the object. An object
that I instantly recognize. Not an object of witchcraft or of
devil worship, but of art. A piece of my artwork. A totem. A
small ceremonial object crafted from thread and twigs into the
shape of a raven. And within the raven, if unraveled, contains a
heart-shaped rose quartz. The memory came back to me from
Sunday night. I was on the beach, tossing this totem into the

water. Releasing a message to my love. Delivering it to my dead partner, in the ocean, where he lies.

I know Mary will make a connection. She's seen my artwork. She will figure out it's mine.

*I am so fucked.*

All I can think of right now is to hurry home to dispose of the gun. Get rid of the evidence.

"Sorry, can you close out my tab?" I ask Aimsley.

"Yeah, of course."

I need a place to dispose of the gun. A place where it won't wash up like the totem. Water without a sweeping tide. And I need an alibi. I've come up with a crazy plan, but desperate times call for desperate measures.

"Hey, you want to hang out?" I ask as Aimsley hands me the tablet to sign my bill. She looks as if she didn't hear me right, so I ask again, "Do you want to hang out later? When do you get off?"

"Yeah! Hold on, let me find out."

Not even a minute later, she returns with the news that she can close up the bar early. She immediately begins plugging the taps and cleaning behind the bar. "I just need a few minutes."

"Great. I'll go fetch the car and pick you up out front?"

"Oh, yeah. Sure!" Her cheeks blush pink under her tanned skin. The poor thing is so excited to be off work to hang out with me, but I fear she'll find out it's only to create an alibi. Her friendship is special to me. The only friend I have right now, but it's obvious she's crushing on me. Her intention is more, but I'll have to use it to my advantage, because I'm not going to jail.

*A life sentence.*

I picture myself behind bars, fighting my cellmates over the top bunk. I'd be sleeping on a thin, dirty mattress while listening to the snores of another convict or several. All I'd have to look forward to is scoring ramen noodles from the commissary. And no alcohol ever again. I could get creative and learn how to make toilet bowl wine. The absolute worst thing about it all would be losing Chico. He already lost Christian. I can't bear the thought of him living with my mother. She's always gone. I can see him curled up by the door, weeping as she leaves, wondering if I've abandoned him. The thought, I can't bear it. I can't wait to unburden myself from this weapon that could change everything.

*I will not go to prison!*

Chico and I run on the beach the whole way home. He sticks his tongue out and scoots his butt around me, darting forward and then waiting and darting forward again to keep up with my slower pace. He thinks it's a game. What a clueless babe, getting the zoomies on the way to dispose of mommy's murder weapon.

From inside my garage, I yank the dust cover off the car, unveiling the shiny grill on my 1969 Ford Mustang. Purchased in poor condition, it was a gift from my love for our one-year dating anniversary. He managed to keep it a secret from me for months, working on it in my dad's garage when I thought he was taking a class for his sailing. Instead, he was greased up, leaning over this grill, making it perfect for me.

I can feel him in everything I have. This car. This garage. This house. He's a part of every aspect of my life. I feel bad for what I've become without him, and I wonder if he'd be ashamed of what I'll have to do. I'd hope he would understand that I'm trying to protect myself, as he would have done for me.

I walk around to open up the compact trunk and shove the gun case into the wheel well of the spare tire.

# Aimsley August

***If I weren't outside of work, I'd spark up this joint right now.*** I'd planned on saving it for when we get there. *Where are we going?* I know I'll need something to take the edge off. My palms are slick, and my neck is glistening with sweat. Even with the sun starting to settle, the heat in me will not subside.

The shaky feeling in my gut is a combination of nerves, knowing I'm about to hang out with Elizabeth finally, and the consequences dangling over my head if Brooke were to find out. Maybe she doesn't need to know.

"Whoa!" My mouth involuntarily drops.

The low rumble of Elizabeth's classic sports car hums in my chest as she pulls up in front of the restaurant. I feel like I'm on the set of a movie scene, and I forgot my lines.

Elizabeth rolls down the window and shouts, "You comin'?"

Shuffling in my sandals over to the humming car, I push in the button on the passenger side door. The interior is supreme:

black leather seats, wood paneling above the door's armrest, a plush dash with circular gauges, a thin wooden steering wheel and a matching round ball adorning the long stick shift in the center.

"Damn, this car is so cool!" As I sit down and shut the door, Elizabeth smirks and asks me to buckle up. She shifts into gear, driving towards town and down Main Street. She drives quickly, but with purpose. She stops all the way at a stop sign, but takes off rather fast. Her arm moves ruthlessly on the stick shift as her undulating knees shift, pressing on the clutch and the gas. It's like a dance; she's operating the car with finesse.

I'm starting to rethink getting my license. I try to keep my head forward, focused on the road, but can't help looking over to her thigh from the corner of my eye.

The lace slit of her dress hikes up as she shifts gears.

"So, I was thinking we could try to walk by the bridge, if I can find a place to pull off."

"Yeah, actually, if you take a left at the end of the bridge, you can park back in there. People fish there sometimes. It's a good smoke spot." I take the joint from my pocket and wave it out for Elizabeth to see.

"Oh." She stops closely behind the car in front of her. Traffic is backed up and moving rather slowly. Although she doesn't mention it, I can tell the traffic is irritating her. I question if bringing up the joint was a bad topic of conversation. Maybe she's not into it. My anxiety flares through my arm and chest muscles.

"Sorry, I guess I didn't ask you. Do you, uh, smoke?"

"Come on!" Elizabeth slams on her brakes and throws up her arms as a car cuts us off. "What weed? I have, on occasion, just haven't really since I left Oregon." She doesn't seem too interested in the topic. She's more distracted about getting to our destination.

I wonder if I should stay quiet, but the silence makes my thoughts race between imaginative scenes of her and arguments with Brooke. "So, does Oregon have the good shit? I bet they had some really good pot out there."

"Yes, they did." She replies while spurring forward to make the light.

Her short answer has my leg shaking, violently tapping the floorboard. I try to think of something better to talk about, but watching her skirt hike up further, inches from my hand gripping the side of my seat, I feel I might explode into a million pieces if I can't hit this joint soon.

"Guess this explains the slowdown," she mentions as we pass the end of traffic turning into the marina just before the bridge.

*The lantern memorial.*

We cruise over the bridge with ease. The warm pink sky on the right is being chased by the dark blue coming from the left. A few stars have already made an appearance. A calm and clear night. The river and marshes are in full view. Trails of water wind through patches of tall grasses, reflecting the color of the sky. We are almost to the turn at the bottom of the bridge. The calm views couldn't be more polarizing than the butterflies raging in my stomach. I'm unsure of her intention, but I hope for the best and I hope for the conversation to go more smoothly once we're out of this car.

I loosen my grip from the sides of the seat as we park at the end of a small turn around spot in the grass that had been made by other cars. No one's in sight. It's just us and the river.

The roaring car engine comes to a halt, replacing the air between us with a thick silence. She takes the keys out of the ignition and points, "Let's go over there. Under the bridge by the water."

"Sure." We get out of the car. Elizabeth follows me past the concrete barricades, under the bridge's abutments. Sounds of cars passing over echo against the concrete ceiling. I make a seat on the seawall that's up against large rocks leading down to the water's edge. She looks around and paces for a bit, checking out each side of the platform before taking a seat next to me. The light grows dim with the setting sun. The dark blue sky now engulfs almost all of the pink sky. At the marina across the river, dock lights illuminate rows of parked boats. A sizable group of people gathers at the end of one of the docks where a lantern is being lit. I flick my lighter and puff onto the end of my joint until smoke fills my lungs.

My muscles finally begin to relax as the relief of the hit washes over me. From my head to my fingers and toes, the weight of my body rests into my hip bones, grounding me into the concrete. I can't help but notice Elizabeth squirming, restless as she sits.

She scratches at her arms and looks around until. Then, to my surprise, she asks, "Can I hit that?"

"Yeah, of course!" I pass her the end of the joint, and she takes a long drag, coughing out hard, causing us both to laugh.

"Sorry, I haven't done that in a while. Those Old Fashioneds are wearing off. I'm just so stressed, if I had been smart, I'd have packed a bottle of wine." If only this were a planned date, I would have packed us a full picnic, filled with anything she liked.

Elizabeth bows her head, caressing a large cut on her hand. "I must seem like such an alcoholic."

She seems embarrassed, but I say, "No, you're good. I drink too. Trust me. Hey, what happened to your hand?"

She offers her open hand to me, to inspect. I lightly rub my thumb over the wound. "I don't even remember. I think I cut it on a broken wine glass. I've been drinking a lot more lately. It's been really hard." She retracts her hand and combs her hair back with her long-pointed fingernails. They weave through the strands of her hair like spider legs.

"I can't imagine. I'm sorry to hear about your partner." Quiet as the night, she looks out towards the marina. The subject of death and mourning floats in lanterns, ebbing out to the center of the river. I wish I could comfort her, but I won't dare make a move, even if I want to.

"How's that joint making you feel? It always helps me relax."

Her response is to scoot closer to me, leaning back into her locked arm. Her icy blue eyes land on mine. "I actually feel really great right now. Thank you."

She feels close, eating up any personal space I had before.

I gulp hard. "Yeah, no problem." All I want to do right now is slide my fingers through the back of her long black hair, grip the strands of it and guide her onto my lips. I can't help but think that her closeness is a sign of chemistry. A spark. A connection between us pulls taut like a string coiling at both ends. The space between our mouths grows smaller. I want to ask her how she's feeling. I want to know if she feels the same way, but I can't. I have no words.

Before I have to say anything, she mutters, "I really like you, Aimsley."

My breath freezes, but a warmth oozes over the top of my head and down my shoulders. I try to hold back the grin pulling at the corners of my mouth. I know I'm going to regret this, but I don't care. Even as an image of Brooke flashes into my mind, all I can see is the man at the bar touching her thigh and her bright red hair tossing back as she laughed. She enjoyed it. My mind is made up, and I don't know if it will ever change. I've been fighting it long enough. Regret or not, I lean into the feeling of this moment and into the space between us as she does the same.

"I really like you too," I whisper.

I can feel my heart beating in my chest. A wave of goosebumps forms over my skin. She tilts her head, landing her lips on mine, inviting a long, locking kiss. She grabs my arm, pulling me in closer. Bourbon and cherries on her tongue. My blood is warm and rapid. Hunger drives me from my core. I kiss and grab her harder. She pulls back, taking a breath, and I latch onto her neck like a thirsty vampire in need of replenishment.

# Elizabeth Corey

**No one's touched me in so long.** Aimsley's lips suctioned to my neck sends me spiraling. One second it feels like ecstasy, and the next like a leech. I miss intimacy. I miss being wanted and hungered for, but I miss it from my love. From Christian.

Oh, how this feels like a betrayal. Regret begins to sink, as I remember why I'm here. It had almost slipped my mind for a moment. *The gun. I need to get rid of the gun.*

As I still my movements, Aimsley detaches from my neck. Even though her face is dark, the light of her eyes sparkles in the moonlight. It's as if I went into that kiss in the day and came out in the night. I wonder how much time has passed, or if the joint is messing with my perception.

Aimsley's face fills with worry, "Are you okay? I'm sorry. Was I too much? I shouldn't have..." Her words blubber from her mouth, but this isn't her fault. I was on a mission, not to make out with my friend, but to distract her. I need to keep her occupied while I dispose of the weapon, but not like this.

I hadn't fleshed out all of the details. How could I? I'm only improvising as I go.

*Dispose of the weapon.*

A weapon traceable to a murder. A murder, I'm not sure if I committed. Either way, Aimsley's face is becoming more concerned, and I fear I'm stalling and making it worse. Not sure what else to do, I lean back into her, kissing her more. Sucking and biting on her bottom lip. Sliding my hand over her thigh while I think.

How am I going to do this? I need an excuse to get into the trunk. Her hands clasp the back of my neck, and I feel her hand falling from my shoulder, taking my dress strap with it. Trying to avoid the next base, I grip her thigh harder, but she takes it as an approving cue and successfully pulls down the front of my dress and exposes me to the darkness around us. She kisses down my sternum, advancing lower. I need a plan. I wish I could focus, but this does feel nice. My head rolls back, but as I pull it back up, I see my distraction.

"Look!" I say, pointing to the group of glowing lanterns floating in the current, underneath the bridge.

Aimsley looks up in a daze. "Shit! They must have released them on an incoming tide. The ocean is the other way. Damn, they are all floating right towards us." A group of fifty or more lanterns knock into one another and bash into the side of the rocks below us.

"That was poor and unfortunate planning," I say. Across the river, the crowd faces us, and their muffled voices become louder. "Do you think they can see us?" I pull the straps of my dress up to their normal position.

Aimsley's face becomes bright, a light illuminating her face, then the light moves onto me, blinding me.

I hold my arm up over my eyes to shield them.

The flashlight illuminates the ceiling, as if the lights had suddenly turned on. A husky man in his fifties wearing a polo, jeans and white sneakers walks towards us from underneath the bridge. His hand hovers over a holster on his belt.

*He's a cop?*

"It's not what it looks like," Aimsley explains, putting up her arms and bowing her head.

"You," the cop says, pointing his flashlight in my face as he nears, "Stand up. Now!"

I immediately freeze, putting my hands up too. I'm sure this is it. They've come to arrest me because of what Mary Pearly posted. Caught red-handed with the murder weapon in my trunk. Only one routine search away from being discovered.

"Look, officer, Aimsley has nothing to do with it." I can't involve her.

"Aimsley?" His deep, assertive voice commands, approaching us swiftly. "What's going on here?" he questions. Aimsley stands, the light beaming on her face. "What are you doing here with her?" Aimsley's face wilts with fright. Her eyes appear watery in the light from the flashlight.

"Alright, both of you in the back of my car now," he says as he points his flashlight towards where we had parked. He waits for us to walk shamefully past him and out to his police car with the guidance of his bobbing light on the path in front of us.

As he opens the door, Aimsley contests, "I didn't do anything."

*No, you didn't. I did.*

He puts the flashlight directly into her eyes, "Aimsley, I'm not going to ask you again. Get in the car." She lets out a gasp and shields herself from the light before falling down into the backseat. I join in after her. The officer leans over the car door and commands me, "Need your identification." He holds out his hand.

Words stutter from my mouth, "I, uh, don't have my ID on me."

He scowls, "Oh, is that so? So, you were driving without your license then?" He gestures to my parked car.

"No."

"So, you're telling me that's not your car?"

"No, it is my car."

"Okay, so you're lying to me."

"No, I mean, I had my license when I drove my car. My license is in the car."

"Well, why didn't you start with that?"

"Sorry, Officer. I can go get it."

"Nope, you're not going anywhere. Hand over the keys." With hesitation in my gut, I wish I'd have thrown the keys into the river the moment he approached us. At least then it could remain locked, but there's no way of getting out of it at this point. Why do I feel as if shakily handing over these keys is equivalent to the last day of my life as I know it, the exchange that will take away my freedom and change my life forever?

The officer slams the door, and I let my head fall into my hands.

"Fuck!" Aimsley beats her fist against the back of the driver's seat. Suddenly, I am more confused.

"How does the officer know your name? I'm the one in trouble here, not you."

"It's Brooke's dad. My girlfriend's dad. I'm in such deep shit." Her tightly clamped fist bangs up and down on the top of her thigh. Her long curls hang over her face like a curtain.

This moment might seem bad for her, but she doesn't understand how much worse it is for me. If I had known her girlfriend had a cop for a dad, I might have scratched this whole plan.

"Wait... What do you mean you're in trouble?" Her fist unclenches, and she comes from beneath the curtain in confusion.

"I'm sorry I didn't tell you before, but I think I..." I pause as I hear the mumble of the officer on the radio. We both listened.

"Yeah, there's access to the lanterns from over here. Just give it a few more minutes before you send the clean-up crew. Wait until the crowd clears out of the marina." He then mentions my name. He must have found my license in the car.

He opens up the door on Aimsley's side, pulling her out. I scoot towards the door, but he slams it in my face and proceeds to talk to Aimsley, his tone growing angrier, and I feel the car jut forward. Looking out the back window, he holds Aimsley's arm, pinning her against the trunk.

"What do you think you're doing here? Hanging out with your little pot smoking friend? I've about had enough of you. You think Brooke would like to hear that you're hanging all over this girl? You don't deserve my daughter, you piece of shit."

Aimsley pleads, "It's not what it looks like. Please don't say anything to Brooke. We're just friends. We were just hanging out."

"Yeah, you've got quite the taste in friends, don't you? You're not allowed to come near my daughter again. You're done." He shoves her body again against the car. It feels wrong. He can't handle her this way. It can't be legal.

Aimsley groans. "You can't tell me what to do."

"What did you say to me? The hell I can. You come near Brooke again, and I'll lock your ass up."

Aimsley isn't backing down. She pushes forward, pulling her arm from his grip. "Who are you to judge? You're no saint, are you?"

"Excuse me?" The officer's voice cracks.

"You accuse me of going behind Brooke's back, but I'm not the one with the burner phone. Don't you think that makes you a hypocrite?" My jaw falls to the floor, and so does Aimsley. She lets out a loud grunt, and I see the officer on top of her, throwing his fists onto her.

"Hey! Stop that!" I shout, and the officer backs off from Aimsley. He opens the driver's side door, sits down, and slams it shut, peeling his tires through the grass as we drive away. He huffs his breath, either from anger or exhaustion or both. From the back window, I can see my car illuminated by the red of his taillights fading in the darkness, along with Aimsley lying on the ground, clutching her stomach.

---

**This is the first time I've been in the back of a police car.** And it may be the last time I'm in the back of any car ever. The possibility of a permanent consequence is eating me alive.

*My car...my car.*

He hadn't searched through my trunk, so I knew he hadn't found the gun, but it's probably only a matter of time before it's towed and someone searches it.

*It's hopeless. I'm hopeless.*

The officer's eyes sneer at me through the visor mirror. Disgusting eyes. How could he assault Aimsley like that? What gives him the right to treat her that way? Because he's a cop? I dare not say a word right now, I've seen his lack of concern for laws, and I'm not about to push any buttons of his, but when I get to the station, I'm reporting it. Until then, I'm quiet as a mouse.

As we speed up the bridge, all I can think about is the walk Aimsley will have to take after her beating. We pass the marina, which is empty of traffic now. I look back before we leave the bridge, and I can see the small cluster of glowing lanterns where Aimsley is. I hope she's alright. I feel awful that I was using her. Putting her into this situation was all my fault. If it weren't for me, she'd never have been there in the first place.

"10-31 over," the officer says.

The dispatcher responds over the radio, "10-4."

"Transporting Elizabeth Corey to the station for investigative detention."

"10-4 over," they respond, and the radio cuts back to silence.

Once again, the officer looks at me in the mirror, so I look out the window until we arrive at the police station. The building is tucked away off Main Street with a tiny parking lot that's well-lit. There are only a few other police cars in the lot.

"This way," the officer leads me in through the double steel doors. My heart starts to flutter, and my legs feel weak and wobbly the further we go in. He tells me to take a seat in the waiting area, pointing towards a metal-framed chair with a hard plastic seat. The walls in the station are all white with grey trim. The floor tiles are cool grey. It smells of burnt coffee and cleaning solution. This place is sterile, cold and unwelcoming. I don't want to be here. I wonder what would happen if I simply got up and ran out the front door. Maybe I could run and hide, make it to my car somehow, jump-start it and skip town. Go back to Oregon, cross the Canadian border and start a new life. I'd have to grab Chico somehow. I wouldn't leave without him.

"Welp, you guys have a good night. I'm heading home," the officer says to another uniformed, larger man sitting behind the front desk as he leaves through the front doors. I decide my plan of escape might be too complicated, and now, with that officer out of the building, I may have a better chance of getting out of this. Maybe I should wait it out and see what they have to say. I'm not handcuffed. That's got to mean something positive. *Right?*

Only the large officer and I are in the building, or at least in this room; I'm not positive what exists beyond the doors that are beyond the front desk. I could assume maybe offices and jail cells. I wonder where I'm headed. I stare down the man at the front desk to see if I'll get acknowledged, but he looks at his phone, periodically chuckling under his breath. I'm not sure what I'm waiting for or for how long, because no one has told me anything, and this man doesn't seem to be doing any actual work or have any actual concern in the world for anything but his phone screen.

It dawns on me that my phone is still in my back pocket. I contemplate if this officer does look over, he might take it away from me, but I can't stare at him any longer. I unlock my screen and read the newest posts on the Vigil app:

**A New Suspect!**

**Mary Pearly, South Island**

*1 hr ago*

*The information is with the police. A new suspect will be in custody soon! It's a very strong possibility we have figured out who murdered Jim. I hope his family gets the justice they deserve, and this evil person will be punished for what they did. No matter what, they will have to face GOD with the truth on judgment day.*

This confirms why I'm here. Mary reported me. That bitch!

The post has hundreds of likes and many comments:

> *Prayers! God will bring this criminal to justice!*
>
> *This town is going to hell! Ever since all these northerners moved down here, the crime has gone way up. Go back to where you came from!!*
>
> *Does anyone know who it is?*

This is ridiculous. I haven't done anything or anything that I can remember, at least. I think of Chico's bloody paws, seeing Aimsley in the lightning. I remember standing in the tide, tossing the totem in the water. I wish I could remember anything after that, but I can't. At least I wouldn't be able to fail a lie detector test since I can't remember doing it.

I clear my throat, trying to get the attention of the officer at the desk. He continues to stare at his phone and laugh. My patience is wearing thin. I need to know what is going on here and what they think my involvement is. I have to let them know about Aimsley's assault. I can't wait any longer. I grip my phone tightly, splitting part of the cut on my hand open. A droplet of blood oozes out and onto the floor. I sit up and shout at the officer, "Excuse me?"

He doesn't budge. He doesn't look up from his phone. He clearly can hear me; I am the only other person in this room, but he simply chooses not to acknowledge me. I grit my teeth, stand from my chair clenching my hand tighter. As I open my mouth, a door from behind the front desk opens, and a new officer says my name.

"Yes, that's me."

"Follow me, we're going to have a chat," the officer says as he holds open the door for me to pass through.

I follow him down the hall into a small room.

This officer is young, maybe even younger than I am. He still has his boyish features, no facial hair, and taut skin. He is rather handsome, with short dark brown hair and green eyes. He's tall and built, but his movements are youthful, like he's still getting used to his body. In the room is a small desk with two more of the metal and plastic chairs. The wall has a large glass panel, like the double-sided glass windows you'd see on detective shows. It's definitely an interrogation room. Taking a seat, I cross my legs and put my arms under the desk.

The officer lays out a folder on the desk, takes the seat across from me, and rests on his elbows, interlocking his fingers. "How are you doing, Elizabeth? I'm Officer Rodger Macon. I see Chief Duncan brought you in tonight?" His voice is deep, but I can't tell if he's making it deeper than it actually is.

"Hi. I'm alright, I guess. I'm not exactly sure who brought me in. I never caught his name. Does he have a daughter named Brooke?" I ask.

"Yes, he does. Why? Do you know her?"

"No, not really. I just know of her. My friend Aimsley dates her. She just told me tonight, before he brought me here."

"You're friends with Aimsley, huh?"

"Ugh, yeah."

He squints his eyes and keeps them focused on me. "You don't say," he pauses, seeming to contemplate my answer. "So, I have a few questions I need to ask you about. Do you know why you were brought in tonight?"

"No, I don't," I say, surely, although I have a few ideas.

He slides over the manila folder and opens it, taking out a couple of pictures. One picture is of the ceremonial totem I made sitting on the sand, the other picture is a close-up of the totem on a metal surface. He asks, "Do you recognize this object?"

It makes me sad to see it like this. It was meant for the ocean, and now it probably lies in some plastic bag in a bin in the back of an evidence room.

I answer, "Yes."

"Okay." Officer Macon pulls out another sheet of paper with a map of the beach. He pops the cap off a marker and marks an *"X"* over my house. He looks at me and asks, "Do you recognize this location?"

It feels like a question he already knows the answer to, but I understand there is a point to be made. I answer, "I live there. It's my house."

"Okay." He then draws another *"X"* on the beach just a little north of my house and makes a line connecting the two *"X's"*. "This other location is where we found the object that you say you recognize. A very short distance from your house, wouldn't you say?"

I feel like rolling my eyes. I know he is trying to connect the dots for some sort of dramatic effect, but I've seen too many detective shows to feel convinced. As much as I want him to get to the point, I refrain and answer clearly, "Yes."

"This object pictured here was found last Monday morning. Do you have any idea how it got there?" Now he goes back to interlocking his fingers, resting them on the table in front of me as he slightly leans in, waiting for my reply.

Instead of entertaining more of the questioning, I figure I would just give him the full explanation. I explain, "Yes." I tap on the picture of the totem. "This is a ceremonial totem. I tossed it in the tide early Monday morning. I lost my partner to the sea a few months ago. You might have seen it on the news. The captain who was taken by pirates in Africa? I made this raven, and wrapped inside of it is a small rose quartz stone. A way to send my love to him because his body was never recovered."

Officer Macon tilts his head, clearly not expecting what I had told him. "So this isn't witchcraft?"

"Ugh! I know who called in the tip. Let me guess, Mary Pearly?"

He straightens up. He looks even more confused now, probably wondering how I could have guessed.

"Look, I'm an artist, not a *witch*. When I first moved here, I tried to get into the art markets, but Mary Pearly didn't like my art and basically shunned me from participating in the art community here. So, I sent her a rather nasty email. My guess is she has something personal against me. But there's nothing evil about it. The totem is a message of love. The totem is art. Mary knows this is my art."

He appears slightly disappointed that it wasn't an object of witchcraft. After a moment, he says, "Oh, I was just at the art market today, actually. Bought something for the wife. And I'm sorry to hear about your partner." He takes a second to think, bringing his thumb and index finger to grip the bottom of his chin. "But wait, you said you threw it into the ocean early Monday morning?"

He's not completely dense. He's sticking to his timeline. I honestly thought he would overlook the connection, but he appeared to be smarter than I thought.

All I can do is be honest about what I already stated and say, "Yes."

"What exact time were you on the beach Monday morning?" He gets out a small notepad and pen.

"Between two and three in the morning, I believe." He scribbles down the number two and a dash and the number three.

"The reason you were brought here for questioning is because we are investigating the murder of Jim Crowley. Now, I don't believe this art object of yours is really a connection after hearing your side, but you also happened to be on the beach around the same time he was murdered. As of right now, you are the only person we can place near the crime scene at that time. Either you are a possible witness, or you could be considered a possible suspect. Were you with anyone else who can confirm the time and what you were doing? Did you see anything that night?"

Without much thought, I blurt out, "Aimsley." I instantly regret telling him this. Between getting her into the situation with Chief Duncan and now mentioning her name to the police, she might have to be my alibi after all. Even though I feel bad, I need her to be. She was the only one. She might just be my saving grace.

"Aimsley? August? You don't say." His eyebrows rise, and he squints his eyes again in contemplation.

"Yep."

# Aimsley August

**Maybe this was karma.** Maybe I deserved it.

Karma or not, I don't regret what I said to that bastard. He wasn't any better than me. He was only more brutal. More angry. More devious.

My stomach is sore, my muscles flinching, but my body hurts less than my mind does, because things between Brooke and me are surely through.

*It's over.*

Deep down, I think the end of us was coming all along. We fight constantly. Her parents hate me. Her dad just punched and kicked me. I cheated. I'm convinced she cheated. Everything between us is broken now.

Hopefully, Duncan won't rat me out to Brooke, knowing I have dirt on him, too. If he wants to avoid looking foolish, he won't bring it up. I'm just not sure what to do now. What if he did tell her? I can't go home now. And I'm practically under the bridge. My knees are cut up from being punched to the ground. I can't drive. I don't have my skateboard.

*Guess I'm walking.*

I gather myself and start walking up the gravel road towards the street and onto the sidewalk of the bridge. With each step, my stomach muscles wince. He got me damn good.

*The bastard!*

It crosses my mind that I could text Jada. She doesn't live far from here at all. But I know she will only lecture me to high hell. That's not the kind of support I need right now. The only support I feel I need is from the glass rim of a strong drink. Maybe one of those Old Fashioneds that Elizabeth drinks.

I only hope Duncan isn't treating her like he's just treated me. I'm not even sure why she was taken in the first place. She mentioned being in trouble, but what for? The night with her was going so well before he had to ruin it. I felt a real spark with her. There was a flame, a passion I haven't felt in a long time, especially not from Brooke.

I stop at the top of the bridge, looking over the railing. The night is eerily dark and quiet, still air even from this height, and the sky is clear as far as I can see. The moon sits low on the horizon. A few stars sparkle. The water is an endless pit of darkness, below me. There is no definition of where it ends or begins until a boat appears from under the bridge. It stops near the cluster of lanterns, now stuck in the marsh grasses. How sad to see this side of the lantern memorial. The burning flame, some sort of symbol for everlasting memories of Jim, that will float out to sea, only to be tangled further into the island. The flames were doused and the lanterns removed by state workers.

I start walking down the bridge when my phone buzzes in my pocket. I feared it was Brooke, but I'm surprised to see it's Officer Macon. I answer, "Hello?"

"Aimsley, are you okay? It's Rodger. Officer Rodger Macon." He sounds concerned.

"Hey, Rodger. Yeah, I'm alright."

On the other line, he sighs in relief and says, "Where are you right now? Do you need a ride?"

"Yeah, actually, I'm on the bridge, walking towards town."

"Ok, I'll be right there," he says and hangs up.

I watch every last one of the lanterns being pulled from the water as time passes. Finally, a pair of headlights flash me as Officer Macon pulls over on the side of the bridge and stops so that I can get in.

Putting on my seatbelt strikes a pain in my side, causing me to moan out.

"Hey, kid. Are you hurt?"

I grab my stomach and answer, "Yeah, I'll be okay though. I'm tough." I let out a little laugh, which makes the pain strike again.

Rodger shakes his head and asks, "Figured I could give you a ride home?"

"Actually, I was just on my way to have a drink."

"I'm off duty. How about I buy you a beer?"

"Thanks, but I think I'll need something stronger."

We ride in silence over to Eddy's, the only dive bar open after nine o'clock off the beach. It sits by its lonesome in a small vacant shopping center, the name scribbled in red neon light above the opening of the bar. A garage door rolled up. Over one side is a tiki hut style grass roof and high-top wooden tables where a group of smokers sit and swig bottle neck beers. The crowd turns and looks at us as we move into the bar. The volume of everyone's conversations lower. I recognize a few faces, but not the normal crowd I get at Breaker's. Most of the people are in their sixties and seventies with leathery skin, and there are some younger people who look rough around the edges. I'm sure Rodger's uniform is the cause of the disruption, but I don't care what they think. I need a drink.

1980s rock music blares from the speakers. The bar is decently full of people at different stages of drunkenness. The walls are packed with cheesy sayings painted on driftwood and neon beer signs. A full mirror wall along the back of the space makes it appear larger and more crowded than it really is. We walk over to the U-shaped bar to order our drinks. Rodger puts mine on his tab, and we make our way to the back corner, past the pool tables, to sit at a high-top for two. I take a long, hard sip of my whiskey and Coke. This was not the place for an Old Fashioned, but it will do the trick.

Rodger swigs his drink, looking around the bar, scoping out our surroundings. "So, I met your friend tonight...Elizabeth."

I suck on the straw in my glass, emptying a good portion of my drink. "Yeah, I figured you did. Is she in trouble?"

"Well, I was questioning her as a possible suspect."

"Suspect? For what?"

"For the murder."

"What? No way. She'd never do anything like that."

"Turns out the tip we received about her was nothing but small-town drama, but I think I need you to clarify something for me...to help eliminate her for good."

"Oh, yeah, sure. Whatever I can do to help."

"Did you see Elizabeth on Monday between two and three in the morning?"

Instantly, the image of her silhouette cast by the lightning came to mind. I say, "Yes. She was near the tide. I was walking back from a night out. Brooke and I were fighting, so I ended up outside her house." I hope telling him this won't get me involved in some sort of investigation. I already have enough drama on my plate.

"Ok. That's the same thing she told me. I just wanted to be sure. But why didn't you tell me before when I was at the bookstore?"

I grip my glass nervously and say, "I just didn't think it was relevant, so I didn't want to bring it up and confuse the situation. Sorry, I guess I should have." I lower my head, bowing in apology.

"It's alright." He swigs his drink and turns to look at a drunk couple arguing at the jukebox. I wonder if this is what people see when Brooke and I argue. It's actually embarrassing.

"I'm just glad you're okay. I mean, are you okay? I can't believe he did that to you. You know Duncan is such an asshole. I don't understand how he's even still Chief. He thinks he can get away with anything."

"So, Elizabeth told you everything?" I wonder how much she talked. This is embarrassing.

Rodger gives me a sympathetic look. He says, "Look, I'm not judging you. And if you want to write a report, it wouldn't be easy, but I could take it above his head."

His concern is sweet, but I wasn't looking for sympathy or even to pursue any more drama than I had to. "Thanks, Rodger, but I'm just going to stay out of it. Plus, I don't want you to sacrifice your job. There's no proof."

We sit in silence for a bit, draining our drinks and watching two younger males strike balls across the pool table. I wasn't really focusing on their game; rather, zoning out. Thinking about our kiss. Reimagining how Elizabeth felt. Seeing her naked skin.

*I want more.*

"So did you let her go?" I ask Rodger.

"Elizabeth? Oh yeah, of course. Someone came and picked her up. Her mom, I believe."

From behind me, I heard a familiar laugh coming from the bar. I turn around and see Tiffany sitting at the bar with some of her friends. "Hey, do you want another round? I can buy this time."

Rodger shook his head, "No kid. I better be heading home. Already getting texts from the wife. We're starting a new series tonight. Can't miss out. But hey, I'll give you a ride wherever you're staying."

"Oh, thanks. I actually have a friend here. I'll probably stay for a few more. But thanks for the ride onto the island. I really appreciate it."

"No problem, Aimsley. Stay safe tonight. You have my

number, remember?" We both stand up from the table and make our separate ways.

"Hey, Tiff."

"Aims! What is up?" She smiles and hugs me, squeezing the nerves from me.

I shake off the hug and lean against the bar, feeling some relief to be with a close friend. "Not much, just came out for some drinks."

"Yeah, drinking with your cop buddy, I see. What's that about? Not going straight on me, are you?" She chuckles and leans into my shoulder. Her long, dark brown hair wisps into my face.

"Yeah, right. No. He's just a friend. He gave me a ride." I chuckle and think about Elizabeth, wondering if she'd enjoy hanging out with Tiffany. The thought makes me realize how intertwined our friend group is and how Tiffany would never hang out with Elizabeth. None of my friends would, and if I do break it off with Brooke, they may never want to hang out with me again, either. I could lose all of my friends.

"Okay, well, next drink is on me!" She waves down the bartender. Smiling at me, she says, "Brooke's meeting me."

My chest shrivels.

*Of course she is.*

Tiffany and Brooke are best friends, so it shouldn't be a surprise, but I can't see her right now. Not tonight.

"Hey, I'm good on the drink. I was just heading out, actually."

"Oh, no. Really?" She frowns deeply. "Well, wait, are you

coming to the hotel tomorrow?" She crosses her fingers, brings her knuckles under her chin, and pouts her lips.

I ask, "What hotel?"

"Didn't Brooke tell you? Dean got us a room. Hurricane party baby!" She throws her arm up into the air and flicks her wrist.

"Oh yeah, sweet. Yeah, I'll be there. But hey, I'll talk to you tomorrow, okay?" I lean into give her a side hug and again she squeezes hard causing my stomach muscles to wince painfully before I can get away.

I wonder if they will talk about me, or if it was just a usual drink meet-up. I guess I'd normally be at work, so I wouldn't know if this was a regular hangout. I guess I don't really know what Brooke does in her free time, which is only further validation of my suspicions that she has been cheating on me. Or I'm only assuming she is because I did.

*I cheated.*

Either way, my heart aches. My body aches. My brain aches.

Even if this hurricane doesn't come, a storm in my love life will, sooner or later.

# Elizabeth Corey

*I'm never asking my mother for another favor.*

She had the audacity to lecture me the entire car ride from the police station to the bridge. About how I've inconvenienced her life, how I'm putting a mark on her reputation, even after I explained I hadn't done anything, and that they only wanted to question me. She almost didn't let me drive my car home, accusing me of being too drunk to drive, when in fact, I hadn't had a drop of alcohol for hours. My own mother, who was supposed to be supportive and on my side, accuses me of putting myself in this situation. Even after I mention the corrupt cop and what he did to Aimsley, her only response is to "stay away from troublemakers". Why does she think she can still treat me like a teenager? Maybe because she was never in my life to harass me before? I'm through with her. And I'm through with everyone on this god-forsaken island!

*I need a smoke.*

I don't normally, but there's a hidden stash with my name

on it somewhere in this house. I fear they could be in the art studio, which I barely go into anymore. I rummage through boxes while averting my eyes from my painting on the wall. Chico follows me, wagging his tail and sniffing into the boxes as I throw things out of them.

"Ugh!" I shout, rubbing my temples.

*The coffee table drawer...*

Finally, I remember where I stashed them last. I trudge my feet into the living room and discover the crumpled pack of smokes and a lonely lighter. A small win. A relief that couldn't come any sooner. I move to the balcony with the remainder of the bottle of wine I've been drinking. Chico's at my heels, anxious to come with me. I open the door and gesture for him to pass. "Come on then." I'm frustrated, but not at him. Of course, he can come sit with me. I wouldn't have it any other way. He's the only living thing that gives a shit about me right now.

I plop down in my Adirondack chair, picturing my love cutting the beveled edge of this armrest every time my fingers grace the end of it. A brighter time, in a different place. I flick the lighter and take a long, deep drag. The cigarette end crackles. Nicotine rushes down my spine, and I exhale the frustrations from my mouth loudly. I don't like to smoke. I hate the smell, how the burnt tobacco sticks to my clothes and tongue, but right now, the relief is worth the stench.

I puff on the filter as the bright orange end smolders against the pitch-black sky. The sound of the waves are soft and subtle. A calm night, unlike me. Now that I am alone and without cops or my mother, I try to let the night take me. Let the wine slide down my throat and coat my emotions. Let the cigarette relax my shoulders. Let my back lie into the chair, resting both limbs on the armrests with my cigarette in one hand and a bottle in the other. My head tilts back slightly, looking into the faint stars above me. I wish one of the speckles were an alien ship on its way to beam me up. Chico's warm body leans against my legs that dangle, tiptoes touching the footrest.

At least for now, the police aren't looking at me. I somehow managed to get myself out of that one. My car is back to its resting place in the garage, harboring the gun that I never managed to dispose of, even though I think I still should.

The wine is rich on my tongue. My lips feel dry. I feel Aimsley on them as I bite and suck in the bottom one.

What have I done? What have I become? Right now, I feel like a monster. I don't recognize myself anymore. The misplaced gun and make-out sessions. Who am I? I'm completely reckless and acting on pure instinct at this point. I'm so close to giving in to pure destructiveness. What does it matter anyway? I could be anything, do anything. No matter what happens, I'm not going to prison. No way. It's my life.

*My fuck up of a life.*

I finish off the final swig of the bottle. It feels empty like me. I think about smashing it, but my energy for aggression has passed. My mind is finally shutting down. The alcohol has coated my rash heart, so I carefully set it down on the deck beside my chair. The anger turns to a dull numbness. I am alone.

Figuring I could tease my feelings once more by reading the latest posts on the Vigil app:

**Shame on PBPD!**

**Mary Pearly, South Island**

*20 min ago*

*The police have ignored my warning. They let the suspect be free to sleep in her own bed tonight, or worse, to hurt someone else. I know exactly who made this witchcraft. She should be behind bars! You know who you are! Your spells may have worked on the police, but they don't work on me. I will find out more. You'll see!*

Instinctively, my head falls back into hysteria. Laughing loudly, devilishly to the sky. I'm so moved by her words, I could summon a broom and fly around the sky, laughing for the whole island to hear. The laughs become quieter, as hot tears force themselves from the ducts in the corner of my eyes. What would my love say about the mess I've become? How would I know? He abandoned me. Us. Chico and I. This house. Our dream. And he's not coming back.

"Fuck him!" I shout and flick the cigarette from the balcony. Watching the orange end float down to the backyard beneath me. My eyes well up with tears, painfully pushing through the dead expression on my face. I'm tired of crying. I'm tired of being sad. I'm tired of being.

*What's the point?*

A shadow passes in the backyard. I become alert but stay still, trying to focus my eyes, ears, and mind. I feel my mind is making me see someone. I question if the dark shadow outside of the gate is a person or a shadow cast by the tall grass. It's too dark to tell, and my mind seems to be playing tricks on me lately. My heart beats heavily in my chest. The blood pools in my head, and a cold sweat comes over my skin. I stare at the shadow. I stare hard and with intent. I want it to move. I want it to be someone. I'll face my demons if I have to. I've had enough. I grip the armrests with my fingers, my nails digging into the surface. I hold my breath.

*Fuck with me.*

Chico shifts from my legs, feeling my tension. He peers in between the wooden pillars and growls deeply. His tail sticks straight out, and one paw lifts. He's pointing. My heart pounds in my chest now, and I grow faint in my head. The edge of the shadow shifts, and I hear, "Elizabeth?"

I recognize that voice. The hair on my arms rises. A shiver runs down my spine as I squint hard to make out what I see, but it's too dark. I don't respond.

"It's me, Aimsley."

The breath I was holding rushes from my full chest and out of my mouth, "Fuck! You scared the shit out of me!"

She doesn't say anything, and the shadow doesn't move. I hold my breath again. Is she really there? I freeze again, staring hard into the darkness.

"Sorry. Can I come up?" The shadow moves over the gate. I hate that I can't see her, but I think Chico does. He stops growling and wags his tail, setting down his paw. I stand up from my chair.

I say to the darkness, "Yeah, hold on. I can't see a fucking thing."

She doesn't respond, still making me wary, but I rush inside and down the stairs to the back door. I let Chico hold his presence in front of me, tail still wagging. I take another deep breath and unlock the door, letting him run out into the yard. To my surprise, he doesn't bark but instead disappears into the darkness of the backyard. I still see a shadow at the gate, but it's clearer now. As I walk into the sand and my eyes adjust, I see the shadow leaning over the fence and petting Chico.

"Good boy," she says as she pets him. "Hey, sorry. I would have called, but I never got your number."

I feel for the latch and unlock it to let her in. "It's ok, come inside."

Ahead of me, Chico runs inside, through the back door. The light from the house draws me back through the darkness of the backyard.

"Sorry, I couldn't tell it was you." I walk up the first few steps. I don't hear the door shut behind me or any footsteps on the stairs behind me. When I turn around, the door is wide open. Aimsley isn't behind me.

*What the hell?*

I walk back down, asking, "Aimsley?" I don't hear her or see anything or anyone. I shut the door quickly and lock the deadbolt. Chico is on the top step, staring down and wagging his tail. He turns and runs off, hearing his footsteps race across the kitchen. I run up the stairs after him. "Chico. Wait."

From the top of the stairs, my heart pounds and my vision

grows slightly blurry. I grasp the railing, holding on to steady the stairway from spinning. The wine's got hold of me. I force two more steps to the top and peer into the kitchen to see it empty and no Chico.

I shout again, "Chico!"

He doesn't come, so I turn the corner through the doorway into the living room and through it. I see the tip of his tail slip past the balcony doors. I follow. Pushing open the cracked door to the balcony, I see Chico's feet.

"Hey, are you okay?"

"Fuck!" I shout and jump from my toes at the sight of Aimsley emerging from the side of the balcony. She stands with a look of concern on her face.

"Is this some kind of joke?" I ask her.

"What?" She looks at me blankly.

I feel faint and grasp the side of my chair, shifting my weight to sit on it. She continues to stare at me, looking confused. I shake my head.

She asks me again, "Are you alright?" She places her hand on my arm, lightly grasping it. Closing in on me, she stands between my legs that dangle from the chair. She moves a lock of hair from my face, and I realize I must have blacked out for a moment. My mind swirls, and I say, "Yeah, I just thought you were downstairs, and now you're here. Sorry, I don't know."

She grips my arm harder and lifts my chin to look into my eyes. "Hey, it's okay. You were going to get us drinks. Remember? I'll get them."

Through the balcony doors, she reaches out her arm and

hands me a drink, saying, "Guess we've both had a really stressful night."

Embarrassed, I extend my glass to the air in between us and say, "Cheers to that."

# Aimsley August

**It may have been a terrible idea coming here, but I don't care.** The moment she let me in, I instantly felt the outside world leave my mind. I was finally getting to enter the house. The inner walls of the tall, dark and mysterious house that's held my fascination for all these months. I'm finally *inside* Elizabeth's space.

She seems disheveled. Her appearance is no longer clean and confident, as it was a few hours before. Her cat-eye eyeliner now runs in squiggly lines down the sides of her cheeks. She has obviously been crying. I wonder what happened at the police station. I wonder if Rodger had worn her down. Was that what drove the black eyeliner from the creases of her eyes, or was it something else? Either way, I have entered her territory, and any feelings of worry I had before have evolved into excitement. My emotions have found a second wind as I observe the grandiose staircase, the high ceilings, wooden framed doorways, and dramatic chandeliers. I wonder how many rooms there are and what treasures they hold. I can now see firsthand the projects that she told me about. There are walls with only small swatches of color on them, surrounded by tarps with cans of paint and dried-up paint trays.

Sipping wine on this balcony with her is what I had imagined before. I'm finally here. I didn't arrive in quite the same way I'd fantasized, but I've made it. I can't help but smile. I wonder where the night could take us. *Us.* Maybe this could become something. Maybe all the struggles with Brooke had led me here to Elizabeth's home to start something new. I could help her finish painting these walls. I could live here.

As I sip my wine and pet her dog that circles my calves, I realize Elizabeth doesn't show the same enthusiasm I have. Her gaze is distant, looking out to the darkness. Her eyes are dark with speckles, like the stars. She looks out to the sea with an endless longing. "What do you see out there?" I ask her.

She blinks, noticeably from the lack of blinking before. She continues to look out, "Well, nothing now." She peers out, as if in a trance, but says, "I'm looking for him."

I look out into the darkness, knowing I can't see anything, but I do it anyway.

She stares out for some time before quietly speaking again. "He's everything. The water as it crashes, the tide as it swells over the sand, the back and forth that keeps rushing. He's in there, lost, forever. My love.

"I've had this thought. If I keep looking out there, one day he'll come walking out of the tide, through the waves and up this sand dune. He'll come through the gate and up to me.

He'll come home to me. I know it's foolish, but I think about it all the time."

"It's not foolish."

Here I had been so googly-eyed, I didn't realize the whole truth of her situation. She was grieving and grieving *hard*. I was lucky not to know the feeling. I've never lost anyone very close to me, to death. All I can think to say is, "I'm so sorry."

She breaks her gaze and drinks from her glass. Before I can offer another pour, she gets up and grabs the whole bottle from the kitchen. Flipping open a box of cigarettes, she pulls two out and offers me one. We both sit on the balcony, indulging in nicotine and wine. She looks over to me. Smoke empties slowly from her mouth as she asks, "You doing alright? That guy hit you pretty hard today. I was really worried."

I grip my stomach and lift the edge of my shirt, but it's too dark to see any bruising.

"I'll be alright. I'd rather just forget about it, to be honest."

"He can't treat you like that. It's not right."

As much as I appreciate her concern, I know there's nothing that can be done when dealing with him. I'm the only one who can make this go away.

"I know. I think Brooke and I are through."

She nods her head, listening.

"I was going to propose to her."

Elizabeth's eyes light up unexpectedly. She replies, "I didn't know you were in such a serious relationship."

Her comment makes my cheeks warm with guilt. I explain, "Things have been really rocky lately."

"I can see where that father-in-law relationship could definitely complicate things."

Her comment makes me laugh. "You have no idea."

"Okay, let's change the subject to something lighter. What do you like to do?" Elizabeth asks.

I smirk. "What do you mean?"

She smiles softly back at me and says, "What do you like to do for fun? Like, do you have a hobby?"

"Yeah. I like to write."

"Really?" She perks up at my response, engaging in what I have to say next.

"Yeah. I want to be an author. You know, write a book. I've actually started something new." I think about my book sitting in the front windows of Book & Brew, even though it hasn't been written.

"You should totally write that book. I can see it makes you smile when you talk about it. That's how I feel about my art. Well, used to anyway."

I feel her peering into my soul. Exposing a side of me that rarely shows itself to others. This woman has me wanting her. She's dark, intriguing, broken, but passionate and a little lost like me. I want to see her smile. I want to make her feel good. Like I had earlier today. Touching her made her feel that way.

My wine glass clinks as I set it on the balcony handrail. I move closer to her, sitting on her throne. My dark queen. I place my hand on her thigh resting bare against the hardwood of the chair. She looks down at my hand and back up at me as she tosses back the rest of her wine and sets her glass on the handrail next to mine. I move my thumb across the burgundy stain on her bottom lip. She stares at me deeply, as if searching endlessly as she does towards the shoreline. Her watery, dark, twinkling eyes open up as a million stars fill them, pouring out down her cheeks.

She asks softly, "Why me?"

She asks the question like she can't believe I want her attention. Or maybe she asks it, pained with tragedy. Nonetheless, all I can do is smile and lean in, where she meets me for a gentle and slow kiss. Hunger pains me. I want more, so much *more*, but I retract, wiping the dampness from the corners of her eyes, cleaning the eyeliner smears away.

# PART II

# WEDNESDAY

# Aimsley August

*Once she had a taste, she could no longer feed on others. Her heart had transformed into something altogether unusual.*

I ponder in the shallow light and the small pitter-patter of rain hitting the thin windows in Elizabeth's living room. Like a sprinkler, waves of raindrops hit the glass, pause, and then start again. The wind shakes the pine trees. Their needles peck at the glass, asking to come inside. This old house is showing its age as the elements outside feel closer than they should be. Judging by the rain and the dim light, weather bands from the hurricane are finally here. As much as I'd like to check my phone sitting on the coffee table for any weather updates, my arm is trapped under the weight of Elizabeth's snoring head.

Last night, after indulging in too many glasses of wine, we made our way to the couch and only spoke briefly before succumbing to an inevitable sleep. It had been a long day for both of us. A mentally exhausting day. Elizabeth lay soundly, clutching my arm. She holds me while sleeping like she's afraid I'd sneak off in the morning. I don't want to disturb her, but I attempt to slightly lean over, reaching with my right arm to the coffee table. My fingernails can barely grip the edge of my phone. With a few tries, I'm able to quietly slide it into my hand and relax back onto the couch without waking her.

My phone is full of notifications. The news, the Vigil app, and my friend group chat. Firstly, I read the updates in the Vigil app. The post titles stick out like a sore thumb:

***I'm Not Giving Up on Jim!***
***Mary Pearly, South Island***

*2 hrs ago*

*If the PBPD can't bring Jim justice, I'll make it my duty to find more evidence and bring her down! She is over there living her life, while Jim's family is left suffering every day.*

***SAY HER NAME!***
***Mary Pearly, South Island***

*1 hr ago*

*I have decided to warn the people. Everyone has a right to know that ELIZABETH COREY is a murderer. SAY HER NAME! GUILTY WITCH! You won't get away with this.*

***!!Reminder!!***
***Mary Pearly, South Island***

*30 mins ago*

*Don't trust anyone who associates with ELIZABETH COREY!*

*Oh my god.*

There's a tightness in my chest. I'm aching from the letdown this will bring Elizabeth when she sees it. I wish there were a way for me to remove the posts to keep her from reading them. I select at the bottom of the posts to report it as inappropriate, but I'm not sure it'll be taken down, and most people have probably already read it. At least Elizabeth is still asleep for now. The publicity also doesn't do any favors for my reputation. If anyone sees me leaving this house, I could be in serious trouble.

Elizabeth shifts slightly, making a grunting noise. Chico perks up from his bed on the living room floor, coming over to sniff her. This dog cares so much for her. He's probably been watching over us all night to make sure the new stranger wasn't a threat to his mom. He sniffs my toes, pausing to give me a judgmental look, as if giving me a warning, before he struts back over to lie in his bed.

I'm disappointed I didn't have any texts from Brooke. Maybe she got wasted at the bar with Tiffany last night, or maybe she's waiting to attack me in front of everyone at the hurricane party. The texts I did receive are all from my friend group chat:

**Dean:** *Brace yourselves! Amelia's coming to give us a big ol' spanking! HAHA*

*Cameron: Dude! CAT 4...legendary!*

*Tiffany: Who's at Breakers? Can you fill up a couple of ice coolers?*

*Dean: Been done! Boss closed the bar. NO WORK for two days!*

*Brooke: WOOT WOOT! What about booze??*

*Cameron: You already know I got the deals from the truck this morning...slid that man that good tip $$*

*Dean: Bet you did Cameron... 4 PM. FLAMINGO INN ROOM #24*

*Garnet: GUYS! It's the curse!! Are we going to die??*

*Jada: I'm actually low-key freaking out. I'm really worried about my house. I'm in line to get sandbags at the park. Can someone help me put up boards?*

*Cameron: It'll be fine Jada... but ya I'll help*

It looks like I'm the only one who hasn't had input on this conversation yet. And it's clear that Brooke actively decided not to text me, which doesn't feel good. I'm not even sure what to say. I'm also afraid of being confronted. Maybe Brooke's dad didn't say anything. Maybe he's too busy with his affair to really care, or maybe he's busy with hurricane prep.

Every headline is some similar form of panicked warning

like "Category 4 Hurricane Amelia, headed straight for the Painter's Beach area". It's strange to see, because only yesterday the storm was supposed to be shifting away. Being a local, I want to brush it off as nothing, like we normally do, but they don't normally mention our island so specifically. That's actually concerning. The news articles seem very certain that the path is set. We have never had a storm that looked like this, so certain and so direct. I just hope the news is wrong. As long as I'm with my close friends, everything should be okay, but what about Elizabeth? What will she do? She can't stay here in this house by herself.

Suddenly, her phone buzzes from beneath us. It must be lodged in the couch cushions. I shake Elizabeth lightly, encouraging her to wake up.

She mutters and then opens her eyes, "Huh?"

She looks adorable with her dark hair all disheveled from sleeping on the couch. I can't help but smile before saying, "Good morning. Your phone is ringing."

Sleepily, she asks, "What? Where is it?"

The buzzing continues, and I say, "I think it's lost to the couch monster."

She rubs her eyes and laughs, releasing my arm, still warm from her body. I help remove couch cushions to discover her phone. She sits cross-legged on the couch next to me, looking at her phone inside a tent made of tangled hair. She lets out a frustrated sigh, "Ugh! Not answering that. My mother's probably just trying to start an early morning lecture."

"Well, to be fair, it is the afternoon."

She looks at me crossly with one eye through an opening in her hair. I almost question if that made her mad, but she raises both of her arms, stretching them as high as they could go, and yawns loudly before giggling.

"What can I say? I'm a night owl."

She smacks her lips, as if her mouth is dry. Before pursing her lips and mimicking an owl noise, "Whooo!" We both laugh. It's nice to see her in a better mood, which makes me feel awful to break it with the news. I get up to get us some water. When I hand her the glass, she chugs it down like she hadn't drunk anything in days. I do the same. Before she has the chance to find out for herself, I say, "Hey, so I have some news."

She slumps over her crossed legs, burying her head in her hands. She replies, "If it's bad, I don't want to hear it."

I know she doesn't want to hear it, but it'd be better coming from me than the phone.

"I'm sorry to break it to you, but that Mary lady posted again. And it's not good."

Elizabeth perks up, grabbing her phone. The energy in her movements suddenly isn't sleepy. As she opens her phone to find the posts, I tell her, "She named you on there. Accusing you on Vigil of murdering that guy."

I grit my teeth in anticipation of her reaction. I wait to hear her call Mary names and toss things about, but to my surprise, she sets her phone aside and stares at the rain outside the window, gripping her water glass and taking small sips. She seems to be zoning out again.

"What does it matter? Everyone hates me on this stupid island already," she states plainly.

Hearing her say that makes me want to fix it. I'm just not sure how. I take her glass and set it on the coffee table, bracing her in a hug. She feels resistant at first, but then she gives in, resting her open mouth on my shoulder. If I had no shirt on, her teeth would be digging into my skin. "That's not true. I don't hate you."

"Aimsley, you seem to be the only one who doesn't."

"Well, one is better than none." I am trying my best to turn the situation into a positive one. I want her to smile, to be happy, but I have to tell her the other bad news too. "There's one more thing," I say as she still rests heavily in my arms, "Hurricane Amelia is supposed to be here tonight. It's a category four, and they predict we are in the direct path."

She pulls back from me and combs her fingers through her hair, untangling the knots.

"Of course it is."

Pine trees dance in the reflection of her eyes.

"Do you have somewhere you can go? There are already mandatory evacuations for residents on the beach."

Wrapping the stray strands of hair tightly around her fingers, she takes a while to reply. I can almost see the gears turning in her mind with every twirl of her finger.

"Yeah, my mom has a place. Probably why she's calling me."

"Oh, okay. That's good. Have you been through a hurricane before? If you go inland a little, you'll definitely be fine. Hurricanes are really just a bunch of rain and wind."

Being from the Pacific Northwest, I wasn't sure if she had

ever experienced a major weather event like this, or if she was afraid. I can't read any emotion on her face at all. She continues staring off.

I place my hand on her thigh, which finally breaks her stare. She looks into my eyes, deeply. They appear darker than last night. How quickly I've altered her mood. I wish I could fix it. All I want to do is love her, make her feel better, but I can see her spiraling into her own mind.

She places her hand on top of mine, preventing it from moving anywhere else. After gripping it tightly, she claims, "I'll be alright. Do you have somewhere to go?"

"Yeah, actually. My friends got us a place at this motel on the island."

I feel guilty that I can't invite her. She doesn't know any of my friends, and I don't think they would really get along. They are so different from Elizabeth. That's why I like her, because she's unique, smart and creative. She probably also knows that if I am with my friends, I'll also be with Brooke. I feel bad, but what choice do I have? It'll be strange spending the night with Brooke after all this time with Elizabeth. Leaving her feels strange, like I'm failing her. All I can hope is that we can continue to hang out and that she believes me when I say I'm breaking up with Brooke.

She says nothing more. She gets up from the couch to feed and water Chico. She busies herself by picking up the kitchen. I take the silence as a hint to leave. She seems like she might be getting ready for her mom to pick her up. I pat Chico on the head in the kitchen and put my hands in my pockets.

"Hey, you guys stay safe. When this is over, maybe we can hang out again?" I ask.

She forces a smile, which makes me wonder if we ever will. A shallow pain twinges in my gut, but this time it's the pain from a metaphorical punch. I walk down the stairs and out through the gate. I climb to the very top of the dune, but before I descend to the beach, I look back one last time. Like nothing's changed, I see Elizabeth and Chico sitting on the balcony, looking out at the sea.

# Elizabeth Corey

**I thought Florida was supposed to be this sunny paradise, but it's been quite the opposite.** Maybe I should have stayed in the Pacific Northwest. Maybe I should have never taken that cross-country ride.

*Oh, how different life would be.*

I'm glad Aimsley's gone. I don't want to burden her anymore with my sorrow. I'd rather wallow in it by myself. She means well, but the look in her eyes and the way she touches me, I can tell she wants so much more. Much more than I have the space left in my heart to give. And to further involve her in this drama with Mary... I can't. She doesn't deserve it.

I couldn't bear to tell her the truth. The truth that I'm not one hundred percent sure if I was truly responsible for the murder or not. That I only used her to try to dispose of a weapon. That I used her name for the sake of my own alibi. That I can't trust myself or my mind, so why should she have to?

Maybe it's better that this hurricane is coming. The storm

can sweep me away. I'm not calling my mother back. I refuse to go anywhere with her. I'd rather go out to the sea to be with my love, where my true happiness lies, at the depths of the ocean with him. It's where I'm meant to be. Maybe this is the universe's way of bringing us together again. If the universe calls for it, I'll let it.

My phone continues to ring. My mother. I decide to pick up because I'm tired of her calling. "Hello?"

"Why aren't you picking up your phone? Are you coming to stay?" Her voice is demanding.

Instead of arguing or having her worry about me, I make up a lie. "No, I'm going to stay with friends, actually. In a hotel."

"Not that girl you were involved with yesterday, I hope. She's obviously trouble."

"Mom." I pause and wait for her to stop lecturing me. Then I say, "I'm good, Mom. I have to get going."

"Ok, honey. And don't worry about the house. That's what insurance is for."

I stay silent.

"I just know how you get with storms. Be safe, okay?"

"Thanks, I'll be fine," I reply and hang up the phone.

I feel bad that I didn't speak to her more. I want to believe that deep down, underneath the layer of pettiness, she is concerned for me. Maybe I should have given her more, but I'm too tired to. My mind is exhausted. My body is weak. I just want to curl into a ball with my Chico baby.

We curl up on the couch together. His thick fur acts as a blanket, as he drapes the weight of his body over my lap. I pet his head and down his back as he holds his head up and looks into my eyes. He lets out a small whimper, almost as if he knows what's happening.

"Shh, we'll be ok."

It's a lie, but Chico doesn't need to know that. In this moment, I only want to embrace his comforting cuddles. The noise of the rain showers against the windows. The living room light is low. A warm yellow tint comes in from the windows against the cool, dim blue walls.

Falling into a daydream, I think about the last time I saw my love. His smile. I can still see it. As much as it pains me to remember when I found out what happened to him, anytime a storm comes, it's all I can think about.

That day, I'd been waiting for an email from my love. I hadn't received anything in a while, which was unusual. I was terribly bothered by it, but I had to keep myself busy, or waiting to hear from him would drive me crazy. This is what I'd always done before, distracted myself from our time apart. So, I made myself a cup of coffee in the kitchen, and Chico followed me into the art studio. Burying myself deep into my practice was what kept my mind busy, preoccupied from worry or boredom that sent my mind into spirals.

While I waited for an email from him, I set up a large piece in the art studio. I wanted to express the frustrations I had been having with the island and my situation. You could say I was, in fact, inspired by Mary. Angered by her. By the people of the island. By the amount of projects looming throughout the house. By the lack of time here with Christian. Having to wait and wait. If Mary didn't want my dark content, it only fueled me to create something darker.

I stapled up a large piece of unprimed canvas on the wall. It was taller than me and almost as wide as the whole wall. I squeezed out large dollops of Lamp Black and Phthalo Blue paints onto a paint palette and, with a large brush, scraped up a heavy portion. I lay in dark blue figures, all representing the people in my life who frustrated me. One for my mother. One for my father. One for Mary. One for my love. I splattered them with dark, running black and red inks. I used my hands and smeared their faces. Covered them, swirling all the paints together, creating maroons and deep purples around their features that bled into the black background. When every inch of the canvas was covered, I took out large bundles of white braided yarn. With a long sharp needle, I threaded the yarn and began to pierce through the canvas. Piercing and pulling through, puncturing the surfaces around their figures, tying them up so they couldn't escape. Locking in the anger and frustration that they had caused me. Punishing them for hurting me.

Threading the needle again in red yarn, I embroidered the words over each of their eyes.

The first one: *"YOU SMOTHERED ME."*

The second: *"YOU DISAPPOINTED ME."*

The third: *"YOU REJECTED ME."*

And lastly: *"YOU ABANDONED ME."*

Hours had gone by. I took a step back to see what I had made. One of my largest and darkest pieces. I almost felt a sense of pride behind the feelings spilled on the canvas before me. Little did I know that the feelings I was having, the relief of pouring out my emotions, were only to become so much worse.

There was a knock on my front door.

My mother had shown up out of the blue. I answered the door in my painting apron, paint covering my hands and arms. She didn't bother observing my appearance; rather, the look on her face told me everything I needed to know. Something was wrong. Something was very, very wrong.

"What is it?" I pleaded.

My mother stepped into the kitchen and, with her arm on my shoulder, she asked, "Oh, honey, haven't you seen the news today? I've been calling you."

"I was painting. You know I don't watch the news."

Tears started to well up in the corner of my eyes, and I had a horrible feeling in the pit of my stomach. A doomed chill ran over my head and down my body to the floor.

When she spoke the words, "Something's happened to Christian," I couldn't process exactly what she was trying to say.

"What do you mean? What happened to him?" She started to pull me into her arms, giving me affection I hadn't had from her before. All the more reason to believe something was very wrong. But what? I couldn't wrap my mind around it.

"Elizabeth, he was taken."

"What do you mean *taken*?"

I turned the news on the TV. The name Astor Odyssey

came across the headline, following the report that the bulk carrier ship had been attacked by pirates. I watched with feverous intent, yelling at the TV to tell me where Christian was. When the anchor finally mentioned that the captain was missing, I collapsed on the floor of the living room.

For days, I waited for an update.

*They have to find him. They have to. They will find him.*

I hadn't eaten, I hadn't moved. I had sat on the couch, clutching Chico, only falling asleep after crying had worn me out.

*How can this be possible? What can I do to fix this? It's not possible. There's no way this is real.*

Mother stayed with me the first week, and on the fifth day, the news finally came that they found pieces of the pirate ship on the coastline of Africa. It had likely sunk over ten miles offshore, and there were no survivors. I had a terrible pain in my stomach. A pain that couldn't be undone.

The couch became my new home. I didn't want to exist anymore. The reality was so heartbreaking that I was numb to my existence. It took some coercing from my mother and a watchful eye to get me through that week. She didn't leave my house until I finally started eating and could bathe myself again.

I refused to do a memorial or a service. There wasn't a body. No survivors. All drowned. My love, drowning. It haunted me every day. Every time I heard a storm, my mind created scenarios of him in the water. He was caught in a part of the sinking ship until there was no air left, or he was floating in the open ocean until his body was too exhausted to swim anymore, and the water seeped into his mouth. He had to give up. All alone, dying alone. What a horrible death he had to suffer alone. And all I could do was wait here in our dream house, not knowing what to do next. So, I took the bottle of wine, and I drank from it in front of the painting in my studio, with Chico in my lap. I stared into the words I stitched into his eyes, YOU ABANDONED ME. It was like my subconscious mind had known it had happened before I had even been told. Like I'd stitched Christian's fate into reality. I killed him. I'm a murderer.

# Aimsley August

**The walk of shame. All the way back to my apartment, I feel guilt settling in.** I don't know if I'm in for the wrath of Brooke or not, but her car's not here.

Inside, the apartment is quiet and dark. I open up the curtains on the front windows to bring in some light. I flick on the living room lamp and a light in the kitchen.

I evaluate the apartment, wondering what kind of prep needs to be done. It doesn't look like Brooke did any prepping. I figure it would be a good idea to reach out to her. I finally text Brooke, breaking our long silence:

*Hey babe. Should we prep the apt?*

*Nah. It's probably fine.*

*Oh...you think so?*

*Can you just put stuff up off the ground, just in case?*

*Yeah, sure thing. Wyd?*

*With Tif. Getting ready for the party. C U there?*

The friendly response from Brooke surprises me. Although

it's not much of an interaction, it's more than I expected, and calmer than I anticipated. I can assume she doesn't know anything about me being with Elizabeth, especially if she was out partying last night with Tiffany. Maybe she hadn't given my whereabouts a thought, but my guilty conscience keeps me paranoid.

My mind was made up that I didn't want to be with Brooke anymore, so much so that I rationalized making moves on Elizabeth. But knowing I'll be hanging out with Brooke tonight at the hotel, and how cool she's being right now, makes me want to see her. It makes me doubt if getting wrapped up with Elizabeth was even a good idea. She seemed cold towards me this morning after everything we had been through. I feel like an idiot now, especially being in our apartment, surrounded by all of our things.

I look around the apartment, moving stuff off the ground. In the bedroom, I throw some clothes and a hamper up onto the bed. I move the power cord behind the TV onto the top of the dresser, right next to some picture frames. I pick up the one in front of me. It's a picture of Brooke and me when we first met. We looked so young, even though it was a few years ago. She has her arms wrapped around me. We're sitting at Breaker's. I remember how obsessed I was with her when I first started bartending there. I'd known Brooke since growing up on the island. Cameron and Dean were good friends with her, but I hadn't had the chance to hang around her or get to know her much. She trained me, and then we started working shifts together. We instantly clicked. She always makes work behind the bar fun.

I set the frame down and look at the others. One was of us at the beach when we bought our paddleboards, one was our friends and us at Dean's keg party last year, and the last one was my favorite picture of us. We dressed up really nicely for my birthday. She surprised me with a night at one of the nice resorts on the island. We went to a fancy dinner and pretended to be a rich married couple, calling each other Mrs. Duncan and Mrs. August. At the end of the night, we broke into the pool after hours and got caught by security. Brooke told the guy, "How dare you ruin our honeymoon!"

It feels like we've grown up together. We have a lot of memories. Yes, some spent fighting and arguing, but it wasn't all bad. A lot of fun memories.

Out of the top dresser drawer, wrapped in a sock, I pull out the engagement ring I bought her. I hold it between my two fingers, letting the light catch on the small diamond. I still want to give it to her. I've always wanted to marry Brooke. It just felt like a natural step that we would spend forever together, because we are always together.

I stuff the ring into my pocket. When I see Brooke tonight, if things go well, maybe it's time. I can't wait for her parents' approval, because I'll never get it. If she really wants to be with me, she will say yes and marry me, no matter what they think.

A text comes from Garnet:

*Hey, can you help us at the bookstore?*

*Sure. I'll head that way in a few.*

With as much off the apartment floor as possible, I change clothes and pack a couple of essentials, including a phone charger, a headlamp and a small stash of joints for the party later.

Before I leave, I pull my notebook from my backpack and scribble down:

***Looking in the mirror, she could barely recognize her reflection, for a monster stared back at her.***

**On the way into town, the air is different.** Not only because of the wind gusts that are blowing hair into my face as I skate into downtown, but there's a *feeling*. A panic. Long lines of cars honk and sit idle at the stoplight to take the main road off the island. I scoot by when the light turns, avoiding a car turning. People along the sidewalks are boarding up storefront windows and moving around at a quickened pace. Angry drivers honk at a car blocking traffic in the middle of the two-lane street downtown.

I jump off my skateboard and shuffle past tools and boards on the sidewalks to the bookstore to help Garnet. As I walk up, I see her and the boss are putting up what looks like the last board over the front windows, covering the Book & Brew logo on the glass.

"Hey, how can I help?" I ask.

Garnet turns around and waves, still clutching the side of

a ladder that's supporting our boss while they drill in the last screw. Her usual cheerful smile is replaced with a small frown and a wrinkle on her forehead. She wipes the sweat from the side of her face and says, "Well, we just got the windows done. I could use your help unloading these sandbags to put in front of the door."

"On it!" I say while taking quick action over to the bed of our boss's pickup truck backed up in front of the store.

"Yeah, we were lucky enough to get a spot here. People are going nuts. I doubt Jada is going to get any sandbags. They were almost out when we left early this morning," Garnet says while hugging around the sides of a single sandbag. She lifts it up, walking with a squat from the truck to the front of the bookstore. She drops the sandbag and uses her small arms to drag it into the corner of the door.

I follow behind her with a sandbag in each hand, piling them next to hers, slightly overlapping each one. As I catch my breath and go to the truck bed for more, I say, "Damn, that sucks. Hopefully it's not as serious as they are saying."

Garnet rests her crossed arms on the side of the truck, looking exhausted. She huffs and says, "I don't know Aims. Seems like it's pretty serious. The curse might be coming true."

I chuckle. "It's not the curse. I'm sure we'll be fine. Why don't you take a break? I'll get the rest of these."

She smirks and nods her head, relaxing her shoulders in relief. I hurry myself back and forth, grabbing them from the truck and placing them against the door, until the entrance is fully barricaded.

"Done! Nothing's getting in there."

I sit on the back of the pickup truck, and the boss drives us down the busy street, turning into the alley behind the bookstore. We grab the rest of the sandbags from the truck bed and place them by the back door. Garnet shouts to the boss, "I'll lock up and get these bags. I forgot my stuff inside."

The boss waves and takes off down the alley. Garnet and I walk into the back entrance, past the small office and cleaning closet, up to the front of the store. Only a dim light over the coffee bar is on. The boarded-up windows make the bookstore very dark, almost eerie.

Garnet grabs a book from a shelf and hands it to me, "Check it out. Page thirty."

In my hands is a copy of a book titled *Painter's Beach Odd History*. I open it up to page thirty to find the chapter called *Cursed Lands*. I look up to Garnet, rolling my eyes, but she nods for me to read. Skimming the chapter, it mentions everything she had said before. A few native people were killed on the island, and they cursed the island to someday be destroyed by a powerful storm. The hair on my arm stands up, prickling with goosebumps. For a moment, I wondered if this could be our near future, but I snapped out of it and handed it back.

"We'll be fine. It's just a story," I say.

"Okay, but you have to admit it's freaky."

"Yes, it is strange. But you know what I think is more freaky?"

"What?" Garnet leans in with curiosity.

"This old ass bookstore in the dark. Can we get out of

here?" We both laugh and run out of the dark store through the back door.

With the bookstore secure, we walk down the alleyway and out to Main Street.

With the way people are reacting to this storm, it feels like someone hit the pause button on the remote, changed the channel, and now we're stuck watching a movie we've never seen before. Forced to exist from one moment to the next. Tonight could change everything. My relationship, my island and my future are all on the line, but right now, the next moment will be the hurricane party. Partying through what might be the worst storm Painter's Beach has ever seen. In some ways, it's exhilarating. Not the same as when Elizabeth's lips touched mine, but it's powerful. The energy in the air is strong. The feeling of panic feels more hysterical. Like how it feels in a dream when your situation keeps changing unexpectedly, and you know you were there for a reason, but can't figure out what to do next. All you can do is ride with the chaos until you wake up from the nightmare.

A blast of wind rustles the magnolia trees lining the street, blowing swirling leaves across Main Street. Curly strands of my hair whip into Garnet's face.

We both giggle intensely. Looking at the nervous smile on Garnet's face, I can tell she feels it too. Our pace increases, walking quickly out of downtown, making a beeline for the Flamingo Inn.

## Elizabeth Corey

**The blue of Chico's eyes slowly disappears as he blinks them closed, but only for a moment.** His sweet, softened face quickly becomes alert as a murmur from outside breaks through the silence of the house. His ear shifts towards the door as we both listen. What sounds like a muffled chanting grows louder. I think the strange sound might be the pine trees whipping in the wind, but suddenly the sound turns into fully legible words.

"WITCH! WITCH! WITCH!"

I freeze up, listening carefully. The chant becomes clearer and closer and louder, echoing into my living room.

"GUILTY WITCH! GUILTY WITCH! GUILTY WITCH!"

I pop up from the couch, and Chico runs to the front door barking. I follow after him through the doorway and into the kitchen, where I can see through the front windows. Shadows aggressively move up and down as the chanting gets louder.

Bright burning lights create an orange glow inside my entryway.

*Are those fucking torches?*

"GUILTY WITCH! GUILTY WITCH! GUILTY WITCH!"

The chants grow louder and louder. I peer through the peephole in the front door, trying to avoid being spotted from the windows, to see a group of twenty or so angered people with flares and fists pumping up and down as they continue to chant. I recognize some of the faces. Neighbors from my street. Faces who had previously pointed and stared from golf carts.

From the crowd steps forward a woman holding a megaphone. I recognize her from the picture at the bottom of her email signature.

*Fucking Mary Pearly!*

With the megaphone covering her head, she shouts into it, "ELIZABETH COREY! COME OUT NOW AND TELL THE TRUTH! FACE GOD AND JUSTICE FOR YOUR SINS!"

*You've got to be fucking kidding me.*

She then begins a new chant, "MURDERER! MURDERER! MURDERER!"

The crowd pumps their torches and fists into the air.

My heart is racing. My head is burning hot. The anger swells deep from inside me, aching to be released. Chico continues to bark loudly as I turn my back against the door, trying to figure out what to do as the chanting keeps getting louder and more aggressive.

"MURDERER! MURDERER! MURDERER!"

Again, she shouts into the megaphone.

"TELL THE TRUTH! TURN YOURSELF IN! LIAR! MURDERING WITCH!"

The chants keep roaring.

*But I didn't do anything.*

I think. I'm not sure. Maybe they are right. Maybe I am a murdering witch. As Chico barks into the window, something hits the glass in front of him, and then another.

*Clink! Clack!*

They are throwing rocks at the windows. Chico barks louder, his pitch growing higher. I cover my ears and slink down the door to the floor into a fetal position.

It's not my fault. Any of this. I didn't ask to be here. I didn't ask to lose my love and drink myself into a blackout. I never wanted this to be my life. My life was supposed to be something else. They were supposed to respect me, not hate me. They weren't supposed to make me so angry.

"MURDERING WITCH! CONFESS YOUR SINS!"

Suddenly, a window shatters and glass sprays all over the floor. A large rock flies into the kitchen. Chico lets out a yelp and runs off.

"HEY! WHAT THE FUCK!" I shout out angrily towards the window, but when I do, another rock comes in and pings against my leg, then another at my chest.

"Ouch!" I cover my head as two more rocks pelt my rib cage and my thigh. I run out of the kitchen and up the stairs.

"Chico! Come on!" I shout at him. He follows closely and runs past me with his tail tucked up the stairs. We run into the art studio and crouch in the corner behind my easels. Gripping my legs and holding Chico tightly with my fingers in his fur, I can still hear the sounds of chanting and more glass breaking.

*They're destroying our house.*

"Please stop! Please go away!"

A wall of rain hits the house along with a heavy gust of wind that whistles through the single-pane glass windows. The rain smacks the side of the house again, and again. With the heavy rain, the chanting stops. I hear commotion, but then it fades into the swirling sounds of wind and rain battering the walls.

An alert blares from my phone. A long and high-pitched beep, and then a pause, and then another long and high-pitched beep. A warning from the National Hurricane Center:

**Emergency Alert**

*National Weather Service: A HURRICANE WARNING is in effect for this area for dangerous and damaging winds and life-threatening storm surge. At this time, EVACUATION ORDERS have been issued for Painter's Beach. If you are in an evacuation zone, gather loved ones, pets, and supplies and head to safety. Visit paintersbeach.org for evacuation zones and shelter locations. FOLLOW INSTRUCTIONS FROM LOCAL OFFICIALS.*

I attempt to send a text message to Aimsley, but the message status reads *"Sending"*. It doesn't appear to be going through.

I grab Chico tighter. Closing my eyes, hearing the rain batter the windows. The wind whistles, and I picture Christian bobbing up and down in the ocean, the waves crashing over him. His arms flailing for something to grab, but the ship is down in the water below him. The rain was beating down onto his head, clouding his vision. I see him trying to keep the water out of his mouth, but it keeps getting in, and the sea keeps pulling him down deeper.

My breath is short. My chest is heavy. My hands are cold, and my neck is beading with sweat. I hold Chico tighter while my mind keeps spinning deeper into the scenario, watching him drown, sinking into the sea, all by himself. My breathing is quicker, and the room is spinning. All I can see is the opposite wall from me, and I focus on the figure I painted, his black and blue face smeared around in terror. I try to take deeper breaths as Chico buries his head into my chest.

*Deep breath. Deep breath.*

My heart rate is slowing. The room is steadying.

*Deep breath. Deep breath.*

The rain is lightening up. The wind has calmed. The noises have stopped.

*I can breathe. I can breathe.*

The panic attacks were really bad when I first found out about Christian. I started drinking to avoid them. And to think of it, I haven't had a drink all day. I need to go back downstairs to see if they are gone. I need a drink to calm my nerves. I need to get out of this room.

Down the hallway and to the stairs, Chico and I walk cautiously. I can hear the wind and rain coming through the broken windows in the front of the house, but I don't hear any chanting or people. We walk through the kitchen and to the front door, and the floors are covered in glass and rocks.

Both windows are shattered, and the floor is soaked from the downpour. This is only going to get worse. I can't have Chico cutting his paws, so I sweep up the soupy floor of glass and rainwater the best I can. With this much rain coming through the window now, it's frightening to imagine how much water could come into the house later. For now, I attempt to put up a painting tarp, stapling it to the wall, trying to keep some of the rain out. The wind picks up on the tarp, blowing it in and out of the window like a sail. Almost like the front of the house is breathing. The tarp sucks into the windows and then bellows out into the room and back.

## Aimsley August

**A *"No Vacancy"* sign glows underneath a pair of neon pink flamingos.** Their fluorescent light contrasts against the quickly darkening sky. The large oak trees over the motel sway slightly, and the decorated palm trees in the parking lot move a little faster, bending to the right with every burst of wind. The rain hasn't come yet, but I'm sure the next weather band will hit us anytime now.

"Dean said room number twenty-four. I think it's this way," Garnet says.

She leads the way through the packed parking lot up to the white motel with painted pink doors and staircases. Cars take up every spot, some spilling over into the grass. Music comes from people hanging out in their cars, and more distant music comes from people's rooms as they hang out on the balconies, watching the trees blow, and the sky darken. Rust pokes out from places on the painted cast iron banisters going up the stairs. On the second floor, the door of room twenty-four is propped open. I can hear Dean and Cameron bantering.

"We should be out there hitting the waves, man. Instead, we're in this shit motel," Dean exhaled.

Cameron replied, "They're probably not even that big dude."

"Whatever, I'd be cutting through those breaks. Once in a lifetime waves."

As I walk into the room with Garnet, Dean is standing on top of one of the two double beds with his arms out, pretending to balance on a surfboard. Cameron is making a drink at the room's desk that has been converted into a mini bar.

"Aims! Garnet! Welcome to the party!" Cameron shouted as Dean jumped off of the bed.

"Hey, guys! Wow! Check out this bar." Garnet says as she picks up a couple of bottles from the desk, examining the selection of liquors and drink mixers.

"Awesome! You guys hooked it up," I say.

Looking around the room, a single yellow ochre bucket chair sits next to the air conditioner unit by the front window. The carpets are worn, disguising any possible stains behind the pattern of different shades of greenish grey. I opt to set my backpack on one of the beds.

"That's nothing. Come here, Aims. Check this shit out."

Dean waves over to the bathroom at the back of the room, so I follow him, walking around backpacks and a cooler on the floor.

"Look what I brought!"

Cramming into the small bathroom, Dean leans over the

bathtub full of ice and a pony keg of beer. I can hear Garnet asking about snacks as my mouth drops open.

"You did not!" I shout.

"Better fucking believe it!" Cameron shouts from outside the bathroom.

Dean grabs a plastic cup and pumps the keg up and down before pouring out a golden amber beer that foams a head to the end of the cup. He hands me the beer and demands, "Take a sip of this. Tell me that's not hitting the fucking spot."

I toss back a swig of the ice-cold beer. Coating my tongue is a soft bitter hops with orange citrus. The flavor profile was a perfectly balanced IPA, at least to my standards. Not too bitter, not too hazy, but just enough hops.

"Damn Dean! How? The beer master did it again!"

Dean pumps his fist in the air and pours himself a beer.

"Hell yeah! I was saving this keg for an end-of-summer party, but I thought fuck it, this is it. And I call her," he raises his glass for a cheers, "Amelia."

We all clink glasses at the name, and I indulge in the homebrew knowing we're the only people to get to try this, especially a draught beer, on a night like tonight when everything is closed up. I'm lucky to have the friends I have.

Taking a seat on the side of one of the two bouncy, cheap mattresses, covered in a stiff and coarse red quilted blanket, I ask, "So where is everyone?"

"Brooke and Tiff said they were on their way like an hour ago, but you know how they are. Have to look their best for the hurricane," Dean says in a sarcastic tone.

I was anxious for Brooke to get there. Not sure how our interaction would go after another night of not seeing each other. I wondered if she would ask where I was last night. I hadn't even thought of an excuse yet. Maybe I should have asked Garnet to have my back, but she's too nice. I couldn't drag her into this.

"Wait, where's Jada?" Garnet asks Cameron.

He shakes his head back and forth and says, "Man, I tried to help her with her house today, but she couldn't get sandbags or plywood. Honestly, she was lowkey freaking out. I tried to convince her to come, but she took off to like Ohio or some shit."

"Damn, that's lame," Garnet replies.

"Outie!" Dean shouts as Cameron laughs. Garnet and I try our best not to laugh, but it's true.

Worried about Jada, I take out my phone to text her, asking if she's okay. I keep the message open for a while, but she doesn't respond. I think about texting Elizabeth to see if she got to her mom's okay, but I know it's not really my responsibility. Still, I want her to be okay. I hold off and put my phone away for now.

All I want to do right now is live in this moment. It's not every day you get to experience a hurricane party. We all joke and laugh, becoming loud as Cameron turns up the music on his portable speaker. Nineties hip-hop plays while we get through our first drinks quickly. I'm trying my best to keep my head in the moment, but it's not an easy thing to do. I keep looking at the door for when Brooke will walk in. I'm not sure what I'll do or what I'll say, but I do know I need all the liquid courage I can get. I'll ride out this storm with beer in my belly, friends by my side and a smile on my face.

Cameron and Dean are hyped up, starting a push-up war. I can't help but wonder when the last time this carpet was cleaned as they lie on it, gripping it and getting their face close to it each time they dip down for a push-up. Garnet keeps count as they grunt into the twenties. Dean finally succumbs to his elbows as Cameron does two more solid push-ups. Dean shouts in disappointment before adventuring to the tub for another beer. Cameron stands, flexing his muscles. He proudly shouts, "Hell yeah!"

"Imagine that. The personal trainer wins the push-up contest," Garnet speaks sarcastically, throwing her head back in laughter.

"Come on, you do some," Cameron eggs on Garnet, who refuses the challenge, shaking her head.

"What about you Aims? You could probably outdo these guys." Garnet's comment is too kind to assume.

Truthfully, there's no way I'm touching that carpet. I say, "Nah. I'm good."

"Oh, come on Aims. You're awfully quiet tonight," Dean observes.

"Yeah, what's up with you? Missing Brookie?" Cameron jokes.

With a slight chuckle, I say, "I'm good. I'm good. Just have some shit on my mind, I guess."

Garnet clutches a drink in her hand and looks over at me with pouty lips. "I think I scared her about the hurricane today.

Made her read about the curse in the bookstore."

"No, no. That's not it. I've just been thinking about that murder."

It was the only thing I could come up with to say, but I hadn't really thought much about the murder itself, only more about Elizabeth, who is being accused of it.

Cameron climbs to the back of the bed next to the one I'm sitting on, rests his back against the headboard and says, "I actually found out some crazy shit about that today."

Dean leans against the open doorpost, and Garnet sits crisscrossed next to me, leaning into the conversation.

"What? Tell us the tea!" Garnet demands.

Cameron raises his eyebrows as his grin grows, happy to share with us.

"So, the woman I was training this morning, solid physique by the way, great ass, such an easy client," his eyes begin to wander as he looks off into a daze.

Garnet smacks her hand down on the bed to break Cameron's daydreaming. "Okay, what did you find out?" she asks.

"Sorry, she's just so fine!" We all laugh, but then go quiet again to hear him explain, "So, the dead guy, Jim, his wife Heather or whatever, I guess she's been like banging some dude. Mid squat, my client was talking shit about her, saying there's probably more to the story, if you know what I mean."

Garnet gasps and looks to each of us.

"Oh, so miss perfect church wife isn't who she says she is," Dean comments back.

"Guys. Don't say that. That woman just lost her husband. I'm sure it's just small-town rumor shit," Garnet says defensively, but there's curiosity in her eyes.

"Hey," Cameron throws his hands up in the air, looking around, "I'm only telling you what I heard."

We all mull the thought over for a second before Garnet jumps up from the bed and shouts to the door, "Brooke! Tiff!"

**The moment I've anticipated all night has finally come.** Brooke and Tiffany walk through the doorway of the motel room, bearing heavy bags in the creases of their arms. My immediate reaction is to get up and help. I take the heavy bags from them, which they seem grateful for. Both of them are drenched in rainwater. Hair sticks to their faces, and their shirts cling to their bodies. I hadn't noticed how hard it started to rain because of the volume of our music.

While they busied themselves near the door, I ran to the bathroom to grab them a couple of towels. Brooke wrings her hair into it, patting her face lightly before finally looking at me for the first time in days.

"Thanks, Auggie," she says softly as she smiles her bright white teeth at me.

I instantly feel a pull to her, to hug her and kiss her. I want to, but cautiously, I keep my distance and just smile back at her, waiting for her to make a move. I'm not able to read her just yet.

"Dean brought his homebrew. Do you want one?" I ask Brooke.

Brooke turns to Dean and shouts, "What is this a fucking speakeasy pop-up?" She laughs and moves in to hug Dean and pinches Cameron on the belly. "Hey there, little shits! I see you brought Breaker's Beach Bar to the room. You did good. You did good." She smirks at the guys but says, "But just so you know, I'm not your fucking bartender tonight. So don't ask me to make you a drink."

Everyone laughs as she looks to me with a lust in her eyes and asks, "Auggie? Make me a vodka cran?"

Instantly, she has me at her beck and call. This is what Brooke always does to me. She's a gorgeous monster that I can't help but long for. I'd do anything for her. Even with her hair wet, her makeup hasn't smeared a bit. Her fresh smile, flirty eyes, skintight leggings, and crop top are sending me over the edge. It's almost as if everything that has happened in the last couple of days has just begun to shrivel like a dying flower at the back of my brain. Now a beautiful new bud is emerging, a flower unfolding its petals.

"Of course, babe."

I make her a drink and hand it to her, to my surprise, she pinches my cheeks together, puckering my lips to lay a long, juicy kiss on them. An instant smile plasters across my face. My cheeks warm with a blush from where she pinched them.

"You guys are so cute, it's gross," Cameron says.

"Shut up, Cameron. You're next," Brooke climbs on the bed after Cameron, who jumps up and runs out of the room.

Brooke is always flirting.

"Guys, it's actually starting to look pretty epic out here. Come look!" Cameron shouts from the railing overlooking the parking lot.

We all get up and join him outside the room. The rain is blowing sideways, thick enough to block visibility past the end of the parking lot. The branches of trees whip around in the same direction.

"This is just a band, right?" I ask.

"I don't know. If it is, that's pretty crazy. We can put the weather channel on the TV." Cameron says as he goes back into the room.

The wind whistles and blows through my hair and clothes. Leaning over the railing, I see the rain pooling in the parking lot like mini ponds. At this rate, I wonder if the rain would come up to the first-floor rooms. From beneath my arms, I feel two hands slide around my waist and onto the railings in front of me. Brooke's manicured pink nails matched the painted cast iron. She rubs her body against me, grinding her hips against my backside. I put my hands over hers on the railing, gripping them tightly, leaning back into her body.

"I missed you," Brooke whispers into my ear. Her teeth nibble my earlobe. Her warm breath prickles the skin on my neck.

My insides feel warm and tingly. Her attempt to seduce me is working quickly. However good it feels physically, my mind is telling me this is wrong, dirty. Any time before yesterday, this would have turned me on, but right now I feel disgusted. I turn my body around, facing her now as she pins me up against the railing. I hold my breath and then exhale to say, "Hey."

Searching for words, she maintains deep eye contact. She leans in to kiss me, but I freeze up. Her body language becomes stiff, and she pulls away, looking at me questionably.

"What's the matter with you? Don't you miss me?"

The only thing I can think of is to use the same excuses as I did with my friends earlier and say, "Yeah, sorry, I've just been kind of freaked out about this murder thing."

"Oh, really? Why? It has nothing to do with you," she assures, but she sneaks in a comment that puts me off guard, "unless there's something you're not telling me."

My heart stops for a moment. I wonder if her dad had told her I was with Elizabeth. Everyone knows now that she has been accused of the murder. I hold my breath, trying to figure out the words to say. Her serious glare is causing a cold sweat on my prickled neck.

Brooke changes her glare to a smile, "Jesus, I'm joking. You should see your face."

She lets out a scoffing laugh, and my tightened shoulders relax. She laughs all the way back into the room, while I'm left frozen to the railing, wind whipping rain on my back.

I gather myself and walk back inside to see everyone focusing on the TV.

The news channel shows a live feed of a man right on our beach from the major weather channel. Standing outside of Breaker's, he holds onto the hood of his raincoat and clutches a microphone as he shouts into it. "A very serious storm surge has already started to affect the area, and it's even up to residents' homes here on Painter's Beach," he says.

The cameraman pans to what the weatherman is pointing to.

"As you can see, the water line has already come up past what normally is a beach and way up to the dunes. A house north of here completely lost its back deck not too long ago. For anyone who needs to hear it, please take this storm seriously and get somewhere safely. This storm surge is not a joke, and it will only get worse due to the spring tide, producing an extremely high tide along with the storm surge."

The news coverage pans from the announcer to the beach. I notice one of the houses that's already damaged isn't far from Elizabeth's. I feel so sorry for her. There seems to be a good chance she could lose her house to the flooding. I'm just glad she got out of there and went with her mom, but I know she will be devastated when she sees this. She's already lost so much.

"Damn, dude! Maybe we won't have to go to work for a while now," Dean says.

He laughs and high-fives Cameron, but I don't find it funny and refuse to join in the laughter.

"Are you okay Aims?" Garnet must have been studying the look on my face.

"I just don't find it funny. People's homes could be swept away. Damaged forever."

Cameron asks, "What do you care about those people? Rich fucks anyway..."

I bite my lip and shake my head in disgust.

"Oh, I know, your little witchy friend lives there, huh?"

I glare at Cameron, hoping he can read my mind through my stare.

*Shut the fuck up.*

I don't need this attention right now. Why is everyone so focused on me? Why isn't everyone just drinking and indulging in pointless conversations like usual?

From one of the beds, sitting shoulder-to-shoulder with Tiffany, Brooke stares at me. I can see her in my peripheral vision, but I don't dare make eye contact. Hoping she will turn away, she only keeps staring before saying, "So it's true then, isn't it?"

Everyone is silent, looking at me. I turn to Brooke and ask, "What?" even though the sweat building in my palms tells me I know exactly where this is going.

"You know, I didn't want to believe my asshole of a dad, but he's telling the truth. You and that girl were together. You know, I was so stupid to say, *'No, Dad, that's just Aimsley's spot. She was probably just there.'* I thought he was taking this whole thing out on me, but it's fucking true, isn't it?"

I hold my tongue, as everyone does. The room is filled with only the sounds of rain and an unfitting rap song in the background.

My silence makes Brooke angry; her eyebrows furrow, and the sides of her mouth tighten. She asks again, "Is it? Is it true?"

I feel myself getting hot, but before I have to respond, she raises her arm quickly and chucks her full drink at me.

I put my arm up to block it, but a stream of cranberry vodka runs down my face and arms.

"Are you fucking serious right now?" I shout.

Tiffany smirks. Garnet gasps and holds her hand over her mouth. Dean and Cameron are quiet as mice. I grab a towel from the floor that they used to dry themselves off with and wipe the sticky  liquids from my body. As I wipe my face, Brooke stands up from the bed and rushes over to me, pushing me, yelling at me to tell her the truth. She pushes, and I resist, but her pushing becomes rough, as her hands slam right into my gut that was already sore, knocking me into the door frame. This is the final line being crossed.

"You need to stop touching me right now," I demand.

The guys leap up, looking ready to hold someone back as the tension in the room rises.

"Then why won't you say anything? Because you did something, didn't you?" Brooke accuses.

She stands back but crosses her arms, her eyes flush red and dark.

I lift my shirt slightly, just over my stomach, and say, "Let me guess. He left this part out of his story." I stare into Brooke's eyes as she looks down at the bruising and back to me. Her angered face lightens slightly, now riddled with confusion.

"What do you mean? What's that from?" Brooke demanded an answer.

"I bet he failed to mention that he punched me to the ground and left me at the bridge in the dark. He was pissed because I told him he was a piece of shit for cheating on your mom." I leave out the doorway onto the balcony, searching for the joint in my pocket. When I grab it, I feel the loose engagement ring.

Garnet comes out and shuts the motel door behind her. "What the hell happened? What is she talking about? Did her dad do that to you for real? Are you okay?" Garnet asks.

"No, not really. I'm all fucked up. Yeah, it's true I hung out with Elizabeth yesterday under the bridge. I was being stupid, but her dad caught us and took her away and then punched me, leaving me on the fucking ground." I explain lighting the joint, taking a huge drag.

"Damn Aims. That's serious. Did you report it?"

I scoff through a thick exhale of smoke, causing me to cough.

"Who am I supposed to report it to? He's the fucking Chief of Police. His word against mine. I just don't think I can do this anymore. I think we're done. I was just trying to get through this storm, honestly."

Garnet sighs and puts her hand on my arm, rubbing it with compassion.

"I know I'm a piece of shit." I manage to say through a sob of tears that start coming to my eyes. The tears are hot on my face.

"You're not. People fuck up. And I'm sorry, he should have never touched you. It's not right."

I hand her the joint as she takes a drag and hands it back. Between the silence, the high falls over me, and settles some of the anger.

Garnet asks, "What are you going to do?"

"I don't know. I think I'm going to bail."

All I want to do right now is run. Even if I don't know where. I'd rather risk being flooded in our apartment than stuck in this motel room now that she knows. We will be fighting all night.

"What now? You can't, it's a hurricane," Garnet says.

Dean comes out of the door onto the balcony, reaching his hand out for the joint. He takes a drag and says, "Brooke's really upset in there. Tiffany's telling me you should go, but I told her that's crazy. Everyone just needs to calm down for a little bit, and it'll be fine."

From my pocket, I fiddle with the ring in between my fingers. I haven't found the right time to give this to her since I bought it. Through all the fighting and thinking about Elizabeth, I can't.

"Can you guys just give me a minute?" I ask.

"Yeah, sure," Garnet replies, and Dean nods. They walk back into the room, closing the door behind them. Looking out at the parking lot, the weather lightens up. The rain now is more of a light spray, but the wind still blows hard in gusts. I take out my phone and see a text from Elizabeth:

*I'm sorry. I lied to you. Write to me in prison...if I make it?*

*What do you mean?*

I wait for a response, but I wonder what she could possibly be lying to me about. There's no way she was involved in that murder. And what does she mean by *if she makes it*? Did she stay in her house? If she never went to her mom's and she's in that house, she's in serious trouble. She's alone.

*Please respond.*

Tapping my foot and pacing the balcony, I am becoming anxious. A lump rests in my chest when my text message reads *"Failed to deliver"*.

*Fuck she didn't evacuate.*

Looking around, the lights on the motel sign and the lights on the balcony hallway flicker and then go out.

Cameron shouts, "Yeah, the powers out, guys."

Without thinking it through, I make a quick decision. I storm into the motel room with my hand in my shorts pocket. Standing in front of Brooke, I hold out my clasped hand and say, "Here."

She looks up at me from the bed, squinting her eyes that are puffy with tears. She holds out her hand, and I place the engagement ring in her palm. Her eyes widen, and her bottom lip quivers.

"I've played this out so many different ways in my head. I wanted so badly to give it to you the right way, but I realize the reason I have been holding onto it for so long is that there hasn't been a right time. And I don't think there ever will be. I'm sorry."

I pick up my backpack from the bed and throw it on my shoulders. I run out of the motel, down the hallway and the stairs, through puddles in the parking lot. My name is being shouted out behind me.

But I keep running, and I don't look back.

# Elizabeth Corey

**I need a drink.**

I uncork a bottle of wine while standing on the damp floor in the kitchen. My toes feel clammy on the hardwood. The Florida heat has all but escaped through the front windows, replaced by cooler, stuffy air.

I pour some wine into a glass, tucking the bottle under my arm while walking through the house out to the balcony. From the doors emerges a most unusual sight. The sky is a manganese violet against the phthalo blue ocean. I've never seen a purple sky before. And I'd never seen the ocean look so angry, almost sickly in color. Beyond the sand dune is a much shorter distance from the beach to the ocean than usual. I hadn't noticed the water level earlier. The tide has come up, gulping up the beach in its entirety. The waves are taller than I've ever seen, rolling over themselves violently. The wind rattles the balcony doors. I feel more uneasy than before. How has the weather gotten so much worse in such a short time?

Chico scrapes his paw on my leg. He looks up at me with pouty eyes. I know what that look means. He has to potty. I hadn't thought about it before, that with the storm surge, he might not be able to go outside to relieve himself. The backyard is guarded by the dune, but if the water were to reach over the dune or collapse it, a haunting thought, the yard would be covered in water. My confidence in holding the house down through this storm is waning. This feels like a completely different situation now than it did earlier, when I lied to my mother and Aimsley and said I was with the other.

"Do you have to potty Chico?" I ask shakily. "Come on then."

We hurry down the stairs to the back door, my little shadow following at my heels. As I unlock and open the door, it jerks from my grip, swinging open and slamming against the back of the house. Chico cowers, but with an encouraging tap on his backside, I assure him it's okay to go.

I stand outside with him. The wind whips my hair over my eyes. The pine trees surrounding my house bend slightly, making a constant whirling noise as the wind pushes through their needles. I can hear the rumble of the waves crashing on the other side of the dune.

While Chico finds a spot, I walk through my back gate and up the dune to get a better look. Still holding onto my glass of wine, I grip the stem to keep it from flying out of my hand. The red liquid sloshes around, and some blows out, spraying me as I ascend. At the top of the dune, I find that only a little bit of beach is revealed as the wave recedes, but the water comes forward and rams into the dune, covering it entirely. Small grains of sand pelt my skin as the wind sprays them around like a fine mist. I close my mouth but can taste the salty grit in my teeth. I hold my arm over my face, trying to wipe it clean, but the sand blows into my eyes. I observe as much as I can through watery eyes. The sheer force of the current each time it recedes and comes back is terrifying. The wind and water are angry. Moving quickly, crashing hard, and blowing violently.

Water slams into the back of a house north of me. The waves hit their siding over and over again, so much that their back decking is ripping itself from the house, falling into the ocean. The debris sweeps out and then back, colliding with the house and back into the tide again.

"Holy shit! Chico!" I yell as I run back down the dune. With all the sand in my eyes, I can't see the path and misjudge my footing. I fall forward. My hands hit the sand. Luckily, my glass doesn't break, but the contents spill out. Slugging through the sand, I help myself back to my feet and run through my back gate, slamming it shut. Chico is already by the back door, stomping his feet up and down anxiously for me to open it.

The door slams back onto the house again as we shovel ourselves inside. I yank the door closed and secure the lock, protecting us from the elements. The loudness of the air outside is now a quiet muffle. It's much darker in the house than before. In fact, I can barely see the stairs, and there is only a faint light coming from the top. I flick the light switch that had already been in the "on" position and flick it back off and on again. The stairway remains dark.

*The power's out.*

I move cautiously, holding the railing and feeling each step by sliding my feet until they hit the back of the stairs. Into the now darkened living room, I light the candle sitting on the coffee table. The scent of sandalwood drifts through the air, and the candlelight flickers. Shadows of Chico and I dance across the wall. With the constant draft coming through the front windows of the house, the candle struggles to stay lit. It almost goes out, then regains full flame again. The tarp makes a cracking noise each time it whips away from the window.

I thought this storm wasn't making landfall until early in the morning, but by the looks of it, the storm is already here, or at least it's already causing major problems. I attempt to check for a weather update on my phone, but it has no signal.

*Well, this is it. My reality.*

I've locked myself away in an old, worn-down house that's beachfront and facing a direct hit from a hurricane. I can't stop feeling like this is something I deserve. It's the universe's way of punishing me for what I've done, for murdering Jim. If I even make it through this storm, will there be police waiting for me on the other side? Just because I was let go doesn't mean Mary and her posse won't continue to harass me. To do everything in their power to further incriminate me. What do I have to look forward to, prison? Everything has gone to shit. It's all hopeless. For now, I'll drink my wine, I'll smoke a few cigarettes, cuddle Chico, and wait. Wait for what fate has in store for me.

I ditch the sand-covered glass and drink from the neck of the bottle instead, swigging down large gulps of wine. It feels dry on my tongue and warm in my throat. My head feels fuzzy, and my sight is hazy. I drink more.

*Maybe if I get drunk enough, I'll fall asleep and wake up when it's all over.*

The balcony doors swing open and closed as the wind blows through the front windows of the house and out through the back. I lean onto a shelf in the room to steady myself. The wine is hitting me hard now. The room is spinning. As a sudden blast of wind blows, my body plunges out with the doors, and I sway back, pulling them inward, latching them closed. The doors rattle as I rest my forehead against the cool glass. I take another swig of wine and watch everything fall apart. Water rushes over, filling up my backyard like some kind of secret, swirling mystical pool. It violently consumes the dune that I was standing on only minutes before. Waves of ocean slam into the house. The walls shake, and the floors vibrate, knocking me back from the glass door and onto the floor where my head strikes, hard. So hard I can't see. I know it hurts, but the feeling is so intense it almost fades away. Suddenly, I feel cold everywhere but the back of my head. I can't get up. I can't move. I stare up at the ceiling. My vision is mostly black except for the sparkles from the crystal prisms hanging from the chandelier above. They shake and sparkle like stars, but they fade into complete darkness, as if I were seeing the entirety of space before falling into a black hole. It feels so lonely.

"Christian. Help."

I hear the distant sound of Chico whimper, which lets me know I'm not alone, before the musical shattering of glass tinkles around me.

## Aimsley August

**My feet splash in puddles as I run further from the motel, in the direction of the beach.** The road is already scattered with fallen branches and palm fronds. My sandals make it difficult to run through the rainwater. It's already flooded up to my ankles in places. Once I'm out of sight of the motel, I steady my pace to catch my breath.

I can't believe I actually did that. I actually gave her the ring. She ought to be feeling extremely bad by now, knowing that I had planned an engagement. I feel responsible for ruining it, but I think we both did. The only real evidence of cheating was from me, but I assume the worst of her, the way she flirts. I guess I could never really trust her. She never gave me any real assurance. I'm still angry with her, and I know this is only the first of many feelings, that the feelings will only get worse as time goes on. I wonder what this breakup will do to our friend group. I only hope we can all still hang out. At least Garnet has my back.

Trudging through puddles becomes difficult and dirty. My sandals threaten to slip off the longer I walk. The bottom half of my legs are covered in mud spots and grass clippings from someone's yard that must have just been mowed recently. Walking through the HOA neighborhood, I shouldn't be surprised. It's comical seeing the perfectly kept lawns littered with small branches and flooding driveways. I wouldn't be surprised if someone was out picking up debris or using a leaf blower right now. Realistically, most of these people have probably evacuated. It feels like a ghost town out here. I'm sure living in this neighborhood, you'd have the means to do so, or they are sitting in their houses glued to the TV, worrying with every update. It would have been nice to do the same. I should be enjoying a hurricane party right now. The only thing getting me through this trek is the slight buzz clinging on from the few beers I had. At least I got to try some Amelia IPA, but my focus isn't on partying any longer. I'm on a mission to check on Elizabeth. I continuously pull my phone out of my pocket to check for a message from her, but I'm not receiving any. I'm worried that Elizabeth's alone in her house. She'd be insane to stay. I have to help her, because unfortunately, I don't think she has anyone else.

It's beginning to get darker, not only from it getting later, but from the lack of power to any houses or streetlamps. At a cross street, I misjudge my footing where the road abruptly dips. My foot slips in my sandal and I lose my balance. All of my weight is on one ankle as I fall into a puddle of water, instantly twisting it.

"Gah!"

I let out a moan of pain, trying to regain my footing as I feel for the sidewalk underneath me. A curb. I misjudged the curb. One of my sandals came off, and I can't see where it is, so I take the other one off as I stand up and toss it to the side.

*This is going well.*

I feel for the phone still in my pocket, but don't even bother getting it out. My shorts are completely soaked. To add to the chaos of the moment, I hear the rain coming. I hobble as quickly as I can on what I think feels like the sidewalk under the water as the rain starts beating down around me. Soaking wet from falling in the puddle, the rain can't do any more damage except to drench the hair on my head. I only regret not packing away my phone, but at this point, it'll only make everything in my dry bag wet. So, I accept nature's free shower and continue on. All that matters is I get to Elizabeth.

I have to get to her house.

Nearing downtown, I cut through a couple of side streets that look less flooded, making my way around, trying to avoid piercing the bottom of my feet, but failing miserably, stepping on what feels like branches and sharp gravel.

I finally approach Main Street. Its lights shine brighter than everything around, like walking up to a carnival attraction. It seems to be the only area in sight with power. I cut a corner, and the sidewalks are finally in view, higher up, without puddling water.

*About damn time.*

Even with power, Main Street is empty of life. There are only boarded-up businesses and a few abandoned vehicles. Pushing through the tightness in my ankle, I sprint between storefront awnings to catch a break from the rain. The magnolia trees whip around overhead as some of their white-blooming flower buds shed petals around me, like a wedding aisle.

Coming up on my right is the police station where the front doors burst open. It's Chief Duncan with a woman. I quickly hide in the alleyway, so they don't see me.

*This island is too damn small.*

Eavesdropping on their conversation, I can hear him trying to comfort her. She sounds panicked. Duncan is the last person I want to see right now, so I'll have to go down the flooded alley, maybe cut over a block. Before I attempt a detour, I peek around the corner to see if he is going to leave. They are still standing on the sidewalk, Duncan with his hand holding the back of her arm in solace.

I hear him say, "I know the storm is messing everything up, but I've got everything figured out. Just please take your kids to the shelter. I promise everything will be fine, my pumpkin."

*My pumpkin?*

What I just heard was probably not supposed to be for my ears, or anyone's, for that matter. A car engine starts, and I can hear it driving towards me. As the car passes, I get a look at the woman driving. It's Heather Crowley.

Duncan stands, opening the door to his police car. Just as I try to duck back around the corner, his eyes look up in my direction.

*Fuck!*

I hope he didn't see me. My heart beats hard in my chest as I look down the alley, wondering if I should make a run for it, but I hear a car door slam and an engine start. A car drives off. I cautiously peer once more, and he is gone. I really hope he didn't see me. I know he didn't intend for anyone to listen to his conversation, but I heard him crystal clear. I remember what Brooke told me:

*"...he took the phone back before she could figure it out, but Mom was reading the messages, and she said he called her 'My Pumpkin'."*

Could it be? Heather Crowley and Brooke's dad? I can't believe my ears or the ideas that are forming in my mind right now. Why Heather? And for how long? Because if they were going behind Mrs. Catherine's back, they were also going behind Jim's back. Jim Crowley, the guy who was murdered. *Whoa.*

One thing I know for sure is that I definitely need to relay this information to Elizabeth. She needs to know that something might have happened between the two of them, so she can quit assuming she's responsible. This doesn't exactly prove her innocence, but it's enough to question other possibilities. It also makes me hate Duncan more. Dean was right. Heather really isn't the innocent church-going lady she portrays.

With both of them out of sight, I continue to walk on the sidewalk to avoid the flooded alleyways. I try to pick up speed, ignoring the pain in my ankle. I hobble as quickly as I can, past the main stoplight downtown and down the road towards the beach. It's a long hike in soaking wet clothes. My skin begins to chafe. The further I get from downtown, the darker it gets. The power is completely out near the beach. Luckily, I've traveled this road so many times that I know where I am without streetlamps. The difficult part is walking the street in bare feet through puddling water. I try to stay as close to the middle of the road as possible. The gusts of wind grow stronger the closer I get.

The first houses in the beachfront neighborhood come into sight. Unlike the pooling water I've been trekking through, I notice the water getting deeper and having almost a wave to it. It swells over my feet. I've crossed from puddles of rainwater into storm surge from the ocean. I cautiously step forward as each placement of my foot gets deeper. On the next block, the water is almost halfway up my calves. The surge splashes up to my face from the wind. The water is warm and salty on my lips. My eyes sting from the rain that's mixed with the saltwater.

Judging my location right now, I'm three blocks away from Elizabeth's house. Assessing the storm surge ahead of me, the even deeper water, I'm hesitant to swim in it. Between debris and possible downed powerlines, the risk is daunting. I need a plan B.

I turn right, in the direction of my apartment. I justify a side quest to see if my building has taken on water and possibly grab some supplies. I think I have just the thing to make this easier. Maybe.

Our neighborhood is out of power as well. Everything

is pitch black. All I can see in the dark is the faint outline of black houses against the dark grey of the sky. I finally reach our apartment, where the depth of the storm surge is half a foot up to my door. It's already flooded.

*Fuck.*

I force open the door and push it shut behind me. It's even darker in the apartment than outside, but with the front door closed, it's the first break from the wind and rain I've had since I left the motel. The windows howl with each blow of wind outside.

I take the lighter from my pocket and flick it until a flame comes out, lighting up the room. My coffee table and couch are slightly floating off the ground. Everything I own is in water. In the kitchen, I look through a drawer to find a head lamp, and from the bedroom closet, I stuff a small knife and some cording, a flashlight, cash and a change of clothes into my dry bag backpack. I attempt to wipe off my phone and turn it on, but I see it has only one bar of power left, so to conserve energy, I power it down and stuff it in the bag. I throw on a jacket and a hat in hopes they will help block some of the rain from my face. I think I am as prepared as I'll ever be to go check on Elizabeth. The last thing I grab is a paddle, and from the hooks underneath a tarp outside of the door, I pull down my paddleboard.

If I can't swim there, I'll paddle there.

*Am I really doing this? Dean, you would be so jealous right now.*

I make myself laugh at the ridiculousness of this moment,

but like a true Floridian, I walk out in the storm surge with my flotation device and make my way back north to Elizabeth's neighborhood. My headlamp illuminates the surge sloshing through my knees as I straddle the board. My toes grip the ground to steady myself. I quickly shift into a kneeling position and pop up onto the board. After adjusting my position a few times, I'm balanced the best I can be. Using my paddle to straighten out in the right direction, I push myself against the wind and waves. My paddle sweeps hard against the current, much harder than any paddle I've ever done. My forearms and thigh muscles burn deep into my core, but somehow, I push past it and reach Elizabeth's street. I tilt my head up towards the house to get a glimpse of it through the rain. It's so dark I can only distinguish which house is hers by the faint silhouette of its pointed peak. Elizabeth's house is on stilts, normally appearing to have the height of a three-story home. Her front door is up a flight of stairs on the second story, but as I get closer to her house, the stairs are completely gone, hidden under the water. The house sits at water level as if it's floating. With my board moving and the water moving around me, it's hard to tell if the house might be moving as well.

With a post in arm's reach, I grab on and use it to cautiously lower myself down onto the porch while keeping my feet firm on my board as it bobs with the waves. When I'm finally seated, I secure my board and paddle by dragging them onto the porch with me. I let out a long, exhausted breath. My arms are spent, my stomach pains in soreness and my ankle stings, shooting a pain up my leg that I can feel in my teeth, but I have to gather my strength. This isn't over. I have to find Elizabeth.

I bang the back of my fist on Elizabeth's door, even though it feels silly to knock at a time like this. I wonder if she can even hear it amongst all of the wind and waves.

"Elizabeth?" I yell out, but I still question whether she can even hear me.

I twist the door handle, but it's locked. I bang on the door again and then hear barking. Chico is barking, but the barking sounds so clear, like he's right outside on the porch with me. I move over to the window to realize it's broken in. As I stick my head into the window to look for them, a tarp whips into my face, almost knocking me over. This time, I grab the tarp and push it aside as I climb through the window to get inside.

# PART III

# Elizabeth Corey

**This is the worst hurricane party I've ever been to.**
Well, I guess it's technically the only one I've ever been to. I'd
probably be having more fun with Aimsley right now, even if
her girlfriend is there. At least it would be entertaining.

I've gotten myself in quite a mess. The house is falling apart,
and so am I. I pick shards of glass from my hair, pondering
what to do with my time now that I'm cut off from the world.
Chico stays close, holding his ears back. I feel horrible that he
is experiencing this with me. I'm a terrible dog mom for doing
this to him. I honestly didn't think it would ever get this bad.
Everyone seems to underplay the significance of a hurricane
here, using it as an excuse for a party. My mother is probably
knee deep in cocktails and gossip by now, without a worry in
the world. Little does she know that her daughter lied to her
and is in the ultimate danger zone.

"It's just the wind, buddy," I tell Chico, petting down his
perked-up ears.

Chico leaps from the couch and stands alert towards the front of the house. The flame of the candle whips around, this time blowing it out completely. A huge gust of wind comes through the house, causing a cracking noise from the loose painting tarp on the front window. Then, I hear the sound of the front door slamming.

Chico jumps back on the couch next to me. The dark room sounds of ferocious wind and hard rain. My eyes adjust to the dark as I feel around the coffee table in front of me for the lighter. Chico wedges his body between me and the couch. He growls.

Against the purple haze in the living room, a dark figure forms in the entryway. Instantly, my heart drops. Chico whines in fear.

"Who's there?"

I fear one of Mary's followers has broken in to seek revenge. I can't tell if someone's there or my eyes are playing tricks on me. Frantically, I search for the lighter as the sound of footsteps walk into the room. The dark shadow covers all the purple as the figure grows closer.

"No, no, no!"

My eyes start to swell, painfully. Tears of fear form in the corners of my eyes, blurring the figure more as it sways in my vision from the booze.

"You're not real! You're not real!" I plead, hoping the figure will vanish from my sight if I will it, but it only inches closer.

With the lighter in my hand stretched out in front of me, I flick the flint wheel down hard. Threatened by my quickened breath, the flame dances in front of me again, illuminating the ghostly figure pulling a hood down from its head to reveal a face.

*It can't be.*

Towering over me is a man with long, red hair and dark eyes. A silver anchor pendant dangles from his neck.

Chico jumps from the couch, whimpering in circles around his feet. The man opens his mouth as he reaches his arms out to me.

He pleads, "Lizzy, baby, it's me."

My knees fall weak. The floor tilts towards the ceiling. I almost feel his arms catch me before my sight goes black.

**A whistle.** Wind gusts push against glass. Chico whines. Happy whines. Velvet fabric on my fingertips. A flickering light. A candle. The candlelight is bright, then it's covered in shadow. A figure, once again, right in front of me. I let out a screech and jolt up from the lounger.

"Lizzy, it's ok. It's me... It's me." A flashlight illuminates his face in front of me.

*It is you.*

"Christian!" I scream.

I flail my arms at him, tossing them into his sides. I beat on his chest, shoving him away from me as he grabs my arms, pulling me in. He holds my wrists as my fists loosen and my arms collapse to my sides with his. He wraps his arms around my shoulders and pulls me in further, burying my head into his chest. His soft, warm, comforting chest.

I sob violently, "I don't understand. I, I...I thought you were dead."

Christian kisses my forehead, holding me tightly, so tightly that the squeeze keeps breath from entering my lungs. After a long time, he releases me, and I take a deep breath. He sits down on the lounger, pulling me down next to him. I look into his eyes. His dark brown pupils are red and veiny around the edges

"I'm here. Everything is okay." I hug hard against him again as he hushes me. "Shh... It's okay."

Debris knocks on the windows. Swishing wind rattles the balcony doors as if they are ready to burst open. I pull back from him, wiping my eyes with the back of my hands. Christian takes his thumb and wipes from the corners of my tear duct and down my cheek, brushing away my tears.

"Why didn't you leave Lizzy? Why are you here?" Christian holds my hands in grave concern. It takes me a second to collect my thoughts as he feels the freshly healing laceration on my palm. "Jesus, what happened here?"

"Leave?" I ask.

"Yes, why didn't you go to a shelter? Or to your mom's?" He looks at me quizzically, followed by a deeply furrowed brow, before looking back at my palm, examining it.

"Christian," I beg, taking my palm and resting it against his face, feeling the coarseness of his beard. My fingernails tangle in it as I look upon the face I never imagined I'd see again, and it's so clearly in front of me, as the day I saw him last.

"How are you here right now?" I ask.

The corners of his mouth turn downward. He bows his head with a deep sigh. He looks back up, locking his gaze into mine. His eyes are deeply saddened, darker than I'd ever seen. His hand rests on my stomach, feeling it softly as he says, "Oh, Lizzy. We've both been through so much. I'm going to tell you everything. You might not even believe half of the things I have been through, but what's important is we are together now."

"Well, tell me. What happened? Tell me everything!" I plead.

Just as eager as I am to know what happened and how he's here right now, I can't come up with any scenarios in my mind that would have allowed him to go without contacting me this long, without anyone notifying me. My mind is reeling at the possibilities, full of questions and disbelief all at once.

Christian pulls a small, ragged pocketbook from inside his jacket and hands it to me. With a reassuring nod, I open the first page. In his handwriting, it reads, *"Captain's Log"*. Knowing it holds the answers I'm desperate to find, I begin to read.

# Captain's Log

**February 16th**

PDX > JAX. Busy first day, but I made it aboard the Astor Odyssey at around 1300 hours. Her hull is slightly longer than what I'm used to, but it has a similar cargo load. An old, ugly thing. Moss green. Rust at every corner. I've already assigned several work orders for the crew to get her all cleaned up. Let's hope her outside isn't matching her insides.

The change of command was quick and cordial, although there was not much direction or overlap to get started. It seems Astor Lines doesn't mind throwing a captain aboard a new ship assignment with zero overhead, but it was the only open job on such short notice. A highly dangerous route and low pay kind of job. Just my luck. In contrast, the young Third Mate, Aiden, has been helpful enough to show me around. My quarters are decent, but I'll need to get some new pillows, or my neck may never turn over my shoulder again.

Loading is in progress, 60,000 tons of grain. I sure hope

they properly inspected the hold before filling it. I don't want to deal with the smell of spoiled corn all the way to Africa.

We should be ready to sail in a day or two. Just waiting to hear the "all clear" from the Astor representative. In the meantime, I'll be finding the best chair on the bridge for my morning coffee and continue to organize the chaos of crew files.

**February 17th**

Getting settled in today. I did find the perfect spot on the bridge for my coffee. I sat in all the office chairs in the lounge and found the perfect balance of back support with a slightly broken-in cushion. I hauled that chair over my shoulder, up the four flights of stairs to the bridge, and set it in front of a large wheelhouse window portside. I may have startled the crew a bit, but they'll get used to me.

Breakfast was pleasant. Eggs. Bacon. French toast. I had to yell at Chief Mate Ben. I caught him eating a banana. Upon further inspection of our dry food storage with the steward, I discovered a whole box of the damn things. Doesn't anyone care about bad sea omens anymore?

**February 18th**

Astor Odyssey is underway. Conditions are fair. Projected to reach the Port of Tema, Ghana, in 20 days as long as everything goes smoothly. At least that's the date I prepared the mates for this morning. We won't know how long the clearance for docking will take yet. I'm sure Africa does things a little differently than what I'm used to state-side. Guess I'll find out sooner or later.

All the crew files are organized alphabetically and in a dedicated file cabinet, as they should have been all along. Overlooking last year's shipyard orders, I have discovered that the workers in Turkey failed to complete about half of the tasks on the list, which included painting and sealing rusty handrails. It's a good thing I located plenty of good paint on my tour around the ship yesterday. In fact, I'm going to have all the handrails painted red, and on the list for next year's shipyard maintenance, the hull will be repainted a crisp, clean white. Astor Odyssey's going to clean up real nice!

Although maybe by next year, I won't be the captain of Astor Odyssey.

## February 20th

It's already 2300 hours, and I'm only finally back to my room from giving night orders to the crew. It's been a rough couple of days. The bilge pump has been acting up. The age of the ship is starting to show. Yesterday, when checking the cargo hold, a few of the door seals were cracked and rotting out, not to mention we had to replace several corroded cleats holding the hatch covers in place. We had to expose the cargo for some time to fix the issue, which was what I was trying to avoid, but either way, water is going to get in anyway if we run into any weather. Hopefully, we won't until after we unload. Maybe with the hold empty, I can get a better assessment of any issues.

Astor Lines heard an earful from me, and all I got were

excuses and scripted answers.

*"We will talk to our supervisors and find a solution. In the meantime, please continue with the cargo as planned."*

I see now why this was the only captain's job available on short notice.

After everything today, I kicked my feet up on my desk and took a long look at the picture of Elizabeth to remember what I'm doing this for. I still can't believe I'm going to be a father. I wonder if parenting will be as hard as taking care of a ship. I have to find it. I have to get off this ship and take care of them. It's the only way. I just hope it's where I think it is.

**February 21st**

Surprisingly, it's a calmer day in terms of mechanical issues, however the seas have started picking up. Swells are up to 12 ft. We're crossing the Atlantic and battling some of the northeast trade winds.

Today is also the day Elizabeth officially moves us out of our apartment. I wish I could be there to help. I know she sees this as a fun road trip, but I told her I didn't want her to go on that cross-country drive while pregnant. What if something happens?

I hate feeling helpless.

As a young sailor, I never had plans for myself other than getting a career. Going to sailing school was the best option for me after leaving foster care. I'd been alone my whole life. I figured the lifestyle of a sailor would suit me well, never knowing any of my own family. I wasn't needed or expected to be anywhere, but all that changed when I met Lizzy. Now all I want to do is be with her all the time. And now with the baby, well, I've got to figure this out.

I think the crew has noticed my off mood. Aiden knocked on my door after dinner and asked me to watch a movie he had downloaded. Watching Alien was a good distraction, but the content made for a strange theme. I never realized the movie was about motherhood. Strange.

He brought his video game console on board, so we agreed to do some gaming next time. It's been nice having someone to unwind with, after all the overthinking I've been doing. Aiden is doing right by me, and I appreciate him. He's a good kid and means well. He's confident and caring. He could make a great captain someday, but he needs years of roughing those innocent edges first.

## February 24th

It's been quiet here. Quiet is a good thing.

I got an email from Elizabeth today with pictures of her and Chico outside of our new home. What a load off my shoulders to hear she arrived safely! It's been tough to run this place with all the overthinking. I did open up to Aiden about it. He's a little young, fifteen years my junior, so I wondered if he could even relate, but just hearing and offering the *"Ah, don't sweat it. To be with you, she has to be a strong girl, am I right?"* was enough to get me through. I had to give him a little shit because I'm still his captain. I kept a straight face with his response to my troubles, and he puckered up real quick. You could practically see the sweat dripping from his forehead, so I lay the moment on him a little longer, to you know, work on the roughening up. Eventually, I gave him a pat on his shoulder. He laughed unsurely and said, *"Good one, Capt."*

I can't wait to be with her. I want to tell her where to look. The anticipation of finding it is maddening, but I must wait a little longer. I don't want her to think less of me if it isn't there. I rest anxiously, knowing how close we are to freedom. I just have to get through this haul, but at least it's protected for now.

**February 30th**

Crew members are complaining that one of the cabin stewards has been saying some concerning things. I called her to my office to have an evaluation. She appeared to be fine. She complained about missing her kids back at home and how she was feeling anxious. I reported the interview to Astor Lines by email this afternoon, and they suggested I contact one of our on-call physicians on the matter, who then had a phone conversation with the crew member and recommended we keep an eye on her.

I met with the other cabin stewards and asked them to let me know if her state of well-being negatively progresses.

**March 2nd**

Crew member Valerie Fuentes had been found dangling her feet off the side of the starboard aft railing early this morning. Luckily, Aiden was out doing a deck walk and was able to talk her off the ledge, literally. I'd say he's roughing his edges rather quickly.

## March 6th

We arrived at the Port of Tema, Ghana. Docking was a hassle. The dockworkers were not as quick to respond when handing over the mooring line. They tried to argue that our position needed to come forward 20 ft, but my patience was wearing thin. I had to exert some force to get them to cooperate. Luckily, the worst of that is over.

Crew member Valerie Fuentes was escorted off the ship to an agent who was taking her to the local hospital. I feel bad she has to get her medical care in a foreign country, but this is the nature of the job. The crew seemed to feel a lot of relief after she was gone.

## March 8th

45,000 tons have been unloaded, and we're off to the Port of Cotonou in Benin, sailing at 16 knots. After talking to the Astor Line representative, they are pushing us to meet a deadline and get there quickly before the storm comes. They feel staying docked up or anchored outside the Port of Tema for too long could be a safety issue.

The weather radar is not looking too optimal, but all we have to do is make it to the next docking, and we should be safe to sit for a few days if necessary.

**March 11th**

We're experiencing rough seas and fighting the currents. I had expected we would be pulling into the Port of Cotonou by now, but we are only halfway there. The conditions are getting worse. I fear we may need to anchor. There's a call scheduled with the representative this evening to confirm how to move forward.

**March 12th**

Son of a bitch. These assholes screwed us. They made us go forward when I knew we'd have bad weather.

We're anchored 10 miles off the shore of Lome with no visual clearance because of the heavy storm. The ship is rolling like a motherfucker. Now we're getting calls over the radio about a potential threat in close proximity that another ship dodged earlier.

Fucking pirates.

**March 15th**

They weren't kidding about the impermeable waterproof seals on this raincoat. My pocket journal was bone dry when I woke up. Maybe the raincoat company would ask me to be the new face of their brand if I can ever get back to America, but first, it's important I write down what I remember about the event. The sooner, the more accurate.

On March 12th, around 2000 hours, a small vessel was spotted approaching the ship's radar. I called the Astor representative to inform them of the situation. While staying on the line, I directed the crew to go through with protocol by sounding the emergency alarm and locking down all doors. The Chief Mate, 2nd Mate, and I all stayed on the bridge to continue evaluating the situation with Astor. The head engineer assisted in getting all the crew to safety in the citadel.

With the weather, we couldn't maneuver the ship or reinforce any anti-pirate razor wire or anything like that. I thought the rolling of the ship might keep them off of us, making it too difficult to board, but somehow, they found a way.

I called the lead engineer over the radio, asking for a headcount. He was short one. The Third Mate, Aiden, wasn't accounted for. I called over the radio to him, but no answer.

Looking down at the deck, the pirates were mere shadows passing through bouts of heavy rainfall. I used a pair of binoculars to try to get a closer look. I spotted them. The pirates had captured Aiden.

I ordered the Chief Mate and the 2nd Mate to go to the citadel right away, and I waited as the pirates approached, holding Aiden hostage with rifles in their hands, demanding to be let in.

Through communication with Astor, I asked how to move forward. They simply said, *"Don't let them in,"* but there was no way I was going to leave him out there like that. No way. I breached protocol and offered myself to the pirates in exchange for Aiden. I couldn't go on with a clear conscience unless I knew everyone on that ship was alive and safe. In training, I'd been told pirates mainly capture the captain for ransom, so I knew there was a chance if I cooperated with them and the company met their demands, I'd be returned safely. Well, it didn't go exactly how I'd thought. I went for the ride of my life after I disembarked that ship and climbed onto their watercraft. I won't call it a boat because it was a poor excuse for one. They tied me up and forced me to speak demands into the radio, but as we cleared a distance away from the ship, the waves became greater than I'd ever seen. The watercraft couldn't take the beating, and the hull began to crack. The water washed the pirates from the deck, but I was stuck, thrashing up and down with the ship until it completely ripped from the seams, tearing it in half. I had tossed and turned, going under the water. I took my last breath in such haste that I thought to myself, this was it; once I let out this last breath, all I could do was drown. I thought of Lizzy and our unborn child.

Then, I woke up.

I opened my eyes to a clear blue sky on the polished teak surface of a 40 ft schooner. Staring at billowing sails hung from two masts, I couldn't tell if I was alive or dreaming. Was this heaven? I thought it might be until I came face to face with Sage and Skye, my rescuers. Sage is a leathery-skinned man, shirtless, with a visor tangled into his dreadlocked hair. I can't tell if he's older or younger than me because the sun and salt look to have worn him years older than he might actually be. Skye is questionably young, dark-skinned, bearing dreadlocks that are tied into a bun on top of her head. She wears so many necklaces and bracelets on her wrists that they appear to slightly pull her posture down. They cheered when I woke up and danced around in circles, handing me food and drink and asking me questions like, *"Dude, where did you come from?"* and stating, *"We thought you were a goner for sure."*

I explained everything, to which the responses were *"Whoa"* and *"No way, man!"* I asked for their radio to call for help, but they insisted it hadn't worked since they bought the vessel, and that they had no EPIRB because they were sailing *"all natural"* and *"on a mission to find the true meaning of life"*, or something like that. I had to lecture them about basic boater safety. They only shrugged their shoulders and insisted that, *"It's all good, man."*

I'm currently trying to manually chart our location so I can get back to civilization as soon as possible, before Elizabeth worries about me.

## March 16th

Sage says that before they found me, he and Skye had tried to sail to Ascension Island in the Atlantic but were run off due to illegal mooring. Then, they sailed to Africa, thinking they'd go to Lamin to see the hippos, but the current and storm dragged them into the gulf, which just happened to put them right in my path. It all seems so coincidental, but I can't escape my reality now.

I pulled out their paper charts to find our whereabouts. Their plan was to sail around the world and see where nature would take them, but ultimately, we will all be going in the direction of Florida now, under my command. They fought me on the idea of going to the States. From what I've gathered, neither of them cares to share their true identities and doesn't want to talk about their past. I can assume something strange is going on with these vagabonds. They would only agree to sail to the Florida Keys, where I could get back into the United States, and they could avoid running into customs. We are quite literally in the middle of the ocean right now with no motor power, only the winds to guide us along. I plan to join a shipping route as soon as possible, to maybe get rescued by a passing ship, but for now, I'm stuck eating rice with tuna curry with Sage and Skye.

I wonder if I'll ever make it back home.

**March 23rd**

The first week with Sage and Skye has had its ups and downs. There's something about the peace and solitude, along with the terribly frightening feeling of being out in the middle of nowhere. I'd been out many times before, but never with a disconnection to the outside world. Just me and these two people on a tiny vessel, no cell phones, or emails, or radios, or life other than the sun, moon and stars in the sky, the currents, wind and waves, the fish and sea birds. Without knowledge of any civilization besides our own, the world could be falling apart, and I'd never know, just up until the moment it came to swallow us whole, too. All I can do is hope that Elizabeth is okay, and that someone is out looking for me, and that this will all be over soon.

I used to feel similar to this, alone and helpless, as a child. I felt I had no one in the world to relate to, or anyone that may actually care about me. The idea of a mother and father was a foreign concept. I'd see other children with their parents. The love they shared was so obvious. A special bond I never had, until I met Elizabeth. I never imagined I'd feel this way about family until the possibility of creating my own started becoming a reality.

I did search for my birth parents, as most foster children do. When you become old enough, curiosity eats at you, no matter how hard you try to ignore it. I started with my genetic heritage. I took a DNA test to discover my ancestry, where I was from, and to see if anyone was out there that I could relate to. I remember sitting at the desk in my dormitory when I opened the results of my test. To my surprise, the results led me to more questions than answers. 100% Minorcan. What was that? What did it mean?

It was clear I belonged somewhere. I researched the history of Minorcan people. I learned that Minorca, a small island off the coast of Spain, went back to the Roman Era. After the fall of Rome, it went under Moorish rule until Christian forces conquered it, making it part of Spain. Later, the island was occupied by Britain and then France and then Britain again, before ultimately returning to Spanish rule. So how did someone like me come to America? Well, it was all thanks to Dr. Andrew Turnbull, an indigo plantation owner, who brought indentured servants from Minorca to work for him. Thus, leading to a rich history of our people in northern Florida. Learning about this history sparked excitement in me. I found out that I might have people to belong to, and

I wanted to know more. I wanted to know about my family. How was their story related to all of this? Where are they now? But I wanted to know most, why did they give me up?

**March 30th**

I'd only sailed a couple of times in my life. Like *real* sailing. I learned how during my first summer in college at the academy. I met a lot of people from a lot of different places. Not everyone was poor like me. I actually made a lot of rich friends who had been sailing since they were children. One cadet I spent a lot of time with had a slip rented on the bay. His sailboat was an excuse for us to get off campus and party, or more commonly for him to impress the ladies. Though there were a few days that summer that he took it out on the bay and showed me how to sail. It was a rush, tracking and jibbing, manning the ropes, knowing when to maneuver the sails for different wind directions. It made me feel very close to the sea, a part of the elements. Sailing on a large ship is a lot different. It's more mechanical and systematic. Barking commands, following orders, monitoring, shifting, making small adjustments, and a lot of planning.

I watch Sage and his movements, how at ease he is to let go of the reins. I can't tell whether he's extremely experienced or a complete idiot. I guess the time I've had on cargo ships has forced me to become so structured that I can't do it *"the natural way"*. Letting go of control makes me anxious. It makes me angry that Sage doesn't seem to care, and he gets away with it. I've never been allowed to be so careless.

Carelessness was never an option in my life. I had to take care of everything, do everything right, or I would become nothing. I didn't want to be poor anymore. I wanted to be in control of my life. Sometimes it still feels that I'm fighting to win control, but I've never felt this close to it before. When I move into our new house with Elizabeth, and soon find what I've been looking for. It's the reason I took this job and bought that house. What lies in Painter's Beach is the answer to everything.

**April 6th**

I've never felt so hungry in my life. I'd die for a cheeseburger and fries right now. Maybe a large pepperoni pizza from that hole-in-the-wall joint back in Portland. The rice, the lentils, the dried fruits and nuts, it's all rabbit food. If I had planned this sailing trip, I would have done everything differently. You could still have nice meals if you prepare properly. I'd at least have a jar of peanut butter and loaves of bread. I'd seriously kill for a peanut butter sandwich right now. Instead, I'm chewing on enough trail mix, grinding it with my teeth slowly enough, that the flavor almost teases me into believing it could be a peanut butter sandwich.

We're running low on protein, but Sage says they planned on catching their meals *"the natural way."* If I hear that phrase one more time, I might strangle the guy. I only hope that my navigations are accurate enough, because we should be approaching a shipping lane soon. Then I can get out of this hellhole and back to some normalcy.

## April 13th

When I last wrote, I'd assumed we'd be in a shipping lane by now. I swear we are tracking one, but I haven't seen a ship this whole time we've been out here. I've been at sea sharing this sailboat with Sage and Skye for almost a month now. It's hard to believe.

On a positive note, we did catch some fish this week. I've been eating pretty well, or at least a hell of a lot better than before, with the trail mix. I'd never fished before. It's not that I didn't have an interest in it; it's just that no one had ever taught me. We came across some disturbance on the surface of the calm water. Sage rushed to pull out his cast net. He held a corner of the net in his mouth and meticulously gathered the net, over and over again. He reached some of the remaining slack of the net on the ground and coiled himself before tossing it, releasing it into the air, where it formed a perfect circle before dropping into the water. He pulled in the net quickly and brought it aboard. Tens of fish thrashed inside the net. I thought we'd be eating them, but to my surprise, he said, *"Get the poles ready, Skye. The sea gods are gifting us today."*

He sliced the bait fish into pieces, and we hooked the chunks of their bodies onto the fishing line before tossing them into the water. It didn't take long for us to start reeling them in. The first tug on my line was sudden and jerked me forward with more force than I expected. I did everything in my power to reel in, but the line became loose, and I lost the fish. Sage said I'd reeled too eagerly. Skye said, *"The idea is to tire the fish, to wear it out, not wear ourselves out, for we have to save our energy to clean and cook them too."*

I hooked the next chunk of fish body and tossed it again into the deep blue and waited. Not long after, my line tugged again.

Sage shouted, *"Set the hook, give it a good yank! Then steady your reeling as they pull, and as they slow, reel harder."*

I did as he said, and after a good fight back and forth, I pulled in a huge mahi-mahi. I yelled with excitement, pumping my fist. Catching that fish, cleaning it, and cooking it made it taste like nothing I'd ever had before.

**April 20th**

Things have gotten better on here. I feel the roles on the sailboat are better established now that Sage has given me more control of the sailing. He's stepped back, but I think he's enjoying the downtime, spending more time in the cabin with Skye.

Seeing them together hurts me, though. I can't stop thinking about Elizabeth and wondering what she might be thinking now. So much time has passed, I'd wondered if she'd given up hope for me. There's no way they'd still be looking for me at this point.

We're still so far from land. The days at sea are all running together; no matter how long, they all feel the same. I've thought a lot about the journey Minorcans took, as they crossed the sea to get to Florida. They thought they would leave what they knew behind, to start a better life, to have an opportunity. I can't help but feel for them, as I too am on my journey to more opportunities. To find what they left behind.

When I turned eighteen, I knew I wanted to find out more about my parents, but I wasn't ready. It was when I took my first sail on a cargo ship out of the academy that I looked out at the vast emptiness of the ocean. The miles and miles of nothing but water. It was feeling how vast our world was, and how far my heritage was from Florida, that made me become more fascinated with the idea. My ancestors were great travelers, and now so was I. But I still wasn't sure what exactly had happened. I let my curiosity take hold, and I requested information about my birth parents. With my new job, although I didn't make much, I did have the money finally to hire someone, to find my birth parents. I waited a long time, but eventually I got the call I wasn't expecting. I knew any information I could find about my parents would have been possibly shocking, but I hadn't prepared myself for the idea that they might not actually be alive. The same day I found out my parents' real names, where they had lived, what they had done in their lives, I had also found out when they died and where they were buried. That was a complete shock.

Margarita and Ramon Ponce were their names. They lived in a small apartment in St. Augustine, Florida. Margarita was a seamstress, and Ramon worked in a mechanics shop. Both of my parents were very young when they gave me up for adoption. My mother was only nineteen, my father twenty. It seems that they had tried to raise me. They had me until I was two years old before they chose to give me up. The private investigator explained that in a case like mine, unfortunately, it's common with young parents who can't afford to raise a child to give them up, to give them a better chance at life. I'm saddened at the thought that our traveling ancestors came all this way for better opportunities, but my parents knew nothing of the sea or travel, and their opportunities were so limited that they had to give up their own son. Looking at the bigger picture was devastating. Realizing I had spent two years in their care, but having no memory of that time together. If they hadn't died, maybe we could have had a relationship, because I could feel they still loved me. Loved me enough to make such a difficult decision. I had grieved them all my life, only to grieve them for an eternity.

**April 27th**

Still no sign of any ships. It seems impossible, but maybe I've been spoiled with the perspective of being in a large vessel with access to radar and digital charting. Maybe every single ship on this ocean has been just far enough away in any given direction that we've passed them. Maybe this is life's funny way of mocking me. Forcing me to become friends with people I loathe. Forcing me to sit with the quiet of the sea, staring at beautiful sunrises and sunsets, left me only to sit and think about everything I've been trying not to think about for years. It's like I'm stuck on a level of a video game that I can't get out of. There's a special item I need to collect, or a path I need to find, but I'm just going around in circles with no end in sight. I'm stuck.

I'm stuck thinking about the pages of my father's journal.

Trying to remember each page. The feeling of tracing his initials carved into the inside of its leather cover. Feeling the R and P imprint was the closest I'd ever feel to his actual presence.

I got hold of his journal because I was still curious. I couldn't accept that finding out their lives were over meant that was the end of it. I'd come too far and lived too long without my parents. There had to be more. I added my parents' names to my DNA profile and was able to populate a relative. My father's brother, Luiz Ponce. I had an uncle. One day, I'm all alone, and the next I have an uncle. I was nervous about reaching out. I wasn't sure about the relationship that he had with my father or if he'd have any interest in meeting me, but I found his number and gave him a call. The response was again shocking. He'd invited me to come to his house in St. Augustine. At the time, I was working out of New York, so I wasn't exactly close, but since it was my time off the ship, I made the long road trip to Florida anyway. As I pulled up to the house, it was very quaint and old, in a part of town with a lot of other older houses. There was lawn equipment scattered in the front yard. A group of people was sitting around a plastic table and chairs. As I walked up, a tall, older man with much darker tanned skin than I and long, coarse grey hair, said my name like he knew exactly who I was. His family all greeted me cheerfully and offered me a bottled beer from their cooler in the yard. I took a seat around the plastic table, and we talked for hours. It was a strange feeling to meet family I had never known. Part of me felt they looked sort of like me, but I didn't feel they acted anything like me. They were very content with a simple life. I got the feeling they hadn't known much else, but they didn't complain. They seemed happy. I only wondered if I were raised by my parents, if I'd be the same man I am today. If I felt the same way I do, like I didn't quite fit in with them. Would I still have wanted more?

Through stories of my mother and father, though few, I learned they were hardworking and struggled to make ends meet. They didn't expect to have me, but they tried everything to make it work. They both worked long hours, and I spent a lot of time being watched by different family members and even neighbors. When it came to their death, it was only shortly after they gave me up that they were in a horrible car accident. I guess if I'd still been in their lives, I might have been in the accident with them. Maybe giving me up for adoption really did save my life.

After a long day spent with my uncle's family, I thanked them all and promised to stay in touch, but as much as it was nice to finally meet them, I didn't feel I belonged as I had hoped. Before I got back into the car, my uncle handed me my father's journal. He said it was all he had left, so he thought I should have it. I was grateful to my uncle for this gesture, for he knew him better than I did. It's hard to tell if this journal was a blessing or a curse, because what I was about to find out would change the course of my life forever.

**May 4th**

Yesterday at midday we saw a ship.

The minute it started peaking over the horizon, all the

contentment I had with my situation shook from my core. The excitement of getting back home, the reality of being with Elizabeth again, was pulsing through my veins. I shouted at the ship, even so far away, but I remained patient, turning our boat against the wind, so the ship could catch up quicker. Of course, there were no flares on board. I had to get as close as possible, so there was no way they couldn't see us.

That big, beautiful ship shone in front of me like a lucky golden ticket. But as it neared, and the ship was in full view, I realized it wasn't gleaming of gold, it was tinted orange and flakey. The hull was completely rusted, railings broken, no signs of life. It wasn't running, it was drifting. It was a ghost ship. I had heard of them before, but I'd never seen one with my own eyes. I cursed at the ship. I beat my fists on the deck. Sage and Skye sat quietly, in horror of my cries. It was the first time they had seen any emotion from me. I'd been keeping it inside this whole journey.

They gave me space as I watched the ghost ship taunt me through angry tears. Why has the world been so cruel? What had I done to deserve this fate?

After the ghost ship had moved on and the stars began to show, Skye put her hand on my shoulder, trying to console me.

She said, *"I think I have something to ease you."*

I wasn't in the mood for their hippy cures or words of wisdom. I wanted to leave, I wanted to go home, but to my surprise, Sage came out of the cabin with a bottle of whiskey and three tin cups. An item that spoke my language.

*"I'd been saving this for a special occasion, but sometimes the*

*occasion doesn't have to be so special at all, it just needs to be."*

Sage handed me a cupful, and we drank and drank until my anger dissipated and I even began to laugh. I hadn't grown too fond of them, but they had grown on me. We've managed to tolerate our existence because we share at least one commonality: we're human.

After a story of the time they'd thought they'd seen the Kraken, they asked me if I had any wild stories to share. After some coercion and another whiskey, I told them about what I found in my father's journal.

After acquiring it that summer in St. Augustine, I'd spent my entire next hitch obsessing over its pages. While standing watch on the deck as a cadet, I'd open up the journal and read it over and over again, until I'd almost memorized it. My father's words. Not only could I hear him talking to me, but it was as if he was giving me a gift. Inside the pages of the journal, he went into detail about the owner of a car he worked on at the mechanic's shop. This man he met, whom he calls John, had been a treasure hunter. He was looking for the famous lost Spanish treasures of the 1715 Fleet Disaster. Eleven ships sank in a hurricane off the east coast of Florida, scattering gold and silver along its shores. John was getting his tire fixed before going on a road trip to meet with a person who might potentially have a collection of the original coins. My father became so fascinated with the idea of this treasure that he followed John on his road trip without his knowledge. He watched from a distance as John shook hands with a man on the front porch of a beach house, before going inside. He wanted so badly to know if they were inside looking at the treasure. So bad, that coincidence or not, John ended up in my father's shop again with another flat tire. This time it was punctured and needed a replacement. My father questioned John extensively, begging to find out if he'd seen any real coins. Although John was hesitant, he agreed to meet my father for dinner and talk with him about it.

At their dinner, John explained he had authenticated a real gold coin from the 1715 Fleet Disaster and that the owner of the coin mentioned he had found it on his property. John had a suspicion that there was more, but that the man only wanted to check if it was authentic or not. This lit a fire under my father. He drove back and forth on weekends to sit in front of this man's house, wondering if the treasure was there. He paced the beach behind it, searching the sand for gold, but no matter how much sand he sifted, he never found anything but shells and sharks' teeth. Until his last entry. The last page of his journal was written the day before he died. He wrote that he had found a coin. He described it as a golden imperfect circle weighing 27 grams. Stamped on one side was the Spanish Habsburg shield with a capital *"L"* and an *"8"* and a capital *"M"*, and the other side had a cross, two lions and two castles. He said this coin would change his and Margarita's lives forever. He wrote that he would drive her to the same spot this weekend to look for more.

Although I found my father's story tragic, his story intrigued me. The coins fascinated me. It may have been too late for my father to save his family, but it wasn't for me.

## May 11th

We should have reached Florida by now. I can't help but feel I'm navigating us in the wrong direction, or maybe we've been going in circles. Part of me wonders if when I fall asleep, maybe Sage routes us back in a different direction. The other day, I woke up to him sleeping at the wheel, and we'd been sailing almost completely due west when we were meant to be northeast. I can't explain all of this lost time other than they're altering our position, plotting against me, to prevent us from going to Florida. My patience is wearing thin. My rage is building. All I can think about is Elizabeth and our baby and getting home to them. I confronted Sage about our direction and how I can't account for our mileage, and he insists that he isn't trying to slow us down. But something in my gut makes me think we haven't moved. Maybe it's the calmer-than-normal seas, the lack of favorable winds. After such a horrible storm I was in, to think of it, we haven't had a single drop of rain since. Every day has been the same. Always warm, always clear skies, sunrises, long days, sunsets, stars. The skyline is always water as far as I can see in every direction I look. Nothing changes, everything is always the same.

I just want Elizabeth to know I am trying so hard to get back to her. If I could sail right up to our house and beach this god damn boat, I would. But I can't.

## Elizabeth Corey

**A loud crashing noise came from the kitchen.** Broken glass flew across the room as a pine tree branch penetrated the window above the sink. The wind swirled up around the room, blowing out the candle. The rain mists the counter and floors in waves. The tree pulls back out with the wind, grinding against the window frame.

"Holy shit!" I shout.

We both stand up.

"Stay over here with Chico. There's glass everywhere. I don't want you to get hurt." Christian orders me. I do as I am told, feeling helpless and dumbfounded in this moment. My brain is overwhelmed. All I can think about is needing a drink to calm my nerves. I scan the dark living room, only seeing the faint outline of a wine bottle toppled over on the rug.

"I'm going to have to get some tools and wood from the garage." Christian throws on a heavy raincoat before opening the front door. The wind throws it open, slamming it into the wall. With a flashlight in hand, I can see that the water is growing closer to our front door before he pulls the door closed behind him. Ignoring the request, I tiptoe over to the door as Chico hides under the coffee table. I try to stay far from the kitchen sink and far from any broken glass to look out the front window, dodging the painting tarp whipping up towards me.

It's difficult to make out anything past the staircase leading to the driveway, where I can see the storm surge has come up to the stairs, covering all but two or three of the bottom steps. I imagine the garage is flooded, wondering how he will manage to get to anything.

I make my way upstairs to my art studio, where I remember I might have a flashlight. Stumbling over my stool, fell onto the hardwood, feeling a puddle on the floor soak into my shirt. Picking myself back up, I feel for the drawer and find the flashlight. I click it on to find the floor is wet, a leak pouring down from the roof. My artwork that was sitting on the floor is now sopping wet. I pick up a weaving that drips onto the floor. Its threads are saturated and heavy with water.

Great!

Angered at the sheer destruction of my art studio, I throw the piece down and walk back out to the kitchen. My wet feet slip slightly on the staircase, so I clutch the railing to keep from falling. Taking better caution, I slip on shoes from the rack at the front door and step widely, crunching across the glass-ridden floor. As the rain comes in from the window, wetting my shirt further, I grab a bottle of wine off the wine rack with a twist-off cap. I undo the top and chug right from the neck of the bottle, when the front door swings open violently, crashing into the wall again. Christian, soaking wet, holds a piece of wood, a drill and a small saw. Just like a few minutes ago, again I am in shock that he is here in our house.

He secures the front door shut and goes straight to the kitchen window while I'm left frozen, watching his every move, studying him, like trying to puzzle pieces of him together I hadn't seen in so long. Sticking his arms and head slightly outside the window, he uses the saw to cut away at a piece of a pine tree branch as it sways back towards the window, rain battering him in the face. His long hair drapes over his face like a mop. He cuts the branch loose and tosses it back out the window, then grabs the piece of wood, drill, and a box of screws.

"I'm going to need your help, Lizzy." He climbs onto the counter below the window and starts to prop up the piece of wood against the window, covering the opening. He struggles to hold it in place as the wind pushes against the board. The opening sounds of rain and rushing wind subsides within the kitchen. I haven't moved. I'm still frozen.

"Honey, put the wine bottle down and come here," he asserts in the sweetest of tones, given the situation.

"I'm sorry." My eyes start to swell with heat, and I sob.

Still holding the board, he turns his head towards me and assures, "It's ok. Just focus. We can do this."

I set the bottle down and put my hands up against the board, leaning over the sink. Trying to pull myself together.

"Yeah, hold it just like that, nice and firm against the window while I secure it." I use all my strength to hold the board in place, my head feeling hot from the wine I chugged a minute ago. Christian drills screws right through the board and into the window frame at the top, bottom and sides. "Okay. You can let go now."

I step back and breathe a sigh of relief.

The window is boarded up.

Christian jumps down from the counter and looks around the room. "My god! This place is a mess. Are you alright?"

"Yeah, I'm okay."

"This house was not ready for this storm. No boards on the windows, no sandbags, not to mention the roof needs to be replaced. I can't believe you stayed here. It's only going to get worse. This is an evacuation zone. The storm surge could reach the front door in a matter of hours. What were you thinking?" he lectures me sternly.

"I'm sorry. I'm really not okay. I've been a mess without you." Bowing my head in embarrassment, I knew I had given up and hoped the storm might just wash my problems right out to sea. Christian knows I was being reckless. He knows I was giving up and I'm ashamed.

Crunching broken glass beneath him as he walks over to me, he holds me once more, whimpering softly. "I'm sorry too. I've been a wreck without you. I've been so worried about you."

We embrace each other, softly weeping for a while. He whimpers in my arms like a child. We cry until the chest heaving slows and the sounds soften. Our sobs turn into chuckles, which turn into laughter and then muted laughter as our lips meet. Kisses that are gentle, with a longing. Kisses that become deeper, wetter, with passion. Until our mouths are devouring one another, hard and breathless. I can only mouth through the exchanges, "I missed you so much."

He pulls away and looks down into my eyes, brushing the strands of hair from my face, "I missed you more," he paused, gripping the back of my hair softly, "my dark moon, my love, my Lizzy."

He grabs me from around my waist and pulls me in, picking me up off my feet. I wrap my legs around him as he holds me up.

"I want to see our bedroom," he demands.

I couldn't agree more.

"Come on, Chico." His claws click on the floor, and from behind he follows. Without another word, Christian leads me down the dark hallway, with our mouths still entangled. He sets me down and holds his hand as we walk up the stairs. And through the door frame of our bedroom, he picks me up again and sets me onto the edge of the bed.

"Lay down, Chico. Daddy's here now."

Christian closes the bedroom door so we are all here in one room, safe together.

He removes his sopping wet clothes, tossing them on the floor. All I can see is his silhouette through the flashes of lightning coming from the window. His hands makes it's way up my shirt, taking it off above my head. Then his hands remove my bottoms, until there's nothing left between us.

I can feel his weight crawling over me, onto the bed, hoisting me onto the pillows. His smooth, warm skin against mine. I forgot how strong he is and how heavy his body is. I forgot how he smells. His unique scent brings me right back to our memories of where we left off.

Mouth to mouth, we kiss as the rain drips onto our bodies from the leaking ceiling. The wind pounds the glass windows that face the ocean. Sounds of the storm beat on our house, but all the noise fades out with our breath.

--

**If someone were to tell me that I would be cuddled up in my bed next to Christian and Chico again, I would never have believed a word.** I can't believe it. There are so many unanswered questions, but all I can do is lay in silence against his chest, while he plays with my hair. I grasp onto him tightly, listening to his heartbeat, feeling his chest rise and lower with every breath. He's a living, breathing person. My person, my love. I never want him out of my sight again.

While the cuddles feel they could last forever, my mind weighs heavily with questions. I didn't know where to begin, or how to explain everything I've been through these months since he's been gone. We have so much to catch up on.

We both wait for the other to begin a conversation. Soaking in the moment, the embrace of being together at last, but with the sounds of the storm shaking the old bones of this house and the steady dripping from the ceiling onto the bed, we cannot deny our reality much longer.

Although I can fill the space by venting everything to him, I long to hear his voice. I waited for him to speak. As elated as I am he's here, resentment grows in my gut. Why hadn't I known he was alive all this time, and did he know how much I had to deal with thinking he was dead? All the grieving and feelings of being close to death were now completely invalid. All that pain and suffering was for nothing.

With a tone of frustration, I speak first, "I thought you were dead. This whole time."

I lift myself from his chest and rest on my elbow to talk to him. He sits up and turns towards me. After a lengthy pause, filling the moist warm air between us, he says, "I know. I can't imagine how bad that must have felt. But I assure you there is a reason."

"A reason? What do you mean? Where have you been?"

"Listen, Lizzy, listen. I came as soon as I could. I'm glad we're finally together, but I am upset with you. Why were you sheltering from the hurricane here? You know that's practically a death wish."

"Well, I really didn't know. I've never been in a hurricane," I recoil.

"Don't downplay this. You're a smart girl. We're in danger being here, and you know that."

The tone in my voice becomes shrill as I say, "I'm sorry. I don't know, I just didn't know what to do."

His tone elevates in seriousness. "What do you mean? You

could have evacuated. That's what everyone was ordered to do. You would just throw your life away because I'm not here? That's horrible. That's selfish."

I sit all the way up in bed to respond. "Selfish? What about you? Where the hell were you? What happened?"

Christian grips his hand around my arm. "I called you Lizzy. You were drunk and irrational and wouldn't speak to me."

Yanking my arm back, I huff, "Wait, what? That was you?" I think back to the night I fell asleep in the sand, thinking I was imagining it.

"What have you been doing? Drinking yourself to death? I mean, the house is in horrible shape. You're skin and bones. Why would you want to kill yourself?"

With a louder voice, I speak, "You left me! You died! That's why!"

Through the shaking of the house, the squealing of the wind against the windows, the door handle shakes. A faint noise comes from the door before it's thrown open.

"Elizabeth?"

A light illuminated the room, blinding my eyes from the doorway. I throw up my hands over my eyes.

I know that voice.

"Aimsley?" I question.

Christian turns on a flashlight, and the room brightens.

Aimsley stands in the doorway, drenched from head to toe. Her jaw is dropped. "Oh, my god. I came to rescue you, and you're hooking up with some guy the whole time? Wow." Aimsley leans against the doorway, shaking her head and shielding her eyes from us.

"Some guy, eh?" Christian comments with a heavy, sarcastic tone.

I cover up my naked body with a pillow, and Christian gets up from the bed to put his clothes back on. His bare ass is out as he slides on his boxers and pants.

"Aw man, come on!" Aimsley shields her eyes from looking at Christian as Chico wags his tail.

I feel like I've entered into a strange fever dream.

"This is Christian. My dead partner." I blankly stare at Aimsley, looking for an explanation.

"So, wait, is this what you lied to me about?" Aimsley asks crossly.

"I didn't lie about anything. He just showed up here. Like just now." I look to Christian for an answer as Aimsley is stewing over something I don't understand.

"So wait, how do you two know each other?" Christian asks.

"We're just friends," I answer.

"Just friends?" Aimsley huffs.

I look to Aimsley, who backs down and looks at me with concern. Her appearance is like a drowned rat. I gaze into her eyes, thinking, *I can't believe you came to rescue me.* How she was able to even get here is puzzling. Aimsley reads the look on my face, but then brings her gaze down and away from my lack of clothing. I back into the dark of my closet and feel around for clothes to throw on.

The room is loud with silence. The muffled sound of wind

and rain batters the windows and the walls, but a loudness fills all my thoughts. There is obviously a lot to unpack here.

Christian sits on the side of the bed, and Aimsley stands awkwardly in the middle of the room with a puddle at her feet.

"You're soaking wet," I say as I grab her a towel from the ensuite bathroom and wrap it around her. Feeling bad, I pull her into a hug. "How did you even get here?" I ask.

"I paddled in."

I pull back from the hug as she uses the towel to dry off her hair and face. "What do you mean paddled in?"

"I paddled in from my apartment on my paddleboard. You do realize the storm surge is almost at your front door, right? I saw how bad it was getting on the news and saw your text. I was worried you never left. And you obviously didn't."

"So, you came here just to check up on me? Why would you do that?"

"You know, storm surge is what kills people in hurricanes. I was worried about you." Aimsley's confession of care for me was beyond infatuation. She really would come across town and risk floodwater to make sure I was okay. I feel guilty for not having the courage to do the same for her or even myself.

"I'm sorry. I guess I really didn't know. This is my first hurricane. I didn't think it would be this bad."

Aimsley hangs the wet towel on the corner of the door and sighs, "This is one hell of a first hurricane experience."

I slump down next to Christian on the side of the bed, gripping his hand and looking to Aimsley. With all the attention on me, I attempt an apology, "Look, guys, I'm sorry, okay? I was just feeling so hopeless. I wasn't thinking clearly. I haven't been for a while. But, I'm glad you're both here with me now." My eyes well up, feeling guilty for putting them into this situation with me. Knowing they both were just concerned for my safety. I've been selfish.

Aimsley's eyes soften. "Well, there's something else I need to tell you about. I think it's good news, well, for you. I know the town has put you through a lot with this murder investigation, but I overheard Brooke's dad on the way here talking to Jim's wife. They were talking like they were a couple. I think there's something going on between the two of them. I think something will come out soon. I want to talk to Officer Macon about it. He's on your side. You're not going to go to prison. I won't let that happen."

Christian perks up. "Wait what? Prison?"

I grip Christian's hand tighter. "I haven't gotten to explain, but they took me in for questioning. I have to confess something to you both," I take a deep breath and decide to get it all off my chest. "I did lie to you, but not about Christian. The truth is, I can't be sure I wasn't the one who did it." Both of them looked at me quizzically.

"Why would you think that? What do you mean you can't be sure?" Christian asks.

"I think I might have been the one who shot Jim. I found a gun. Well, Christian's gun. And I think I might have done it when I blacked out. I don't know, but I was trying to get rid of the gun that night before Duncan showed up and took me in."

"My gun? How did you..." Christian asks before Aimsley

interrupts.

"Wait a minute. So, you found a gun, and you think you killed Jim?"

"Yeah, I think I buried it in the sand that night after I shot him. So, I tried to dispose of it. I thought the river would be a good place, but I wasn't sure how to, and then Chief Duncan showed up, and it was too late. And now I think they will search the house and find it. I'm so sorry for involving you, Aimsley. I just didn't know where to go or what to do."

"Was that the only reason you wanted to hang out with me? To use me to get rid of a murder weapon?" Aimsley questions me with her nose scrunched and her eyebrows flared.

"No, Aimsley. Of course not. I mean, yeah, initially. I didn't want to mention that at the time, though. I didn't think you would want any part of it and..."

Christian interrupts, "Where is the gun now?"

"So, was that all some type of game. Were you just playing me? I thought you were actually into me." Aimsley shakes her head side to side. "Damn it, I am so stupid."

I move towards Aimsley, but she backs away from me. "Aimsley."

"What do you mean you thought she was into you? Is there something going on between you two?" Christian waits for an explanation, looking back and forth between us. "Lizzy? Answer me."

Aimsley explains, "We made out. It got intense. I thought she was into me. But don't worry, I see it was just a ploy."

"No, it's not like that. I mean, I did like it." Christian's eyes widen. "I'm sorry, Christian, but I was just confused. I was grieving. It had been a long time since I've had any companionship. I got carried away."

"Wow!" Christian states.

"Don't wow me. You're supposed to be dead! If you were here the whole time and actually came to me, it probably would never have happened."

Aimsley grunts, crossing her arms and biting her lip to hold her speech.

"I told you I have my reasons. Where is my gun, Elizabeth?" He uses my full name. He only does when it's serious.

Chico stands in front of me, on top of my toes, guarding me from the commotion.

"Calm down, please. It's back where you left it."

Christian reaches underneath the bed, where he pulls out the gun case, setting it on top of the bed. He unlocks and opens the case to inspect it. "How did you find it?"

I respond, "I've always known it was there. What do you mean?"

"How did you know it was buried in the sand in the backyard?"

"I didn't. Chico was digging it up."

"He must have smelled me."

And then I realized. "I never said it was in the backyard. How did you know that?"

"You didn't shoot anyone, Elizabeth. I buried that gun there. I was hiding it from you," Christian confesses, "You couldn't be trusted. I was afraid you'd hurt yourself. I mean,

my god, you thought you were capable of murdering someone?"

Staring blankly towards the wall, my vision blurs. My mind begins to spiral. To think this whole time, I thought I could have been responsible for the murder. Then for Christian to have hidden the gun there would mean he had been in the house and didn't bother to let me know he was alive. And to think he hadn't trusted me with the gun, afraid I'd use it. Well, maybe he is right. I thought I might have.

The thoughts weigh heavy and the voices of Christian and Aimsley muffle in the background. I question my reality. I grip my fist and dig my nails into my palm to feel the pain. I need to know this is real. If I can feel the pain, then I know it is. And if this is real, then not only was I deceived by the love of my life, but I was also deceived by my own mind. Trapping me into a false reality. So much about the last few days, hell, the last few *months* have felt wrong. I feel like a fool.

The muttering grows in the room, and I hear, "Elizabeth," and feel Aimsley's hand over my clenched fist, breaking me from my mental spiral.

## Aimsley August

**Elizabeth's eyes look at me with desperation as I grip her hand.** A look that says she wants to be anywhere but here at this moment, a feeling I know all too well, especially after trying to avoid Brooke this week. I can't imagine I would feel great either, knowing someone I thought had been dead for months was really alive and lied to me about it.

It's hard to hear that I might have been lied to, too. Using me after I felt such a deep connection with her, mentally and physically. I may have been wearing rose-colored glasses, but something tells me the connection between us was real, and she's masking it because he's here now. I'm happy for her, but I'm heartbroken too.

The storm outside is growing louder. We're not far from the eye of the storm. Maybe a couple of hours or less at this point. As awkward and frustrating as this situation is right now, I'm stuck here. The flood waters would be too risky to travel through now. We need rescue.

Elizabeth sits hunched at the end of her bed. I ask, "Does your cell phone work?"

She looks confused and then replies, "I mean, it's on, but no service. Why?"

I give Christian a serious look and ask, "How about you? We need to call for a rescue. We're in serious danger here."

"I am aware, but no, my phone has no service. The cell towers are most likely down. We're going to have to ride this one out."

"Great," I exhale.

We all sit in silence. The branches bang against the windows. Waves crash against the first floor of the house. My headlamp illuminates the floor, lighting up whoever has the stage of the discussion we'd been having, like I'm the lighting crew for a B-movie horror film.

"I should probably preserve my headlamp battery. Do you guys have any candles?" I ask, scanning my light over Christian.

He paces the side of the room and then goes over to Elizabeth, who still sits over the side of the bed, seemingly lost in her own thoughts.

*Poor girl.*

"Yeah, in the living room," Elizabeth says. She gets up while Chico follows her ankles closely. As she passes by, her hand grabs mine and squeezes hard on her way out into the dark hallway. I follow her. Christian's footsteps trail closely behind mine.

My headlamp shines on the back of a thin and lengthy Elizabeth who approaches the railing of the stairs, waiting for my light to illuminate her path. Looking down the steps to the first floor, water rushes over the floorboards. Like a small tide, it swishes from the front of the house to the back. We stand at the bottom of the stairs, observing the dark, salty water.

"Everything is ruined," Elizabeth sighs.

"I'll go get the candles," Christian says as he pushes his way past us both and steps down into the ankle-deep water.

I take the headlamp off and hand it to him, "Here."

He takes it willingly and places it over his head. Then we watch as the light fades into the living room and beyond. Elizabeth's silhouette leans against the railing before dropping into a seat on the step. She hugs onto Chico, who willingly accepts her comfort.

I'm trying to remain calm, but I'm reminded of the pressing seriousness of our situation every time a wave of water hits the house. The sounds of the house creaking and cracking are concerning. If I had my light, I would investigate them. I worry the crack sounds are the house breaking around us.

"Do you have a radio?" I ask.

"A radio?"

"Yeah, like to listen to emergency updates?"

"Do you think it would make a difference right now?" she asks hopelessly.

I want to be helpful, but she's right. All I can manage to do is sit on the step next to her and wait for Christian.

The headlamp approaches, and Christian cradles candles and two bottles of wine. Elizabeth's head perks up. The corner of her mouth may even have smiled.

"I've got supplies. Come on, girls and boys, head on up to the art studio. The second floor is our only safe space right now, and I think it's the only room furthest from the trees. I'll be right up." He hands me the wine and Elizabeth the candle, and lights the stairway with his headlamp until we reach the top.

I'm excited to see inside Elizabeth's art studio finally. I've been so curious about its contents, but I've only been able to imagine it. I didn't have the pleasure of seeing it the last time I was in the house. The thought crosses my mind that I might see this space tonight, but it could be gone tomorrow. Her dream home might not be recoverable after this. Hell, my apartment won't be either. After tonight, we might all be displaced. Homeless. The thought makes me eager to open this bottle of wine.

The art studio is dark. I don't know what surrounds me. I can only make out faint shadows of objects around the room.

Elizabeth asks, "Hey, do you have a lighter?"

"Yeah, of course," I say.

I pull the lighter from my damp pocket, hoping it still works. I flick the lighter, but there's no flame. I blow hard into the lighter, trying to get rid of any water. Finally, a flame sparks, and in front of me is Elizabeth, who's much closer than I had realized. She cups the candle in her hands. I put the flame from the lighter onto the wick, which lights immediately, giving a warm, flickering glow to the room. We look at each other in candlelight. Her beautiful face and sad eyes. Desperate eyes. Not the same flirty eyes I saw sitting behind the bar, not the same hungry eyes I saw sitting next to me by the river, but sad eyes, deep and dark.

Behind her, on the wall, is a painting. A large painting of figures without eyes, but with words where the eyes should be.

Elizabeth motioned the light towards the painting, as we both stood in front of it. It's of monumental scale. I've never seen paintings like this, so engulfing and full of darkness. I moved closer to read the words, *"YOU SMOTHERED ME, YOU DISSAPOINTED ME, YOU REJECTED ME, YOU ABANDONDED ME."* I wonder if Christian has seen this. One of these figures could be him, and I hope none of them are me. The painting is powerful and dark and makes me feel even more deeply for her. But before I can comment, Elizabeth places her hand on my shoulder, digging her sharp nails into my shirt, still looking at the painting herself. She asks me if I like it, searching for agreement, like she was proud to call it her masterpiece. How sad that something that caused her so much pain was the same thing that made her an artist. I nod my head *"yes"* while taking it in.

From behind us was the sound of footsteps and a thud on the wall. Christian carries something sizable into the room. Elizabeth's purple chair from the living room. Immediately, she handed me the candle and rushed to Christian to help pull it into the room. I can feel the dents Elizabeth's nails left on my shoulder.

"My lounger! Oh, thank you so much!" Elizabeth throws her arms around Christian, squeezing him into an embrace and a kiss that lasted long enough to make me feel more awkward than I already had.

"Of course, my moon. I know how much it means to you. Even if I can't save anything else." He kisses the top of her forehead and then hands me my headlamp back.

I stretch it back over my head, shining the light into Christian's eyes that gleam dark, almost black. He smiles widely at me before I shut it off.

"Thanks," I mutter.

Elizabeth yanks at my arm towards the lounger. "Come sit with me. Let's drink wine."

Her attitude has quickly flipped with the comfort this piece of furniture brought her. I guess I should feel lucky she asked me to sit beside her when she could have easily asked Christian to. Setting down the candle on her drawing desk, I take a seat next to her as Christian walks out of the room.

"Where are you going now?" Elizabeth shouts at him, but he doesn't reply as he disappears into the dark of the hallway. She shrugs her shoulders and smiles at me. What a light her smile brings to the dark. I think she truly is in love with him, or is this smile for me?

"I'm so happy you're here. Welcome to my dream studio!" she says as she holds out her arm, gesturing to all of her supplies and artwork. Yarn and string dangle from the ceiling. Stacks of canvases and drawing paper pads stack against the walls. Paint litters the floor. Coffee tins of paint brushes ornament her desk. It's chaos, but everything feels intentionally placed. I feel like I'm exploring the insides of Elizabeth's brain. Her art studio is *her*. It's exactly how I had been imagining it.

She looks at peace now with her lounger, her love and her libations. Like she had completely forgotten that we were in a dark room with a life-threatening hurricane outside.

"It's really impressive. How come you didn't show it to me before?" I ask.

She pauses, as if searching for a response, and gulps. "I, uh, it's a very personal space to me. I would have shown you. It wasn't the right time. Better now than never, right?"

I almost feel a sense of denial from her. Her reality has turned from sadness to madness. All I can do is play along. I place my hand on her knee and say, "It's incredible. A dream art studio if I ever saw one."

She places her hand down on top of mine and says, "Thank you, Aimsley," and then she glances at my mouth. For a moment, I think she is leaning in to kiss me.

From out of the dark doorway, Christian pops into the room with three wine glasses. He had gone into the dark, flooded first floor to fetch wine glasses. This really is like a dream, a mad dream, and we were all making the best of it.

I could have been in a rundown motel, slinging back homebrews out of the bathtub keg with Dean and Cameron. I could have been cracking jokes while Brooke and Tiffany laugh and throw pillows at each other, with Garnet giggling and egging them on. But instead, I'm here. I'm stuck on the second floor of a flooded home on the beach with this beautiful, dark, mysterious girl and her dead lover, having wine on an antique chair by candlelight. At this point, I'm not certain that I'd feel better here or there.

Elizabeth smirks as she fills my glass and presses the rim of it against my lips, tilting it back to give me a drink. The swig of wine burns smoothly down my throat. Her image sears into my eyes.

*No matter the beast she had become, a once shy girl now drew her claws, ready to hunt at the dark figure's expense.*

# Elizabeth Corey

**I couldn't be happier right now.**

Christian looks like a little kid, sitting crisscrossed on the floor in front of us. It reminds me of the time we moved into our apartment in Portland. I remember sitting on our living room floor like that, only with boxes piled all around us. I miss our little apartment. It was a quaint one-bedroom on the second floor of an old house. It was in a sort of busy neighborhood, packed tightly next to the others, but the bottom floor was a hair salon. We never had to worry about noisy neighbors, except for the faint sound of a hair dryer sometimes. When Christian was home, we'd spend our days walking Chico together through the neighborhood. A short walk away was our favorite coffee shop. The baristas knew us by name and always gave Chico a pup cup filled with whipped cream and a dog biscuit. We would sit at the café tables along the street and sip cold brew and indulge in breakfast sandwiches. Christian always got the bagel, and I got a croissant. Then, on our way home, we would pick up half a dozen donuts and snack on them at night while watching movies.

And to think, during that time, I was looking forward to something better. Our future dream home and life in Painter's Beach. To think of how much pain and loss we've suffered in such a short time. At least we are together again. And I have also made a friend. A good friend. A friend who came to rescue me. One who really cares about me. Two people who really love and care about me so much are sharing this room with me, and I couldn't be happier.

A loud crash booms through the house.

Aimsley looks concerned.

Christian stays stern and says, "This is going to be a long night, ladies."

A long night indeed.

I reach towards Chico, who jumps onto the lounger between Aimsley and me. I scratch his head and squeeze him firmly against me. He licks my nose and pants slightly. The storm is stressing him out.

*We need a distraction.*

"I have an idea," I say while petting Chico. My hand brushes against Aimsley's hand as she pets Chico, too. The feeling of her skin sends my mind back to our embrace under the bridge. Even with Christian here now, I still feel a slight pull to her. An interest. A curiosity. It feels almost wrong yet thrilling. "I think we should play a game."

"A game? Like what?" Christian asks, sipping from his wine glass. He looks up at me from the floor. His smirk makes me wonder what type of game he has in mind or if he thought it a silly idea.

"Hide and seek," I state.

Christian chuckles, and Aimsley smiles, shaking her head.

"What? Come on. I think it would be fun. We'd have to stay upstairs, obviously, but there are a lot of hiding places. We need something to do to pass the time." I give them a pouted lip, one that is probably stained red from the wine.

"You really want to play?" Christian asks.

"I don't know this house, though," Aimsley says.

"I know which will make it even more fun. How about Christian and I hide, and you seek? We can start in the hallway by the stairs. Close your eyes, count to ten, and then come look."

"What! But it's so dark in here. I'm gonna trip over something. I'm already gimping around."

"You'll have a light, but only the candle. No headlamp, that would be too easy," I instruct.

Aimsley shakes her head no, curls swaying from side to side.

"Please, please," I beg, gripping her hand while my bottom lip pouts out further.

I pout my lip at Christian. He shrugs his shoulders and agrees, "Okay, I'll do it."

Before Aimsley has a chance to agree or contest, I stand up, still holding her hand, and drag her out into the hallway. She says under her breath, "Alright, guess we're doing this."

Christian hands the candle to Aimsley.

"Okay, close your eyes. Oh, and no peeking!" I add.

She turns around to the railing of the stairwell, where the water sloshes below, and starts counting. "Ready? One..." Aimsley says.

Christian and Chico race past the art studio and into our bedroom.

"Two."

I pass him, dragging my hand along the wall, guiding myself down the dark hallway.

"Three."

My fingers graze the doorknob of the second bedroom. I stop and grip the handle, thinking it could be a place to hide, but as I start to turn the nob, my heart sinks.

*I can't go in there.*

My hand releases. I then feel the trim around the door of the bathroom on the left. I know I'm at the end of the hall. I grip the doorknob of the last door.

"Four."

Trying not to make any noise, I slide into the pitch-black space on the other side of it and close it softly behind me.

Muffled now, I hear Aimsley faintly say, "Five."

Bracing the railing, I kick my foot forward to the bottom step of the stairs. I ascend them until I reach another door at the top of the steps leading into the small, square room of the turret. A nook full of windows looking out over the ocean. The storm drowns out any noise from Aimsley. It's the perfect hiding spot.

My pupils dilate to capture any bits of light from outside to look around the room. It's empty besides a pile of boxes that

I hide behind and wait to be found. This turret was supposed to be my library. Christian was going to build me shelves that curved around the whole room so I could fill it with books and sit and read while looking out over the beach. Sounds like a dream. A dream that, even with him here, seems very far away now.

The wind rattles the thin walls and vibrates the windows. The room shakes with each gust, almost feeling like it's swaying slightly. The sound of the powerful waves crashing outside has almost engulfed me entirely. Maybe the whole house is afloat in the ocean now, or maybe the sway is from the red wine. I wait patiently, entranced by the movement and sounds. Only me and the ocean.

I'm not sure how long Aimsley's been seeking, but I want her to find me. I want her to find me in this dark room and corner me. When I hear a clicking of the doorknob turning and releasing from the wall, my heart flutters, and all I can think of is letting her come up to me in the dark, sliding my hands around her, and letting our lips touch again. I see her light and hear her footsteps pacing around the room. But the light she is using must be her headlamp.

*Cheater.*

I'm waiting for her to come behind the boxes, but she doesn't. The light goes towards the door, and the footsteps sound as if she is leaving. I have to drop a hint or she'll miss me completely.

From behind the pile of boxes I whisper, "Thought I said candles only."

The light whirls around, illuminating the box I'm hiding behind. Suddenly the pile is ripped out from in front of me and tossed across the room. The flashlight shines brightly into my eyes. A hand grasps my arm forcibly, and I scream out.

# Aimsley August

"Seven," I count.

Even though this game seems like a ridiculous idea right now, Elizabeth's excited about it, so I'm playing along.

"Eight."

I open my eyes, knowing they probably found hiding places a while ago. Looking down on the first floor, the water is deeper than before. The waves are crashing in and out of the house, reaching halfway up the first set of stairs. It has to be at least a few feet, practically a river flowing through. Objects float back and forth, but I try to keep my head in the game.

"Nine."

I bet Christian is in the bedroom. I heard his heavy feet stop within close range, but Elizabeth might be harder to find.

"Ten. Okay, here I come!"

With the candle in my hand, I walk down to the bedroom.

*He better not try to jump out at me, because I can't guarantee I won't punch him if he startles me.*

The last thing I want right now is to find Christian instead of Elizabeth, but the long bushy tail hanging out from under the bed is a dead giveaway. I lean down and peer under the bed and say, "Found you!" I was assuming Christian was there with Chico, but he isn't. Chico crawls out from under the bed, wagging his tail, and kisses my face as I manage to get back up and continue to look. The only other place he could be is either in the closet or in the bathroom.

"Where is he, Chico? Huh, buddy? Help me find him." Chico looks up at me, tilting his head and trying to figure out what I'm asking. He puts his nose to the floor and sniffs around the room. I walk up to the closet, stepping in slightly. I push clothes around, reaching my hand deeper into the closet, hoping I don't graze Christian somehow. I don't. The closet is clear. I back out and walk into the bathroom, the only other place he could be. With the candlelight, I check behind the door. Nothing. The remaining hiding place is behind the shower curtain.

*I know this motherfucker is in here trying to scare me.*

I give a warning, "Oh, I found you. Come on out," but there is no movement. I reach out to the curtain and grip the side to pull it open. I quickly pull back the curtain to the sight of an empty tub. My vision quickly vanishes as the candlelight blows out.

"Damn it!"

I pull the lighter from my pocket, flicking the spark wheel to ignite a flame, but the spark won't catch. I flick it again and again, until my thumb is raw.

*Great.*

Now I'm curious where they both could be. I've only explored downstairs when there was power and lights. Now I have to find my way down a dark hallway with a mysterious number of doorways that lead to who knows where. I pat the walls as I slug down the hallway, using them as a crutch to baby my ankle until I come across the next doorknob. I throw open the door, trying to startle any unwanted visitors in the room. With what little senses I have left, touch and sound, I am unable to sense any movement. I inch further into the room, until I run straight into an object that's waist high. A wood bar knocks me right in the stomach. I lean over, clutching it, moaning from the sudden, sharp pain.

"Gah! What the hell is this?"

Investigating the bar with my touch, it feels like a gate, but sort of in the air, because there's nothing to touch near my feet. I reach my hand out over the bar, and it hits something soft, dangling. As I feel the items that appear to be suspended from strings, some crinkle and some jingle like bells, I realize what I am touching. It's a mobile.

*This is a crib for a baby.*

Instantly, my mind races. Elizabeth never mentioned a baby.

A noise comes from the hallway. My heightened sense of sound homes in on it. At first, it sounds like the wind and rain are intensifying, but then it gets louder, like a muffled humming.

*Is that a boat engine?*

Quickly, I run out into the hallway to look over the railing of the stairs. Flashing red and blue lights beam into the front of the house. I can't believe my eyes.

*Holy shit! They came to rescue us.*

The boat motor shuts off. I run down the stairs, trying to get a better look. An officer crawls through the front window of the house, sloshing through knee-high water with a flashlight.

I shout, "Hey, over here! We're upstairs!"

"Aimsley, is that you?" The officer says my name, and I immediately recognize his voice. It's Chief Duncan.

Instantly, my blood runs cold. I have to face the man who punched me in the stomach and ratted me out to Brooke. I wonder too if he noticed I saw him talking to Heather today. All I can think about is how pissed he must be. I back up a few stairs as Chico barks from the top of the steps, startling me.

"There you are!" he says as he approaches.

My heart is beating in my ears.

"Brooke said you might be here. You know I wasn't going to come. Honestly, I'd care less to rescue someone who puts themselves in danger like this." He kicks through objects in the water towards the stairs.

I'm against the wall with nowhere to run. My feet are frozen.

"But I have to be the doting father." His pitch changes as he mocks Brooke, "*Daddy, please help Aimsley.*"

He begins to ascend the stairs while I frantically look around, hoping Christian will come out, but he's still hiding somewhere.

"So where is she?" Duncan asks, his soaking wet shoes and pants drenching each carpeted step as he stands at the bottom of the stairs.

"Who?"

"You know who. That *murdering witch*." I run up to the top of the stairs. He climbs the stairs after me, flashing his light around the hallway.

"She didn't murder anyone," I protest, watching him reach the top of the stairs.

His body blocks the space in the hallway between me and an escape. "Tell her to come out. We need to have a little talk."

"About what?" I ask, but before I could get an answer, he lunges out and grabs my shirt. As I try to pull away, he strikes my face with his flashlight right across my cheek. I fall to the ground. There's a sharp, hot pain. My head spins, and a warm ooze of blood falls from my cheek. My sight goes dark and then comes back. Duncan stands over me. I hold my arm up in defense while scooting backwards into the hallway.

Reaching for me again, he yells, "Come here."

I kick my feet and turn over to get up, but he grabs my ankles and yanks me back, dragging me across the floor. I flail my body and let out a scream, "Help!"

Duncan pushes on my flailing legs and kneels on my back. Pushing my face into the hardwood floor, he restrains me, smacking a cuff against each wrist behind my back. I yell again, "Help! Stop!" But as soon as I do, he presses his weight down harder, crushing my lungs, causing me to gasp for air.

*I can't breathe.*

"Shut up," he demands. Chico barks loudly and nips at Duncan's ankle. He lets go of me and swats Chico, causing him to yelp.

"Please don't hurt him," I plead. Chico continues to bark, but backs into the art studio, and Duncan slams the door closed, trapping him in.

"Fucking mutt! Where's your little friend, huh? Where is she hiding?" he asks as I squirm on the floor, trying to get up. "Where do you think you're going to go? You know what, if you don't tell me where she is, I'll find her."

"Let go of me," I shout as he drags me by the shirt into the bedroom. He throws me down as my face smacks the floor, giving me another sharp pain against my cheek that's already gashed open.

I grunt and slowly curl into a fetal position. I feel a piece of duct tape pressed around my mouth, restricting me from calling out.

Duncan pushes on the sides of the tape and presses his finger into my cut cheek, causing an excruciating pain. Without saying another word, he walks out of the room and down the hallway to search for her.

All I can do is hum into this tape until the back of my throat feels raw. I know they are both here somewhere.

*Where the hell are they? Why aren't they helping me?*

He yells through the house, "Elizabeth, this is the police. Come out now."

I can hear him moving things around, opening doors, until I can't hear him anymore. From the doorway, a shadow approaches. Christian sits me up and tugs at my handcuffs.

A high-pitched scream lets out. I know it's Elizabeth. I hear shuffling down the hallway. Christian puts his index finger to his mouth, silently shushing me, and hides behind the bed.

Duncan pushes Elizabeth into the room.

"We just need to have a little talk. So, get in there and sit down," he says as he throws Elizabeth onto the floor. She slams into her shoulder and then quickly sits up next to me, looking frightened.

Wide-eyed, she looks at my bleeding face and the duct tape around my mouth and gasps. "What the hell? Aimsley."

She reaches for my duct tape when Duncan yells, "Don't touch her, get back." His flashlight and the barrel of his gun are pointed directly at Elizabeth. She immediately backs away from me, holding up her thin arms, showing her palms.

"Officer, please, don't hurt us. I won't touch her."

"That's a lie. You two have been doing an awful lot of touching, haven't you?"

We both stay silent. Frozen with the threat of his gun pointing at me and then at her.

"We haven't done anything. Why are you pointing a gun at us?"

Duncan scoffs and holds his arms out, pointing his gun firmly towards Elizabeth. He walks closer. "Haven't done anything? Oh, you know what you did."

He holds the gun closer, tapping the front of the barrel against her head. Elizabeth lets out a shriek and cries out, "Please don't. I didn't do anything, I swear."

"Yes, you did. You murdered Jim Crowley in cold blood. You shot the man on the beach and sacrificed him to your pagan gods." Duncan spits to the ground in front of her.

"But... I don't think I did." Elizabeth bows her head.

Feeling helpless, I look at Duncan with pleading eyes and shake my head, humming "no" into the duct tape, but it doesn't seem to faze him.

"*Murdering witch!* Isn't that what they all were chanting? Everyone on this island believes it was you. So why fight it?" Duncan drops his gun slightly and paces back and forth in the room.

"You know, the two of you couldn't have done a better job of setting this all up for me. Between your recklessness, Aimsley, and Elizabeth over here looking like some drunk freak... Hell, all I have to do is say, '*Welp, I found them, but it was too late. Tragically, Aimsley drowned looking for her new lover in the hurricane like an idiot, and Elizabeth, well... She was feeling so guilty about what she did that she went and offed herself.*"

My eyes widen as I look at Elizabeth. This was part of his plan. We're now at his disposal.

"Everyone already thinks it's you anyway."

"Why? Why are you doing this?" Elizabeth asks, as she begins to sob.

"I was planning to make my way over here regardless, knowing you were here all by yourself. But, unfortunately for Aimsley, she had to come here in the middle of my plan, and now I don't have any choice but to get rid of you both. Plus, I know you heard me with Heather today. I saw you spying on me. You probably think you have it all figured out, don't you?"

All I can do is stare, but if I could respond, I'd tell him that I figured out he's a complete psychopath.

"Since we have some time, why don't I just tell you? You'll both be dead soon anyway. Might as well get it off my chest."

*But to her surprise, the dark figure was everything to her, saving her life whilst consuming it all at once.*

# Elizabeth Corey

**Where the fuck is Christian?**

It's the only question repeating itself over and over again in my mind while listening to this piece of shit explain himself.

*Oh, Christian, please hurry!*

Duncan forces us to listen to his story and how he will resolve all of this once he accomplishes his *plan.*

He says to Aimsley, "I'm sure Brooke told you all about my burner phone. Yeah. It's true. I have been fucking Heather. You know, if Catherine weren't such a fucking bore... I bust my ass working to provide for my family, and what do I get? Not even a decent piece of ass. I've given up and sacrificed my whole life to support them, and all they do is bitch and moan. *'Daddy, can you do this? Daddy, can you do that? Eugene, you never talk to me anymore. You never have any fun with the family. Don't touch me.'* Yeah, well, you know what? I'm fucking tired and deprived." He takes a deep breath and continues to pace the room.

"Heather, now she's a great fuck. Heather's never had a man like me, and I drive her wild. That guy Jim? He was soft. That's no real man. She hated the guy anyway. But I'm not a killer. You probably think I killed the guy, right?" He looks at both of us. I keep my mouth shut.

"No. I've never killed anyone. I have to now. But only because *she* got me into this situation. Women. It's always women. We have to take care of everything. The sacrifices I make for all of you." Duncan pauses his rant and holds his hands up to his head, gripping the sides of his hair.

"If you didn't kill him, then why do you think I did?" I ask.

Duncan tosses his head back, laughing like a madman. "I know you didn't kill him. Because Heather did. Heather shot him. Right there in her living room, while I was still butt ass naked. And I had to help her clean it all up. Figured the river would have swept him out to the ocean with those strong currents, but there he was, washing up on the beach. And if you hadn't thrown your little arts and crafts witch project in the water, we'd probably still have an open investigation. Good for me, bad for you. So, now, here we are."

Duncan points his gun at my forehead. My body shakes violently, and I look at Aimsley, whose eyes are wide and full of tears.

*Where is Christian? I just want Christian.*

"Everyone will know your name. Elizabeth Corey, the Witch of Painter's Beach. And they'll be happy they don't have to spend their tax dollars on you with some lengthy trial or to keep you alive in prison. If anything, I'm doing you a favor."

"Please don't." My final plea.

I hear the gun cock, and I close my eyes, feeling the imprint of the barrel firm against the side of my head. I brace myself as best as I can.

*I just want to see Christian one last time.*

The sound of the gunshot rings through my ears, but I open my eyes. Duncan drops his gun. He falls to his knees in front of me, bowing his head and gripping his chest. I take the gun and turn it on Duncan.

I feel Christian behind me. His arms slide underneath mine. He aims my hands up. My finger is on the trigger. When Duncan lifts his head, I can't pull it. I'm not capable of killing anyone. I never have been.

Duncan's mouth is open. There's blood on his tongue and in his teeth. He begins to raise his arm towards the gun.

Christian squeezes my finger. The trigger clicks. A loud bang explodes in my ear. Duncan's head bounces off the wall behind him. Blood spatters, painting my wall a sickening shade of crimson red. For a second, his body remains upright. His neck holds an unrecognizable head barely pieced together before he falls forward into his lap.

*I killed him.*

I stared at his lifeless body on my bedroom floor. Christian pulls the gun from my hands and sets it on the ground.

"Lizzy." I faintly hear him calling my name over and over, but my ears are ringing.

*I killed him.*

"Lizzy. Lizzy honey. Look at me." Christian shakes me,

and I look up from Duncan's body and into Christian's eyes. "Lizzy. We have to get Aimsley out of the cuffs. Come on. You can do it."

Christian removes the sets of keys from Duncan's waist and hands me the handcuff key. Aimsley angles her body so I can unlock them. With a quick turn, I release each of her hands. She rips the duct tape off her mouth and then holds me, cradling me like a baby.

"It's okay. It's okay. You did the right thing," she says as she holds me tight and rubs circles in my back.

*I killed him.*

"Christian, what do we do now?" Aimsley asks.

"I think these are keys to Duncan's boat." Christian jingles a set of keys in his hand.

"Right. See? We're all going to get out of here." Aimsley rocks me back and forth, looking at me, avoiding looking at Duncan. I know she must be upset about what I did. That was Brooke's father.

"I'm sorry," I say.

"Don't be sorry. You're okay. That's what matters." Aimsley assures me.

"But, I killed him," I said out loud.

Aimsley's tears fall from her face onto mine, and we hold each other tightly.

The house rattles hard. The floor begins to feel like they're shifting.

Christian offers his hands to both of us. "Let's get out of here."

He rushes us out of the room and away from the body. Leaving everything exactly as it is and closing the door behind us. We sit at the top of the steps. Christian opens the door to the art studio and encourages Chico, "Go see your mommy."

Chico walks cautiously over to me after looking both ways as I say, "It's okay, buddy, come here." He wags his tail low and sits on top of my lap on the stairs, licking my face and nuzzling into my neck. I hold onto his fur, gripping it in between my fingers and smelling his coat, "I'm so glad you're okay, Chico."

Christian sits on the step below us, petting Chico and looking up at Aimsley. "Aimsley, can you take Chico to the boat? I'm just going to talk to Elizabeth for just a minute."

Aimsley seems hesitant to go without me, but I reach out for her hand and smile. A smile of reassurance, to let her know that everything will be alright.

"Okay. Come on, Chico. Follow me." Aimsley leads him down the stairs, encouraging him to swim through the water, and hoists him out of the front windows of the house.

My hands shake. My mind is racing. I didn't know why Christian made me pull the trigger, and why he hid from Duncan, and why he came onto the island and avoided me for days. I need an explanation. Everything is strange. Something is not right.

Red and blue lights flicker into the house as Aimsley starts the boat. I can almost hear her shout for us over the wind. Rain pours into the house. Part of the roof is now gone. A crackling sound comes from behind us that travels the length of the hallway. The hardwood boards begin to splinter upwards as if the whole back of the house might split at any moment.

I gasp and get up to run, but Christian grabs my hand, preventing me from leaving the stairs. "Christian, come on! We have to go!"

He doesn't budge. His face is calm and unconcerned. His fingers interlock with mine as he places a kiss on top of them. "Do you trust me, Lizzy?" he asks.

"Of course I do." His eyes worry me. There's something big behind them. I can feel it, but I'm not sure I'm ready to accept whatever it is.

"We can't leave."

# Captain's Log

**May 18th**

Every night I dream of beaching this boat behind our house. I dream of walking up the dune in our backyard and through our gate. I see Elizabeth sitting there on our balcony, holding her belly.

I dream of sifting the sand, searching for coins. Elizabeth watches me, pacing the balcony, refusing to let me inside the house until I find them. Endlessly I search, day and night, but no matter how hard I look, I can't find any. I have this aching feeling that they're inside the house, so I beg her to let me in, but she won't. I know that old man took his gold coins and hid them somewhere, but in my dreams, I can't find them. It's a terrible nightmare that's been wrecking my sleep all week. Sky tells me it's just my subconscious trying to process my situation right now, that soon the dream will pass, and I'll be with Elizabeth forever. I really want that to be true, but it's terribly hard to maintain hope on this boat. It's the reason

I bought this house in the first place. It was the same home that my father wrote about in his journal. The one where he'd found a coin all those years ago. Now all I had to do was get there, and the treasure would be ours. All ours.

It was simple to convince Elizabeth that this house was the one. The hardest part was watching the property, waiting for the old man to die. I checked the house listing every day after I read the address in my father's journal. I obsessed over this property, and once it was listed for sale, I'd already put in an offer above the asking price before showing it to Elizabeth. From the moment I met her in that bar in Portland, when she told me she had grown up in Painter's Beach, I knew my life was fated. Our relationship was like an alignment of the stars. Everything was happening exactly as it was supposed to. This woman and I would fall in love, we'd start our own family, and we'd move into this house in Painter's Beach. I'd find the gold coins, the legacy my father left me. Sure, it might be strange, I never told her about it, but what difference would it make now?

**June 1st**

And just like that, the world opened up to me.

I finally cracked the code, collected the right items, and found my path to the next level in my video game. But as soon as I leveled up, I realized how much time had passed, and things felt very different.

For the first time since the shipwreck, the sky darkened with clouds. A storm was coming. I helped Sage and Sky prepare the boat, securing the hatches and tying the sails. I knew we were headed for danger, but there was no way I could have checked the weather to anticipate it. I have to admit, I was afraid we wouldn't make it through. After all this time at sea, even with feeling like I was so close to home, there was a chance this storm would wipe us out for good. But as the day was reaching its end, just as the clouds and seas darkened, a light shone out in the distance. It was bright and flashed green, as it does in a sunset, right before the sun falls below the horizon. The clouds around us opened up, and they revealed tiny lights ahead. We were looking at a shoreline. I allowed my knees to fall to the teak surface, the same surface I woke up on so many weeks before. I wept with joy, smiling at the sight of it. Sage and Sky were celebrating, dancing around like fools on the deck. They chanted, *"It's time, it's time!"*

As we got closer, I spotted a large container ship. It was the first ship we'd seen besides the ghost ship. I almost felt as if I was in a dream, like reality had a fog over it, but the fog wasn't blocking my view. It covered everything like a veil. It's a feeling deep in my chest, that something was different, something had changed about the world.

Following behind the large ship, we entered a river that headed away from the sea. We eventually hit a fork that headed inland, and after sailing around a bend, the twinkling lights of a marina came into view. I had no idea where we were, but I definitely never expected to read the sign: *"Painter's Beach Marina"*. Not only had we found Florida, but we had pulled into exactly where my destination was. I thought my eyes were deceiving me. I pinched myself to check if I was dreaming. The pinch hurt, but I wondered if I should pinch Sage and Sky, too, just to make sure.

The moment we reached the dock, they huddled together, like a set of parents seeing their kid off to college. It's a sight I'd never witnessed, but it felt like they had given me something close enough to that experience. And just as soon as my feet touched the dock, without tying in, they waved and pushed off, floating away. I shouted for them, trying to come up with something to say to summarize spending so much time together within one phrase that I could shout. *"Thanks!"* was all I could come up with. And just like that, the sailboat blended in with the darkness.

I didn't want to appear suspicious, so I hurried up the dock and out of the marina. My feet touched land. I savored the feeling of my feet in the grass, gravel and pavement. I could have kissed the surfaces for finally being on stable ground, but I just started walking. I walked to the road, and I walked into town. I walked through the cobblestone and the sidewalks until I was on another road that led to the beach. I'd studied the maps of the location of this house so many times that I knew exactly where I was going, even though I'd never been there before. My feet, although tired, pulled me all the way to the front of our house. This was it. I was going to see Elizabeth.

Finally.

But I couldn't.

Time had changed things, and not for the better.

Through the front window of our house, I saw her. Elizabeth stood at the island in the kitchen with a glass of wine in her hand. She looked sad, defeated. Her spirit was gone. When she walked from around the kitchen island, I expected to see her beautiful, round belly that had grown while I was away. The belly I had dreamt of. But it too was gone. She was as thin as a rail. So much had changed, and it was all my fault.

Instead of going up to the house, I walked around the island. I tried to figure out what to say to her, how to explain what happened. But for some strange reason, it never felt like the right time. It feels like it had to happen at the exact right time. I physically can't make myself walk up to her and say, *"Lizzy, I'm home!"* It sounds crazy, and I don't know why.

**June 4th**

On Sunday, I spent most of the night watching Elizabeth. I watched her through the front window, and when she moved to the back of the house, I went around to the beach, and I watched her while she was on the balcony. She sat there with Chico, staring out at the shore. She drank heavily and looked like a shell of the person she once was. I hardly recognized her. I wanted to go up to her, tell her everything would be alright, but as much as I willed my body to, my legs wouldn't move. I felt so terrified. Paralyzed with fear of facing the truth.

The night grew late. A storm was brewing offshore, threatening to come on land. The lightning struck bright and hard. As I watched from the dune, Elizabeth and Chico left the balcony and moved out to the backyard. She went through the gate and over the dune, onto the beach. Lightning was getting close. I wanted to warn her. I yelled out, but my voice wouldn't carry over the crashing thunder. She stood in the tide while Chico barked at her to come back. I was so worried she'd get swept away, but just as the rain began to fall, she turned around and walked back to the house. This time, my feet could move. I followed. Through the back door, up the stairs, into the kitchen, through the living room. I stood before her, but she acted like she couldn't see me. Sitting on the coffee table in front of her was my gun. Her hand was toying with the magazine. Her hair draped wet over her face. Softly, I said, *"Lizzy, please don't."* Her head rose slowly, and the white of her eyes grew wide in fear. Like she'd just seen a ghost.

I watched her sleep all night as the cut from her hand dripped onto the floor. I wanted to hold her hair back while she got sick from the wine. *"Hydrate, Lizzy,"* was all I could get out. I watched as our house was pelted with shells by teenagers who called her horrible names. I stood in the living room, wanting to tell her not to listen to them or that rude officer at the door, but my mouth was zipped up. I only hid the gun from her to protect her from hurting herself. Chico wasn't supposed to dig it up or smell my scent, but somehow, he knew I was there when Elizabeth didn't. These people put the wrong idea in her head. The thoughts I could hear her say as I stood by the shower, behind the curtain, trying to keep her company as I listened to her weep. How could she say such things about herself? I sat in an empty chair at the dinner table while her mom made her feel worse. How could she say such things to her own daughter? I sat with Chico all night in the backyard, petting his fur as we watched his mommy lie helplessly in the sand, passed out again. I had tried to talk to her, *"Lizzy, it's me,"* but it only upset her more. She got ready the next day. She looked so beautiful. I stood in the hallway and watched her look at herself in the mirror. I told her, "You're beautiful, my dark moon," and I thought she almost saw me. I waited in the house, exploring the rooms. Her art studio was amazing, but I saw the words *"YOU ABANDONED ME"* stitched into my face. She was right, I did.

I'm so sorry.

Lizzy, you were right to yell at me from the balcony, screaming, *"Fuck him!"* I know I let you down, and I never wanted to hurt you. All I ever wanted to do was to take care of you. To make you feel loved and happy. I've failed you. So, it's no wonder you'd seek comfort in someone new. You think I'm dead, and I am. But I don't blame you, and I'll stick with you until the very end. Through this storm, I'll watch over you since you're too damn stubborn to leave. I'll do anything I can to protect you from the evil in this world, from them and from yourself, until I can't anymore. And then, Elizabeth, when the time is right, we will be together forever. In this life and in the next.

***Although she feared what came next, they were fated in the stars. She was a dark moon that lit up his whole world.***

# NEXT YEAR

## Aimsley August

**The sound of the doorbell dinging at Book & Brew makes my stomach flutter.** Bittersweet butterflies dance in my gut when I see Garnet smiling at me from behind the café counter.

"Hey, stranger!" Garnet says, wiggling her fingers in a grabbing motion towards the box I'm carrying. I set the weight of its contents down onto the countertop.

"Hey! I know, long time no see," I reply.

"Oh, can I pick which one I want?" she asks as she reaches into the box to pull out a book.

"Actually, that top one is signed just for you! I only need one out of this box, then the rest are yours to sell."

"Aw, Aims! Thank you so much!"

"Well, it's only fair, since you did the same for me," I say as I gesture towards the window display where a stack of her books sits next to a stack of mine.

"That is true, I guess, but anyway, I'm so excited for you!

You did it! We're both published authors now!"

"I know, it's hard to believe. It almost doesn't seem real."

Although I say it doesn't feel real, the nervous excitement in my stomach says otherwise. I never knew I could feel this way about an inanimate object. But holding up one of my hardcover books, velvety to the touch, with the embossment of my name on its spine, I can't deny what an accomplishment it is and the feeling of pure joy it brings me.

"Thanks for bringing these over. I've had a few people coming in asking for signed copies already. They're going to sell fast."

"I sure hope they do! My hand is killing me! I guess I never thought about what kind of damage I could do signing my name that many times. I'm not sure I even recognize my own name anymore. The spelling of it almost took on a whole new meaning of pain and agony. I hope I never have to sign my name again!" I laugh.

Garnet laughs too. Her nose scrunches up, and her nose ring wriggles.

"So, what's the special today?" I ask, eyeballing the shiny coffee machine while breathing in smells of freshly ground beans through my nostrils.

"Today is a butterscotch cream shaken espresso. It sounds super sweet, but with the vanilla cold foam and the dark roast beans, it balances really well," Garnet says as she hands over an almond-colored drink topped with white foam that slowly melts into the coffee.

I know my eyes are probably the size of my head right now

as I take a sip. The flavor is as delicious as it sounds.

"Damn, Garnet. You seriously make the best coffee. I don't know what I'm going to do without you."

The smile fades from Garnet's face. She makes a deep frown with a pouted lip.

"You could stay," she says, doe-eyed. Her lip pouts out further.

I huff, letting out a sigh. I am sad to leave my friends, the island, these places I am so used to and familiar with, but that's all the more reason why I have to go. Garnet already knows this. We've talked about it a bunch of times. She can read my lips before I even say a word.

"I know, I know. It's exciting. I'm happy for you. I'm just going to miss you so much!" Garnet walks around the counter, wrapping her arms around me, hugging me tightly.

I squeeze her back. "I'm going to miss you too, but hey, we still have the party."

Garnet perks up, clapping her hands together in excitement.

"Yes! I can't wait! The whole gang together for one last hoorah."

I leave the box at the counter, grabbing a signed copy of my book with me in one hand and my iced coffee in the other. Walking towards the door, I shout, "Can't wait. I'll see you there!"

I hit the unlock button on the key fob to my little green SUV. It's nothing expensive, or classic, or rumbly, but it gets me around, and Chico likes it. He sticks his head out of the window, whining for me as I walk up to the driver's side. He's officially my passenger princess. Equipped with his own dog seat cover and a stash of treats in the glove box. He scratches his paw at its latch.

"Hey buddy!" I scratch the back of his soft fur while opening the compartment, pulling out a biscuit for him. He crunches with content and looks at me with a reassuring "thank you" in the white of his eyes as he chews.

"What do you say we go to the beach? Want to go to the beach, Chico?" The word *"beach"* instantly triggers excitement in his movements as he stomps his feet up and down and pants. He sits in the seat, almost like a person, and tilts his head towards the window, sniffing the air, as if he's mapping out how to get there.

I back out of my parking spot on Main Street. It looks a little different from what it was a year ago. A few storefront windows are still boarded up. The damage was too much for some businesses to come back from. The large magnolia trees struggle to grow back after they've shed too many branches. Spots where trees used to shade the street reveal obvious patches of sunlight. The town feels smaller, less busy. There are fewer tourists this year.

As we cruise slowly through town, I take a left and pull into the Painter's Beach Police Station. Before I have a chance to text him, Officer Macon comes out of the double doors in a slow sprint up to my passenger side window.

"Hey, kid!" he says cheerfully while petting the top of Chico's head. "How you been?"

"I'm good. I'm really good, actually. I just went by the

bookstore, so I wanted to bring you this," I say and hand him a signed copy of my book.

"Well, would you look at that! See, I knew that signed napkin might come in handy someday."

He traces his hand over the cover, reading it slowly, like for the first time, even though he knew the title of it already: *"The Weight of the Horizon"*.

"It's a signed copy, so you get another one of my signatures," I say.

"Nice. You should be really proud of yourself, Aimsley. Heck, I know I'm proud of you. You've really been through a lot, and you didn't let it drag you down, you know? Made something good out of it all."

His words of sentiment are endearing to me. My stomach shrinks, and my eyes well up, but I force back any tears from falling.

"Thanks, Rodger. That means a lot coming from you."

"I know there've been rumors about everything that happened, but I'll always be on your side. I believe in your story."

He salutes me after one last head rub for Chico, and as I pull away, he shouts, "Don't forget about us when you're a big shot, you hear?"

Chico and I head for the beach, blaring 2000s rock on the radio while the wind whips through our hair and the smell of sea salt fills our nostrils. The music stops for a radio host break:

*"That was your Metallica lunch break, melting your face for an hour every day at noon! Before we crank back up… Here's the latest:*

*Today's warm and sunny with a high of seventy-five degrees. The forecast is clear all week, so make sure to get out there, kick up your feet, and crack open a beer! I know I wish I could right about now. Just remember, North Beach is open and clear for activities, but South Beach still remains closed to the public.*

*Don't want to be a Debbie Downer, but today marks the one-year anniversary of Hurricane Amelia. Don't forget to take a quick moment of silence today for our friends and loved ones who were affected by the storm.*

*You know our saying: Painter's Beach strong! Keep rocking on!*

*In other news, the local police department is still asking for your help in locating Officer Eugene Duncan, who has been missing since Hurricane Amelia. You can visit our website for a full list of missing persons, and feel free to call the station with any tips or leads!*

*Alright, enough of that! Let's get back to the tunes, man!"*

It's hard to believe it's been a year, although so much has changed. The sand piles on the sides of the road, the missing roofs or houses, the torn-up signs and streetlamps. Now every time I drive out to the beach, I'm constantly reminded of what happened.

I picture the trek I made through the floodwaters. I hear the strong winds blowing and the sound of the rain pelting. I can picture the dark sky, the waves rushing in from the storm surge. I still remember the silhouette of the pointed tower of Elizabeth's house, rising tall above me.

As I pull my car up over the sand where her driveway used

to be, I can see the house almost sway in my memory. All that's left of it is a few stilts poking head high out of the beach. Chico and I get out of the car and walk up to where the front steps used to be. I remember grabbing onto the columns of her porch, pulling myself and my board up. I remember climbing into her front window and hearing Chico bark. I was so lucky to find him when I did. When I walked into her living room and saw the water from the ocean sweeping in and out of the balcony doors, I knew it wasn't good.

We walk further, between the stilts. Chico's nose presses to the ground. He wags his tail and looks back at me to make sure I am still behind him, before following his nose again.

I think about Elizabeth's smile when she sat at my bar. I think of her knee moving up and down as she shifted her car. I think of her kissing me beneath the bridge. I think about the mascara running down her cheeks as she sat on her balcony. And the agony in her eyes when she talked about Christian. I only hope that my book gave her the ending she deserved. It was never our story. It was never about me. Elizabeth was meant to be with Christian, even if in another life; at least they had each other.

Chico and I stand in the middle of what was once her home. It was washed away board by board, swallowed by the ocean. It's hard to believe on a beautiful day like today, the forces of nature came and took her away with it. As we reach the last stilts, what was once the back of her house, I think of seeing her up on her balcony that same day, looking out at the sea. How everything progressed so fast. I look out at the ocean, taking in a very different view.

Chico pulls the leash tight, yanking my arm out to the side. He pulls from me, even after I tug back.

"Whoa, Chico! You almost ripped my arm off, buddy."

He relents, tugging and pulling. With his tail sticking out straight, he lifts his front paw underneath him. His whole body looks like a dart, as if he's saying, *"This way, human!"* I decide to entertain him, letting him pull me towards whatever he's pointing at. He sniffs heavily against the sand, pacing in circles.

"Chico, what do you smell, boy?"

He stops.

His nose sniffs hard several times before sand starts flying in the air towards me. I quickly shift to the side of him, away from his back legs that kick sand. He thrusts his body forward into his paws, dragging sand from the ground at an alarming speed. He digs a sizable hole within seconds. I wonder if he found a dead sea creature or an animal under the sand.

*Are there animals that live under the sand?*

Chico steps back, whining, and looks at me.

"What did you find, Chico?"

I further amused him by looking into the hole. I wasn't sure I'd find anything other than a smelly, rotten fish or a burrow of some sort of animal, but to my surprise, something sits at the bottom of the hole. The sun glares against it. It's shiny. I kneel down, reaching into the hole, grabbing a handful of sand at the bottom that feels like it contains something. Something small but surprisingly heavy for its size. The sand filters through my fingers, falling from the sides of my palm, revealing its uneven edges. In my hand is a golden coin with a cross, two lions and two castles.

Jessica Ryan is a writer and an artist with a Bachelor of Fine Arts in Painting and Art History. Fascinated by human nature, she writes thrillers inspired by what horrifying things could occur to anyone at any time. Her background in visual arts share similar themes in her writing such as setting scenes and exploring the emotional imagery behind them. She lives in Florida where nature and personal experiences continue to inspire her work. Painter's Beach is her debut novel.